W9-BDV-804

A KILLING IN CHINA BASIN

Many consider Homicide Inspector Ben Raveneau to be at the tail end of his career – not least his ambitious young partner, Elizabeth la Rosa. But Raveneau's long experience proves invaluable during the pair's investigation of a murder in San Francisco's China Basin district. The body of a young woman has been found in a derelict building, her ankles and wrists tied. Who was she, and what was she doing there? The more Raveneau uncovers, the clearer it becomes that the dead girl was involved in something sinister indeed...

Further Titles from Kirk Russell

The John Marquez series

SHELL GAMES
NIGHT GAMES
DEADGAME
REDBACK*

The Ben Raveneau series

A KILLING IN CHINA BASIN *

* *available from Severn House*

A KILLING IN CHINA BASIN

A Ben Raveneau Thriller

Kirk Russell

Severn House Large Print
London & New York

This first large print edition published 2013
in Great Britain and the USA by
SEVERN HOUSE PUBLISHERS LTD of
9-15 High Street, Sutton, Surrey, SM1 1DF.
First world regular print edition published 2011 by
Severn House Publishers Ltd., London and New York.

British Library Cataloguing in Publication Data

Russell, Kirk, 1954-
  A killing in China Basin.
  1. Raveneau, Ben (Fictitious character)--Fiction.
  2. Police--California--San Francisco--Fiction.
  3. Murder--Investigation--Fiction. 4. Detective and
  mystery stories. 5. Large type books.
  I. Title
  813.6-dc23

  ISBN-13: 978-0-7278-9976-7

Severn House Publishers support The Forest Stewardship Council
[FSC], the leading international forest certification organisation. All
our titles that are printed on Greenpeace-approved FSC-certified paper
carry the FSC logo.

Printed and bound in Great Britain by the
MPG Books Group, Bodmin, Cornwall.

For Philip Spitzer

Acknowledgements

Without the help, guidance, and generosity of spirit of two San Francisco homicide inspectors, Holly Pera and Joe Toomey, this novel would never have happened. In San Francisco it takes thirteen to fifteen years from the time you first apply to join the homicide detail to when your name comes up on the waiting list. Homicide Inspector Joe Toomey's career spans thirty-nine years from Patrol Officer at the Southern Police Station to the last fifteen as a Homicide Inspector. Inspector Sergeant Holly Pera has thirty-one years with SFPD and was the first woman to join the homicide detail. She and Joe worked together as partners. In 2007 they were chosen to form San Francisco's first Cold Case Unit. Joe has since retired but still works twenty hours a week in what's called a 9-60 position that allows the talents of retired officers to be tapped. Both work cold cases. Neither Raveneau nor la Rosa, the fictional inspectors in this novel, resemble or are drawn from either, but I surely drew inspiration.

ONE

Whitacre's salt-faded Buick faced the Golden Gate Bridge from a corner of the Marina Green lot, a blue handicap placard hanging from the rear-view mirror. Whitacre brushed the placard aside as he reached to open the passenger door for Raveneau.

'That door doesn't shut easily, pull it hard.'

As Raveneau did, Whitacre said, 'I'm sorry it's so hot in here. The chemo drugs mess with my body temperature. I'm always cold now, but I am winning this fight, Ben. Last scan, the tumors had shrunk by fifty percent. I've got another this morning and if it's as good as the last one I think they're going to tell me I can go back to work next month.'

'Everybody in the office is waiting to hear that.'

But Raveneau saw that far from gaining weight, Whitacre was losing it. He watched him struggle to unfold a piece of paper and looked out at the bay, dark blue and windswept this morning, the bridge bright orange, whitecaps running toward Alcatraz.

'He drives a late model white Lexus SUV. These are his plates.'

Whitacre handed him the piece of paper. He could have sent a text, email, or called it in yesterday. He was on medical leave but was still very much a San Francisco homicide inspector, same as Ben Raveneau, and could easily have picked up the phone and had the license plates run. He also had much closer friends among the inspectors than Raveneau, any of which would be glad to help him.

After a liver cancer diagnosis late last spring Whitacre used up his sick time, comp time, and vacation pay, then applied to the Catastrophic Illness Program. The program allowed San Francisco Police Department officers to donate time to each other and Raveneau donated half of this year's vacation time. Maybe that figured into Whitacre calling him.

Raveneau glanced at Cody Stoltz's plate numbers. Stoltz was out of prison, had been for several years, and possibly he held a grudge against the homicide inspectors who took him down, Ted Whitacre and Charles Bates, but usually once out of prison they moved on.

'What's your old partner think?'

Whitacre tried to smile, didn't get far with it and said, 'You know how Charles is.'

Raveneau wasn't sure he did and waited.

'Charles thinks the cancer drugs are affecting my mind. My seeing Stoltz is a hallucination or something like that. He doesn't believe any of this, but I'm telling you, Ben, it was definitely Stoltz who followed me last Saturday.'

Whitacre coughed, cleared his throat, and said, 'That's not completely fair. Charles did watch

8

him last week. Stoltz lives in a guest house on his mother's property in Los Altos. He's working again. He's still a Silicon Valley whiz-kid. Charles sat on the house, followed him, and said all Stoltz did was go between work and home.'

Whitacre paused. He turned and stared.

'Stoltz wrote us all those letters. Do you remember?'

Not really, but he'd pulled the case files after Whitacre's call yesterday. In the files he found letters to Whitacre but none to his long-time partner, Charles Bates. He looked over at Whitacre and confirmed, 'Bates told you he sat on Stoltz for two days?'

'Yes.'

Bates was retired. He had his pension but was also doing work for the Alameda County DA. If he'd taken time off to put Stoltz under surveillance, he would have checked out Stoltz other ways as well.

'Other than me, you're the only one left who knows how to knock on a door, Ben. All the rest are modern guys. They'll file a report.'

'Did Bates knock on his door?'

'Charles thinks it's got to come from an active inspector to have any weight.'

Raveneau nodded. So that's what this meeting was about.

'Here's what I can do. I'm on-call this week with my new partner but I'll go see Stoltz Monday or Tuesday. You're sure he's living with his mother?'

'Two-story guest house, painted yellow with a big rose garden behind it, and thank you. I can't

9

tell you how it affects me to know Stoltz is following me and feel I can't do much about it.'

'Walk me through again what happened when you saw him.'

Whitacre seemed agitated by the request but did it anyway. He had spotted Stoltz in a parking lot outside a Belmont hardware store not far from where he lived. Stoltz was watching the front doors and Whitacre came out a side door after buying grape stakes to repair his fence. Stoltz wasn't watching the side of the building and Whitacre got close enough to confirm it was him and get his plates. After recounting this he didn't wait for any more questions.

'I've got to go. This thing is at the med center in half an hour.'

Raveneau called in the plates on the drive back to the Hall of Justice, and then phoned Bates and asked if Stoltz drove a white Lexus SUV.

'He does.'

'The plates I just ran are registered to a San Jose corporation.'

'I don't know about that, but I spent two days on him. He went back and forth from work in a white Lexus RX350. I can read you the plate numbers if you want.'

'Go ahead.'

Bates did and then asked, 'Did Ted tell you he saw Stoltz three or four other times last week, and that one of those times was when I know Stoltz was at work in Palo Alto? Did he tell you that? I'll bet he didn't. I saw Stoltz go into the building where he works an hour before Ted called me. I could see his Lexus in the lot as Ted was talking to me.'

'He talked about the hardware store. He's certain it was Stoltz.'

Bates sighed.

'Look, lately he's calling me in the middle of the night. I mean, two, three o'clock in the morning, anxious and panicked, and it isn't really about Stoltz. It's about dying. It's about needing someone to talk to. With me he's focusing on all the old cases, all the cold ones, and those we screwed up or didn't solve. He's trying to tie up the loose ends. But you saw him this morning so you probably already know what I'm going to tell you now, though you keep this to yourself. They've given him three months max. The priest at his church is counseling him, but you know Ted, he just won't accept it. He's fighting it all the way in.'

'Wouldn't you?'

'At some point, I don't know.' They were both quiet. It was easy to imagine how you would face death, another thing to do it. Bates asked, 'Are you going to knock on Stoltz's door?'

'I told Ted I would.'

'Give me a call when you're ready to and I'll come with you.'

Raveneau would never make that call. When Stoltz opened the door it would just be him standing there looking back at him, and he would make it very clear to Stoltz. He'd make it so clear Stoltz couldn't possibly misunderstand.

TWO

Raveneau was often restless when he was on-call. He ate a late dinner sitting at the bar of a pizza place close to where he lived, and then drove out Fulton Street to the ocean and up the Great Highway past the Cliff House to the Guadalcanal Memorial in the broad lot at the base of Fort Meyers.

He came here occasionally, not as much any more, but it did something for him still, and tonight he remembered the fever and fear after 9/11 and the invasion of Afghanistan when his son, his only child, Chris, eager to get to the front lines of the newly coined War on Terror, became a Marine. Chris had died eight years ago in a firefight in Fallujah, Iraq.

Raveneau parked and walked out to the shrapnel-scarred bow section of the USS *San Francisco* and the plaque reading,

This memorial to Rear Admiral Daniel Judson Callaghan, USN and his officers and men who gave their lives for our country while fighting on board the USS 'San Francisco' in the battle of Guadalcanal on the night of 12–13 November 1942 was formed

from the bridge of their ship and here mounted on the Great Circle Course to Guadalcanal
by the grateful people of San Francisco on 12
November 1950.

Raveneau's father, who was also gone, brought
him here at age five and had him run his fingers
over the names inscribed until they came to rest
on Benjamin Tomlinson. Tomlinson, like Raveneau's father, had also served on the USS *San
Francisco*, but unlike his dad, Tomlinson was
killed in the battle at Guadalcanal.

'I gave you his first name because he was the
kind of man I want you to be.'

After the service for Chris, his dad had suggested coming here, and once here, touched the
etched granite and said, 'All I can say to you is
that after this war ends and the reasons for going
into it and the men who took us there are forgotten, and they will be, remember that Chris
went there for us. Never forget that. In his heart
he was there for us. Always hold that, son. It will
help you.'

Raveneau touched the cold steel bow. Chill air
blew in off a dark ocean. Clouds at horizon left
the sky there starless. He listened to waves break
against the rocks below and then headed back to
his car. As he unlocked the door, his cell phone
rang.

The communications dispatcher's clear dispas-
sionate voice asked, 'Inspector Raveneau?'

'This is Raveneau.'

Raveneau reached for the black leather note-

13

book. He wrote the address of a building in China Basin. The dispatcher would also text it to him, but this was his drill. This was how he started a case. He confirmed now that the responding officers were holding the man who'd flagged down their patrol car on Third Street, and asked what he always did, 'How do we know it's a homicide?'

'The responding officers reported that her ankles and wrists were bound with plastic ties and that there are ligature marks at her neck. The medical examiner has asked that we call homicide. Will you be responding, Inspector?'

'I will, and I'll call Inspector la Rosa. You don't have to call her.'

He woke la Rosa who was momentarily confused, then aware that after a slow week when she'd taken teasing for being on-call at Homicide for the first time and not catching one, it was happening now. The cop in her adjusted rapidly.

'I can pick you up at the Hall or meet you at the scene,' Raveneau said, but knew already what her answer would be. Elizabeth la Rosa was ambitious, independent, and intent on making her mark. She had an angel in the brass and didn't need an aging homicide inspector on what she thought was the tail-end of a career to watch over her. La Rosa wanted to wade into the fray.

'I'll meet you there,' she said. 'I'm out the door.'

THREE

At Vice, Elizabeth la Rosa was a rock star. Successes there got her on to the homicide detail at thirty-two, which was young, unless you looked at what she did orchestrating two significant and complex drug stings that slowed a Mexican cartel's push to establish distribution in the Bay Area. She was taller than average and dark-haired, with a smile that made you want to smile as well. Raveneau liked her, but he was having trouble connecting. She was standing with the responding officers, Taylor and Garcia, when he drove up.

Nearby, though not close enough to overhear them, was the homeless man, Jimmy Deschutes, who'd flagged down the patrol car. Deschutes was thin and wiry with a piece of rope for a belt. His priors were for vagrancy, loitering, panhandling, trespassing, and urinating in public. The responding officers had searched his daypack, a pink plastic bag with a smiling Mickey Mouse.

In the pack they found clothes, small rocks, bottle glass smoothed by the ocean, a flashlight with several extra batteries, two rolls of toilet tissue, and dozens of salt, pepper, mustard, and catsup packets. Asked if he'd taken anything off

15

the victim, he said no.

The building, a two-story white-painted stucco-faced relic, had a rusted link fence surrounding and iron bars protecting the lower windows. A 'For Lease' sign hung from the second floor and had for a while. The responding officers called the real estate agency. They left a message then cut the chain that looped through a padlock holding the gate shut.

They cut it but not before Deschutes showed them how he usually got in, wriggling under a cut flap of chain link along the bay side of the fence. He claimed to sleep in the building regularly and demonstrated how easy it was to jiggle the lock on the door facing the water. Then he led them up to the second floor where her body was and pointed at the mattress, saying, 'Where I sleep most of the time.'

The second floor was brightly lit now. Paramedics brought a generator from the Bluxom Street Fire Station. CSI was on the way. So was a photographer. The medical examiner was inside. Raveneau, with la Rosa standing alongside him, questioned Taylor and Garcia, the responding officers. When they finished they walked down the street to talk privately.

To the northeast, hulking in late night city glow, was the ballpark, home of the baseball team, the Giants. A couple blocks this way was the concrete plant. Businesses in this area had a decidedly industrial tone and most closed at the end of the working day. Not much traffic through here at night, though neglected buildings had a way of getting discovered.

'Let's take Deschutes's tour,' Raveneau said. 'He's not going to contaminate anything. He's already been in there once with Taylor and Garcia.'

Deschutes wore pants with a long tear on one leg and fairly new Nike tennis shoes. The shoes might matter. Raveneau felt sure he recognized Deschutes from the Tenderloin, but could be he moved around regularly. The homeless had encampments and territories and usually didn't wander too far, but some were walkers and Deschutes looked fit enough. Down here the encampment was out along the old railroad tracks, yet Deschutes remained insistent that he often slept here in the building.

As they looked at the loose flap of chain link where Deschutes said he routinely crawled through, Raveneau said, 'We should check it out to make sure it works. Go ahead and slide under, partner. I'll hold the flap.'

She answered sharply. 'I don't need the old school jokes.'

They moved to the back door and Raveneau was last in, turning to look at the line of moonlight on the bay and the gray rocks before entering. The room was stacked with office furniture. Down a hallway a light shone at the bottom of stairs. He let Deschutes lead. Behind him, la Rosa muttered, 'He shouldn't be in here with us.'

They went upstairs to the second floor and walked past rooms that looked like former offices, though ransacked, some even missing their doors. In the room where the victim was, the

17

lights brought from the fire station not only lit the space, but were also heating it. The warming air smelled of urine, mold, and dust, the floor littered with needles and fast food wrappers. In the doorway, the medical examiner stood to one side writing notes.

Deschutes described what he'd seen and confirmed again that he didn't touch her. Raveneau took him back downstairs and la Rosa stayed with the ME. When Raveneau returned he opened his notebook. The victim appeared to be of mixed race, Asian and white, possibly in her early thirties, and was lying on her right side on a mattress on the concrete floor.

White cotton rope, what appeared to be clothesline, was pulled tightly around her neck, the knot surrounded by bruising. The rope extended three feet beyond the mattress, and looked as if it was dropped after she was strangled. Orange ties bound her wrists behind her and held her ankles pressed together. From the position of her body, and that she was dressed, he made a guess that he had no right to make yet, that she hadn't been sexually assaulted. But that didn't mean this wasn't someone's sexual fantasy.

The medical examiner had commented as they arrived that death was probably within the last two hours, so Jimmy Deschutes was either here when she died or very shortly after. Deschutes's reward for flagging down the patrol car was that he became their first suspect.

Drool ran from the victim's mouth. Where it reached the mattress, the mattress was still wet.

He followed the marks on her neck to the purple-colored silk top, the pants, belt, her shoes – the right off her foot and lying on the floor. No coat, no purse, no apparent reason to be here. He saw scuff marks where her shoes had rubbed back and forth on the mattress. He saw struggle. He guessed she was conscious and it looked from how her make-up ran that she had cried. She knew what was happening.

CSI arrived, lugged in their gear, their baggy cargo pants floating around them. The photographer showed up. La Rosa stayed near the CSI team; that's what her generation believed in.

Raveneau walked back outside, walked China Basin Street looking at vehicles, taking down plate numbers in case one of these cars was hers. He studied the handful of spectators, and saw the medical examiner come out and go to his wagon. Raveneau went over to talk to him. In San Francisco the medical examiners were all doctors. This ME would take their victim the distance, doing the autopsy and toxicology.

'Think you can get to her before Monday?'

'I can tell you tomorrow. I don't know tonight.'

After CSI had vacuumed and gone, the photographer finished, and the victim was in the thin white bag that the ME had put his seal on, Raveneau and la Rosa spent another forty minutes in the building before driving back to the Hall of Justice. They rode the elevator up and were quiet for the moment. They ate the egg croissants they picked up on the drive back and made coffee, and went downstairs to the morgue and rolled her prints, putting on latex gloves and inking her fingers with the ME looking over them.

Shortly after nine that morning they ran her prints through the local AFIS system. When they didn't get a hit, they ran them through both the state and the western states systems. Nothing there either and Raveneau suggested they return to China Basin and start knocking on doors.

But no one had a female employee who hadn't showed up this morning, nor had anyone seen anything unusual, though one owner asked, 'What's unusual any more?'

At noon, the bars and clubs began to open their service doors and they questioned the bartenders and owners they could find. No one remembered the shimmering rich purple shirt that they carried in an evidence bag.

Perhaps, Raveneau suggested to an assistant manager at the next club, one of your bartenders remembers two women, one with a purple silk shirt and high Asiatic cheekbones, black hair cut back from her face, a tiny stud in her left nostril, and her friend at the bar with her. Maybe they met a man or a couple of men and paired off.

They worked a wider radius and a bartender on Folsom Street, a young guy with spiked hair and a pallid face, saw something familiar in the shirt, but then couldn't quite find the memory.

When they returned to Homicide they put together a press release without a photo but with a description of the victim and her clothing. La Rosa walked it over to the PIO, the Public Information Officer, so they wouldn't miss the news cycle.

Late in the afternoon Raveneau returned to the building. He might find something. He might not. He didn't expect to. But it had become his habit to return alone when the scene was quiet. Over the years he had even come to the irrational belief that the spirits of the dead linger a short while.

He felt sorrow as he walked through the building trying to see why she was here. If she was local and there was family or others who had cared for her, then there was a good chance they'd hear from someone soon. Bringing her killer to justice was the responsibility he and la Rosa carried. For anyone who had loved her, they could do little more. And a murder conviction seldom brought closure. Closure was a well-meaning idea capitalized on by radio self-help hosts and talk-show psychologists promoting books. The only true way to free your heart from a terrible act was forgiveness, and forgiveness was one of the most difficult things for a human being. It got bandied about as if common, but it wasn't. Forgiveness was a kind of transcendence, beyond justice and maybe beyond most all of us.

FOUR

Toward dusk, as Raveneau returned to the homicide office, Cody Stoltz joked with the staff at a Starbucks in Palo Alto as he waited for his macchiato. Then on his way to a table he stopped briefly to check in with a middle-aged woman who'd been laid off and was looking for a job. He met her last time he was here. Same as today, she'd had her laptop open and was working on her resume. She seemed grateful that he took the time to say hello.

When he sat down it was at a corner table. He pulled out his laptop and used Google Earth to find Whitacre's house. He wasn't necessarily ever going to go anywhere with it, but it gave him pleasure to see Whitacre's dumpy little stucco box with its faux Spanish look. Whitacre's neighborhood wasn't far from the freeway, so maybe the exhaust had caused Whitacre's cancer. He hoped so. The lawn was dry, shrubs ratty, the pine tree sickly and out of place. Whitacre's old American relic of a car sat in the driveway.

Past the car was a fence. On a long bike ride he once checked out the fence and gate. The fence was redwood, silver-gray with age. A couple of flagstones led from the white concrete of the driveway to the gate. Through the gate was a door to the kitchen. It was a nowhere house on a nowhere block in the bleak life Whitacre lived. But none of that changed what Whitacre had done.

FIVE

When the homicide detail moved from Room 450 on the fourth floor to Room 561 on the fifth floor, the difference was more than just moving up a floor in the gray monolith of the Hall of Justice. In the old office, the window behind Raveneau's desk looked northeast over the roof of the morgue, past the county jail, better known as the glass palace, and into the city. Tall cabinets holding case files and nicknamed 'the towers' had loomed over the cramped quarters, but up here the homicide inspectors had a large open room and a row of windows looking southeast toward China Basin. They had a row of computers and new high-tech equipment.

Raveneau's desk backed up to la Rosa's. Nearby was a coat stand, a concept that would have been comic in the closed quarters of the former office. From his desk he watched the dark water of the bay lighten with dawn and the outline of the hills across the bay haloed in crimson light as the sun rose. The door to the homicide office opened and Lieutenant Becker waved at him. Raveneau stood to go talk to him before Becker got too busy.

'Do you remember a shoot-out between two yuppies in the parking lot of an apartment

24

complex out near Golden Gate Park in 2000?'

Raveneau paused to give Becker a chance to remember the case before continuing.

'They were friends, Cody Stoltz and John Reinert. The shooting was after an argument about John Reinert's wife, Erin. Stoltz had an affair with her that Reinert found out about. That led to a confrontation in a parking lot below the Reinerts' apartment and then a shooting that Erin Reinert witnessed from the apartment's kitchen window. She disappeared; moved away somewhere after Stoltz took a plea deal. He did five for voluntary manslaughter.'

'The letter writer?'

Raveneau nodded.

'What about him?'

'Ted Whitacre thinks Stoltz is following him and after revenge. I saw him yesterday morning. He asked me to knock on Stoltz's door and let him know we know he's been tailing Whitacre.'

'That's not how we do it.'

'Maybe not, but I'm going to let him know Whitacre saw him.'

Becker said nothing but shook his head.

'What do you remember about the Reinert killing? I'm looking for what's not in the file.'

Raveneau knew Becker wouldn't really have any problem with him visiting Stoltz. He wasn't going to endorse it, but underneath he was still one of them. Becker knew what a gentle reminder a homicide inspector's knock on the door could be for a guy who'd already done time for murder. Cloud computing or whatever it was he was working on now would look a lot better to

Stoltz after a conversation.

Becker answered, 'I was there when Bates and Whitacre brought Stoltz in. Stoltz was so shocked at what he'd done that in his head I think he tried to turn it into an accidental shooting. He came up with a story of how he wasn't the shooter at all. He needed to transfer it to someone else and created a fictional mugger.'

'I read the interview notes on the mugger. Were you there? Did you listen in?'

'Yeah, I did.'

'Tell me about the mugger.'

'Stoltz claimed that in the middle of his confrontation with Reinert a man with a gun showed up and robbed them. Backed them up at gunpoint and got into Stoltz's glove compartment where he found Stoltz's gun. He took their wallets and then shot John Reinert with Stoltz's gun instead of his own when Reinert tried to prevent him from getting away. Then dropped Stoltz's gun and ran with Stoltz chasing him.'

'Chased him instead of helping Reinert?'

The lieutenant stared at him and asked, 'What are we doing here? You read the file so you know this already.'

'What was he like?'

'Nervous but trying to pull it off. He claimed he chased the mugger because he knew instantly that Reinert was dead.'

'How did he know?'

Becker shrugged. 'He just knew. Maybe he sensed it because he's so bright.'

'You remember that?'

Becker nodded and Raveneau thought about Reinert dying. It wasn't instant. It took him ten to fifteen minutes more to die. A patrol unit picked up Stoltz two miles away walking down Divisadero Street.

'What did you think of the case Whitacre and Bates made?'

'It was solid. They got the right man. Where are you on this China Basin murder?'

'Nowhere yet.'

He left Becker and called the realtor who was trying to lease the building where their China Basin victim died. Yesterday, the realtor was co-operative. This morning he sounded self important as he launched into the city supervisors and the Port Authority, and how he wished he'd never left LA where they knew how to do business. When he finished, Raveneau offered, 'Maybe you should move back there.'

'Believe me, Inspector, I'm thinking about it. About your other questions, let me talk to my attorney and get back to you on who I've showed the building to. I'm not sure it's ethical to provide a list. Some of these clients aren't going to like a call from the police, let alone a homicide detective. You have to understand that if a prostitute breaks into the building at night there's not much we can do. We've got a ten foot fence up with razor wire on top and "No Trespassing" signs posted everywhere.'

Raveneau learned now what he'd suspected last night, that the 'For Lease' sign was up only to demonstrate to the Port Authority and the city that the owners were serious about utilizing the property. That it had no power and smelled of rat droppings and human urine, and that the homeless, runaways, and drug users treated it as a hostel, or that prostitutes in the area were familiar with the building but avoided it because it wasn't clean enough, that didn't matter. The investors were playing a longer game that required a certain kind of negotiation with the Port Authority.

Raveneau was still on the phone with the realtor when Lieutenant Becker came to get him.

'You've got a walk-in. There's a man named Carl Heilbron in the second interview room. He says he's here to see you and la Rosa about your China Basin victim. He claims to have information and knows you and la Rosa are assigned the case.'

'When did he get here?'

'Five minutes ago.'

Raveneau followed Becker to the interview room where they'd parked the guy. He looked like he was in his early thirties with long pencil-thin sideburns and short hair. Black shirt, canvas pants, lime-green tennis shoes, an ornate red tattoo on his right forearm, dressed like an artist but doing auto body work. A Diet Coke sat on the table in front of him and he stared at his right hand resting on the table near the Coke as if it was a phone and he was waiting for it to ring. Physical energy and nervousness emanated from him. He glanced up at the glass several times and brought the hand on the table down to his knee as his knee jiggled, then looked abruptly up at the glass again and smiled, as if spotting Raveneau and Becker standing there.

'Looks like a nice normal guy,' Becker said. 'Let's keep him in there while I find la Rosa.'

SIX

Raveneau and la Rosa studied Carl Heilbron through the one-way glass and Raveneau made sure the audio and video feeds were working before they went in. Heilbron focused immediately on la Rosa, showing her a face that was pleasant and attentive as he said, 'I killed her.'

Raveneau hadn't even sat down yet. He slid a chair out and asked, 'Who did you kill?'

'The one in the building in China Basin and I don't know her name. I never asked her name. I picked her up on Eddy Street. She was there with a couple of other whores. I offered her forty bucks, and after she got in the van I told her we were going to a building I know and that I wanted special sex. But she had a big problem with that. I freaked her out.'

'What's special sex?' la Rosa asked softly.

'Come on, Elizabeth, I know you know what I mean.'

'Inspector la Rosa,' she said, 'and I don't know what you mean. I need you to explain to me.'

It meant binding her wrists and ankles and slipping a piece of wire, not rope, around her neck. He told them he had a key to the padlock at the front gate but evaded telling them how he got the key. Kept answering, 'It's just a common

Master Lock.' He claimed he used the building another time with a young girl, a runaway he'd picked up, and gotten drunk before having sex with her. He talked about driving through the city at night. He liked to drive around at night. He talked about his job at Boyle's Auto Body Shop and then touched the side of his neck and turned to Raveneau.

'Would you mind getting me another Coke?'

Raveneau got him the Coke. When he returned Heilbron had shifted slightly in his chair so he faced la Rosa more directly. He licked his lower lip. He frowned as he explained.

'I told her I was going to cut off her wind for a little while, then release the wire again, but she didn't want to be unconscious. She got scared.'

'When you started choking her?' la Rosa asked, and Raveneau tried to catch her eye, tried to signal, just let him talk.

'Yeah, the wire cut into her neck.' He touched his neck to show where. 'She moved around too much and started crying, and I didn't want her to cry. I didn't go there with her so she could start crying, so I tried to calm her down. I thought if she was unconscious for a little longer than usual she'd calm down.'

'What do you mean more than usual?' la Rosa asked, and Heilbron took a drink of Coke. 'You wanted to relax her?'

'Yes.'

'So what did you do?'

'I pulled the wire tight until she stopped moving.'

'When she stopped moving did you loosen it?'

31

'No, I just kind of watched her.'

'Weren't you worried you would kill her?'

'Not so much.'

'Did you have sex with her?'

'No, she was dead by then.'

'You knew she was dead?'

'Yes.'

'Did you feel for a pulse?'

'No.'

Heilbron turned to Raveneau.

'I threw everything in the bay.'

'Show us where,' Raveneau answered.

But Heilbron had another story to tell them first. He focused on la Rosa again, telling her about a woman he raped in San Jose. Neither Raveneau nor la Rosa revealed that they already knew San Jose detectives had questioned him about a rape two years ago. That came up when they ran his name before walking in to talk to him.

'She had a flat tire. I helped her fix it. That was on a Sunday. She was back in these hills.'

At some point soon they'd have to read him his rights, Mirandize him, and with that he could request a lawyer. Raveneau liked to get the lawyer question out early so a defense lawyer couldn't claim later his client hadn't realized he was entitled to one. He studied Heilbron with a sense that something was off about his story, and Heilbron seemed to pick up on that, taking the conversation back to China Basin, telling them more about the wire around her neck – eye hook on one end of the wire so he could slide the other end through, pull it tight and release it easily.

They Mirandized him and Heilbron waved off having a lawyer. On the drive to China Basin he said he'd bought both the wire and the eye hook he had soldered on to it at Discount Builders on Mission Street. In China Basin he led them upstairs but to the wrong room. Maybe that was because the mattress wasn't there any more. He got agitated. He wanted to leave the building and showed them where he had thrown her purse, phone, and 'other things' into the water.

Raveneau pulled a can of spray paint from the trunk of his car and marked a chunk of broken concrete for divers. Calling the divers in was problematic because now they were very skeptical about Heilbron's account. His description of the victim was off. He dodged details, and on the ride back to the Hall he went dark on them. He went quiet.

But he did sign a confession and they booked him into jail. Raveneau figured they'd hold him all weekend and maybe as long as Tuesday afternoon, depending on what happened after San Jose detectives questioned him. Before they left him, Heilbron turned to la Rosa. 'I read that article about you moving to Homicide.'

Raveneau knew there'd been some puff piece when la Rosa moved over from Vice. La Rosa didn't acknowledge the comment. They left Heilbron with the jailers and upstairs learned that the San Jose police tracked him through one fingerprint left on the rim of a wheel. They were ready eighteen months ago to charge him with the rape of a woman who got a flat returning from a party late at night. He'd stopped and offered to help, assuring the woman that he worked in an auto shop, and then raped her in the back of the vehicle.

All they needed were DNA results from the victim's swab, but somewhere along the way the swab samples taken the night of the rape got lost, and without DNA the district attorney's office didn't want any part of it, so the case went into limbo. A San Jose detective told la Rosa that the victim would no longer take their calls.

When la Rosa got off the phone with San Jose they drove down to meet the divers. Raveneau took his laptop. He filled out the search warrant application for Heilbron's house as they waited and also called the Southern precinct to try to reach the responding officers, Garcia and Taylor, to question them about what spectators they might have talked to. He reached the younger officer, the tow-headed blond, Taylor, who after some coaxing admitted he'd talked to a couple of spectators. Said it was his first murder and he was sorry.

Then, as they were still waiting and walked down the street to get coffee, la Rosa turned and said, 'I have to tell you something about me that happened right at the end of my senior year in high school. I try not to let it, but sometimes it still affects me. It was in late May at the start of the Memorial Day weekend. The weather had turned warm and we had finals ahead of us, but we knew we were done, so the parties were getting a little wild. I had just turned eighteen and there was this guy I'd always had a crush on. I was drunk, so was he, but I wasn't ready to have sex with him. He held me down and raped me. Until you know that feeling of powerlessness and violation, you can't know what rape is.

'The next day I went by his house and when he opened the door I broke his nose with a piece of pipe. I heard he made up a story about falling off his mountain bike and he was such a dipshit he probably forgot about it all by the end of the summer. But me, I'm still angry. If he crossed the street in front of me, I'd run him over.'

'Maybe you should talk to somebody.'

'Yeah, I tried that. I'd rather kill him.'

'Great.'

In China Basin, less than half a mile from the building, Rescue One divers set up to search a grid pattern. Four divers went into the water, their lights glowing from fifteen feet down where they found a black plastic purse that long ago had filled with bay mud. They searched for an hour and a half and didn't find any of the things Heilbron described.

The on-call judge barely looked at the search warrant before signing it. They drove from his house to Heilbron's. They pulled on latex gloves and Raveneau unlocked the front door with the key Heilbron had given them. He turned on a light. Before they stepped over the threshold, la Rosa asked, 'Why did he tell us about the rape?'

'Because it proves he could do the China Basin killing, that he's got the stuff. Or maybe he's testing himself and wants to see what it feels like to take ownership for a killing. I think he knows we'll dead-end and he'll walk.'

'But, why do it? He's going to lose his job. You

know they'll fire him. What's he going to do next?'

'That may be something to worry about. He may have built up to this point and he's ready to move forward.'

'That's what I'm worried about, too.'

Raveneau pointed at the TV. 'Let's turn it on and see if they included our victim on the evening news. I didn't see anything last night. I'll check the refrigerator to see if there's any beer.'

'You don't mean that, do you?'

No, he didn't mean it about the beer, and they'd go methodically room to room. But he was serious about the TV. He found the remote and turned it on.

SEVEN

Raveneau surfed through the local news stations and then left the TV on Channel 4. Near an armchair facing the TV, six porno magazines were stacked under a copy of *Sports Illustrated*. Three of the magazines featured women on women.

'Bed is a like a rat's nest,' la Rosa called. 'Come look at this.'

When he did, Raveneau saw only the rumpled sheets of a man living alone. The oddest thing was how clean the bathroom was. In his medicine cabinet was a prescription for antidepressants. He took a photo of the prescription label and they worked their way slowly through the bedroom again.

When a TV station anchor announced a murder in China Basin they moved out to listen.

'Police are seeking help identifying the body of a woman found in China Basin Wednesday night...'

Pretty good coverage, thirty-five, maybe forty seconds, more than he'd hoped for. Raveneau clicked to Channel 5, listened to part of a report of a three-alarm fire underway in the Richmond, and then started in on a hall closet. They didn't find anything in Heilbron's house, but his van looked promising. The crime lab would go

37

through it on Monday. La Rosa wrote out a receipt for the address book and computer they bagged to take with them. She left the receipt in the kitchen on an ancient Formica counter trimmed in chrome. On the ride back she seemed frustrated.

Raveneau pulled in behind her car outside the Hall of Injustice, as his defense lawyer friends were so fond of saying. He got out as she did.

'Where are you going?' la Rosa asked. 'I thought you were going home.'

'I'm going upstairs for a few minutes first.'

'Is that so you can be the last to leave?'

He didn't pick up on her seriousness and said, 'Yeah, I've always got to be the one to turn the lights out.'

'Not with me.'

'Come, again?'

'I said, not with me. That might have been your style with former partners, but that's not the way it's going down with us. You're not going to paint me as always first out the door.'

This really sideswiped him and he heard his voice rising as he answered, 'Look, I'll leave when I'm ready. I don't need you to tell me when.'

He walked away angry, and upstairs in the office tried to push it aside and studied a sketch of the China Basin crime scene CSI had dropped off. La Rosa's comment surprised him enough to make him lose focus. He was ready to call it a night, ready to leave when water started dripping on to one of the desks nearby. That would be the prisoners on the sixth floor plugging up the toilets.

He phoned upstairs. He found a wastebasket to catch the water and on the way out he took a seat at one of the computers up front and replayed the last part of the interview with Heilbron. He did one final check of his messages before turning out the lights.

There was one new message and he thought it might be la Rosa. But it wasn't. The message began with traffic noise and what sounded like a large truck downshifting on a freeway. A muffled voice, as though speaking with the phone held at a distance, said quietly, 'So you found her.'

Raveneau sat at his desk and listened to it half a dozen times. 'So you found her.' He listened to it again from his car before driving away from the Hall. He swallowed his pride and called la Rosa, but she didn't pick up. It went to voice mail.

EIGHT

La Rosa was at dinner with Deputy-chief Edith Grainer at an Italian place near Grainer's house, so she didn't take Raveneau's call. Part of her irritation with Raveneau going back up to the office tonight was that she was meeting her mentor and didn't want to tell him. And she didn't like keeping secrets, but that's the way Grainer had steered her from the start, saying that if word got out about their friendship, it would give the appearance she was playing favorites. She could call Raveneau back on the way home.

There'd been a period there when la Rosa had wondered if Grainer was hitting on her, but fortunately nothing like that had happened and Grainer's career advice had been sound. She also knew Grainer was in the background when her name had come up on a list of women eligible to make the bump to Homicide.

'Would you like a drink, Elizabeth?' Grainer asked as the waiter returned. Grainer had a vodka martini and preferred not to drink alone. 'I know your regulation about being on-call, but I think you can have one drink with me tonight.'

La Rosa knew Grainer would have a single drink before and then one glass of wine with dinner.

'Sure, I'll have a drink.'

La Rosa felt tired. She rested her elbows on the blue and white checkered tablecloth and looked around. Total retro as a restaurant and she didn't really feel like doing this tonight. She wanted to go home, shower, and think about the China Basin case.

Deputy-chief Grainer's father had been a small-town cop and when they first met la Rosa had told her about her grandfather, a county deputy in Minnesota. They'd found common ground through the memories of the two men. Both had liked to drink after their shifts and la Rosa thought this cocktail together before dinner was Grainer's way of incorporating that.

Grainer kept her brown hair cut short and neat, as though it needed to be that way to avoid interfering with her work. She had a pleasant if unmemorable face and an iron work ethic. She also had a generally empathetic view of the public's complaints about the police department, a view la Rosa didn't particularly agree with, though she'd never said so. One of Grainer's favorite refrains was, we should listen more to what the public is saying, and sometimes she'd cite the example of Chief Gains, the chief of police at the start of her career. Gains had black and white patrol cars repainted blue and re-named 'Police Services'. This was stuff that la Rosa found herself nodding in agreement to but not really agreeing with, and that was a part of herself she didn't like, the same part that showed itself now as she ordered a vodka martini.

'Maybe we should order dinner now,' Grainer

said. 'I have a very busy schedule tomorrow. I'll go first to give you a moment.'

La Rosa glanced at the menu and the phrase 'old school' came to mind for the second time in twenty-four hours. She heard Grainer order 'An iceberg salad with bleu cheese dressing, chicken cacciatore, and garlic bread for the table.' She looked from the waiter to la Rosa and asked, 'Elizabeth, should we have a glass of wine each? Or half a glass for you?'

'Half a glass is plenty for me.'

La Rosa ordered the veal and a salad that she knew would come drenched with dressing. The veal would come with a quart of some rich sauce she didn't need. But who cares about food? That's not why they were here. Her drink came and the chef sent complimentary plates with two raviolis each. She ate both though they were cold and doughy. She sipped the vodka and it hit her right away.

'So how is it going with him?' Grainer asked.

'It's going fine.'

'Was today productive?'

No, a lot of it felt like a waste of time, especially wandering through China Basin knocking on doors. It made no sense. She thought of the construction workers along China Basin Street studying her breasts and Raveneau bantering with them. None of that advanced the investigation and she didn't like it that he'd turned the TV on at Heilbron's house, or that he'd gone back upstairs tonight. Earlier today she'd watched him text messaging back and forth and when she'd gotten tired of waiting on him, asked who he was messaging so urgently. His answer was he'd learned to text drug dealers: 'I'm trying to get this one to come in and talk to us about a drive-by murder he witnessed.'

'Elizabeth?' Grainer asked.

'I'm sorry, chief, it was just a lot today. We caught this case after midnight last night.'

'That's why it's important to talk while it's still fresh. I guess our larger conversation is about the homicide detail, and whether our inspector's methods are modern enough. What are your first impressions of Inspector Raveneau's investigative techniques?'

'There are things I have problems with but I don't know if that's just my inexperience.'

'You know, this is an important moment because your initial observations are much less likely to be clouded by sentiment and that's what I'm interested in. Others are too. There's a lot of concern about the low solve rate, in particular with respect to gang slayings. There's a feeling that not only does that part of the community not trust us, but that we're out of touch with the people living there.'

You've got that right, she thought, and then wondered when Grainer had last been around gangbangers. She thought of Raveneau text messaging the dealer, going back and forth with him, Raveneau with his salt and pepper hair, and no real respect for racial differences. What did he say to her today? That he didn't believe in race, that it didn't matter any more, especially not on the homicide detail. She considered telling that to Grainer, but didn't because she knew

Grainer would hear it differently than Raveneau meant it. La Rosa became aware now that Grainer was talking.

'It's generally understood that inspectors view themselves as untouchable, and in fact, though they may never rise any higher, they are by and large left alone. But there's a perfect storm of political pressures building and I don't know this, but I believe something may happen that hasn't in a very long time. I'm not the only one who views you as a rising star. You have very modern training and you made a point of getting it on your own. We need more like you and with your initiative. You know enough about trace evidence to walk down the hall and work with CSI or out at Hunter's Point in that Quonset hut, though neither of those would be a fit for you. Better that you make your mark at Homicide before moving up. Would you say that your new partner respects the advances in science?'

'Yes, but it can take a long time to get DNA results.'

'That sounds like an excuse, Elizabeth.'

It was more like reality but la Rosa took another sip instead of pointing that out. The vodka was hammering her but she could easily drink another one. She needed a good sleep tonight and hoped the public came through with a tip on their Jane Doe.

'He feels he has to rely on people skills. When we didn't get a hit off AFIS or the western states system this morning, he said 'We're taking the case to the people.''

'Cute.'

44

'It's worked for him for a long time.'

'And he was the top inspector for a long time, but the city has changed. It changes every day. It changes underneath us.'

'He talks about the change.'

'What's he said?'

'That there are twenty-eight ethnicities now but the act of murder hasn't changed.'

Grainer shook her head. 'I don't know what that means.'

'I don't either.'

'I'm relieved to hear that.'

If you weren't loyal to your partner what were you worth? She held Grainer's gaze as she thought that.

'What is this China Basin killing?'

'A homeless individual stopped a patrol car and reported the body of a woman in a room in an unoccupied building for sale. One of the problems I have is he brought this homeless individual back inside to view the body with us.'

'I hope you're joking.'

She wasn't and vodka fueled her indignation.

'This means if any DNA of his is found in the area around her body or on her body, other than from a sexual assault, then a good defense attorney will argue it happened when we brought him back in.'

'Not just a good defense attorney, Elizabeth, any defense attorney. How did he justify doing that?'

'The same homeless individual had led the responding officers in earlier.'

'Had he?'

'Yes, but they didn't let him re-enter the room with the body.'

'But your new partner did?'

'Yes.'

'That's a fairly significant procedural error.'

'I don't know if it's an error or not, or whether he sees things I don't, but it's an example of where I would treat the trace evidence differently.'

'Would you call him willfully ignorant of the advances in science?'

The waiter brought the salads and she pictured Raveneau's face, his eyes as he looked at her.

'He never seems unaware.'

'Then how about careless about procedures and cynical about the investigation's ultimate results?'

'No, that's not him at all. He cares quite a lot.'

'Elizabeth, I can't keep up with you. You're jumping all over the map. Now you sound like you're defending him.'

'He loves the work.' She thought of him going back upstairs tonight and added, 'It's his life.'

'Yes, and in his world he's something of a legend, but he's also emblematic of a problem that's grown in recent years.' She lowered her voice. 'No one is targeting Inspector Raveneau, and it's certainly not limited to him, but good questions are being asked about why we're failing. I, for one, believe we aren't keeping pace with the shift in sensitivities within the micro-environments in the city. What do you think about that?'

She thought it was a bunch of fucking gobbledegook, but said, 'There may be a real truth there, but I'm too new to say.'

'I don't mean to put you in the position of attacking your partner. If I do that, you stop me. That's an order. But the homicide detail is seeing a lot of scrutiny and may need a kind of catharsis.'

La Rosa bit into a piece of garlic bread and nodded. The chief smiled brightly and waved her hand at the room.

'This is what I call authentic,' she said. 'I just love Italian food.'

La Rosa looked around the room. She didn't think it was authentic. She didn't agree at all, but smiled and said, 'Yes, it's wonderful.'

NINE

Raveneau knew the muffled voice might be no more than someone with a grudge against police who was hovering at the edge of a homicide investigation, hoping to screw with them. It happens. But the call had unsettled him and he felt tired and on edge as he drove home. He should have stopped at a grocery store, but didn't. He rode the service elevator to the second floor and climbed the narrow flight of wooden stairs up to the rooftop apartment.

A clean rain-laden wind blew in off the ocean and he left the slider open as he tried to figure out what to eat. Leftover pasta looked like glue, but there wasn't much else. He heated a little olive oil in a sauté pan, slid the pasta in, and was adjusting the burner down as the phone rang. Celeste.

'Hey,' he said.

'Hey, yourself, I'm in San Francisco. I did a wine thing today. What are you doing right now?'

Celeste was a wine broker he'd started going out with about a month ago. He was starting to get the picture about how she organized tastings and sold wine, and in truth, he probably knew more about her job than her. But they were easy about all that and it was good to hear her voice tonight.

'I'm heating up some leftover pasta and it's going to be terrible. Come on over and I'll split it with you. Where are you?'

'On the Embarcadero, but if you just got home you must be exhausted.'

'No, I'm good.'

She called again as she arrived and Raveneau unlocked the gate so she could park next to his unmarked cruiser. That he lived on top of a warehouse with a coffee house on the floor below in the corner of the building was fun to her, and for Raveneau living up here was fine for the moment. He kept an eye on the building for the owner and liked the big roof and the view from the brick parapet. A three foot wide wooden walkway ran from the stairway door to a redwood deck off the apartment.

Raveneau barbecued on the deck regularly. His cop friends called it the rooftop bar and likened the walkway to something you'd see in the Everglades for viewing alligators, and the tar and gravel roof in the September heat to the La Brea tar pits. He laughed along with them, but he wasn't looking to buy another house. He sold his house after Chris was killed, and then the market fell and no one really knew where it was all going to end.

And he didn't know any more where he stood on the homicide detail. He was basically a mostly white older guy on a squad that was trying to become more diverse to better reflect the city. If not for his solve rate he likely would have been bumped out already. A month ago he was approached about partial retirement or early retirement, neither of which he had any interest in, both of which were good reasons not to buy another house.

Celeste was forty-four and never married. She lived with a boyfriend for fifteen years and then the boyfriend left her and married someone else within three months. She drove a Miata with a license plate that read 'No Kids', though when she talked about kids she was wistful and close to sad. She was cheerful tonight though and pulled a bottle of Cristal champagne out of her bag saying, 'Perks.'

Raveneau popped the cork and poured them each a glass. She was a sweet, graceful, hopeful human being, and when he was with her he forgot his own loneliness even as he was seeing it in her. He was very glad she'd called. He watched her step out on the deck and lean to smell the leaves of the potted lemon trees that ringed it.

'I'm going to grill cheese sandwiches,' he said. 'This pasta isn't going to work.'

He scraped it into the garbage as Celeste came back inside and checked out the videos near his TV.

'Are any of these any good?'

'They're from crime scenes. I bring them home to watch and try to figure out what I've missed.'

'But not tonight?'

'Definitely not tonight.'

He refilled her glass but not his own. When the

sandwiches were ready they ate, and Raveneau realized what was causing her nervousness after they were sitting near each other on the couch and the sandwich plates were back in the kitchen. She turned toward him as the first rain pattered on to the deck boards and blew against the slider.

'Rain,' she said, her mouth just inches from his, and then it just kind of unfolded and he tasted the cold, sweet champagne on her lips and tongue. They moved into the bedroom while in the front room Gillian Welch sang a faraway song about a hickory wind. The feeling of being with a woman again almost overwhelmed him. It's funny how you think you know something so well and all the while, every day, you're forgetting what it was.

TEN

It rained steadily during the night and left the asphalt roofing and wooden deck dark-colored, and the leaves of the lemons clean, shiny, and wet in the dawn. Celeste was asleep when Raveneau made coffee and stood at the brick parapet looking out at the city, thinking about where he and la Rosa were at with the China Basin killing.

As the sun rose he made more coffee and read back through the case notes, then heard Celeste moving around. When she walked out she was dressed and already late to a Saturday appointment at a winery in Santa Cruz.

She had just driven away when Lieutenant Becker called, his voice weighed by the message.

'Ted Whitacre is dead. A caretaker found him this morning. The Burlingame police are there and want to call it suicide. I need you to go there, Ben, and represent us. Tell them this is a joint investigation. Make that clear to the detective in charge. His name is Ed Choy. I'll text you his number. Call him on your way down. I'm doing the same with the chief there in Burlingame.'

'Have you called Charles Bates?'

'He's on his way.'

When Raveneau arrived, Whitacre's body was

52

already gone and the Burlingame detective, Ed Choy, was sitting at Whitacre's kitchen table, typing on a laptop. As Choy started to explain, Raveneau realized Burlingame must have waited several hours before calling them.

'The caretaker found him lying on his back in bed with a gunshot wound to the head. She didn't touch anything and called us from her cell phone. We found a gun registered to him lying on the bed and recovered a bullet buried in the headboard. We'll see if we get a match. Were you aware he was terminally ill with cancer?'

Raveneau stared at Choy. He should have called them as soon as he knew Whitacre was on the SF homicide detail. Raveneau looked back at the headboard spattered with blood and fragments of brain. Bed was stripped, sheets taken as evidence.

'His doctor gave him very bad news Wednesday.'

'Did you call the doctor before you called us?'

This time Choy was the one who didn't answer and Raveneau walked outside. He walked the house exterior looking for signs of forced entry and didn't see any. Choy made an assumption about suicide early on after interviewing the caretaker and talking to Whitacre's doctor, so didn't dust anything in the room before removing the body. Basically, he decided it was a suicide, took some photos, and cleaned up.

'It's not my first suicide,' Choy said.

'I'm sure it's not. You have photos, right?'

'I'll show you.'

In the kitchen Choy pulled down the shades

then projected photos on to Whitacre's white-painted kitchen wall. Whitacre was on his back, mouth open, and gun close to his left hand.

'I think he reached into the nightstand drawer with his left hand, pulled out the gun, and then put it in his mouth,' Choy said, and then conducted a PowerPoint slideshow.

'Autopsy is next week, Tuesday or Wednesday. What do you see?'

'Did you find a suicide note?'

'No note, and I understand he was your colleague, but Inspector Whitacre killed himself. His hope was gone. He saw no other choices.' Choy gestured toward the hallway and bedroom. 'He had no one to stop him.'

'I'd like to get on his computer. I want to see if he put his things in order, paid his bills, or whether he left that for his younger sister in Florida.'

Which was something Whitacre wouldn't do. He was very protective of her.

It took an hour to go through the computer files and Bates arrived as Raveneau turned from the screen. Bates was in tears, unashamed to show what he felt. Raveneau walked out to Whitacre's car with him.

'I'm going to give the detective here what I have on Cody Stoltz and we're going to approach this as a joint investigation. But this Choy already settled on suicide. He's seen other suicides. He's a suicide expert.'

Bates didn't seem to hear. He exhaled hard and said, 'God help me if it was Stoltz. I blew off everything Ted said about him. Tell me he just killed himself because he knew it was over. Tell me that.'

It took Raveneau a moment to get what Bates was saying.

'You didn't watch Stoltz those two days?'

Bates shook his head.

'So you lied to Ted, and to me?'

Bates nodded and then turned away.

ELEVEN

From a second floor window of the guest house Stoltz watched the car sweep beneath the big oaks on the long curved drive in front of his mother's house. The knock on his door came less than ten minutes later, but by then he'd turned the music on and was out back starting the gas grill. Beer iced in a galvanized tub on the garden terrace. A second knock now and it brought back a lot of bad stuff and made him angry. He didn't want to deal with this. Before answering the door he pulled sausages from the refrigerator and laid them carefully on the counter.

When he opened the door a San Francisco homicide inspector named Benjamin Raveneau introduced himself and in that cop way, said, 'I'd like to talk with you.'

Fuck you, Stoltz thought, and said, 'Sure.'

Raveneau handed him a card and without looking at the card, Stoltz took in the man. Neither tall nor short, but at least six feet and unconcerned about his size, no gym muscles, no weight lifting bullshit, nothing faked, but obviously comfortable and quick. His stance wasn't confrontational, but there he was, a square-shouldered presence, shoulders that probably

56

had been in his family thousands of years, eyes neither afraid nor flat, but light-hearted and deadly. This guy was the real deal.

'Thought you were a salesman,' Stoltz said. 'You look like a salesman who works in my office and I'm not kidding, you look exactly like him. Do you have a brother in sales?'

'I'm here to talk with you about two San Francisco homicide inspectors, Ted Whitacre and Charles Bates. Do you remember them?'

'Remember them? You're joking, right?'

'When is the last time you saw either one of them?'

'When I saw your car I knew you were police and I was wondering why you were here. I couldn't think of a reason.'

'I'm asking because Inspector Whitacre was shot and killed last night and we're going to talk to anyone who has ever threatened him. You're on that list.'

Stoltz was surprised and said, 'Let me get this straight. He was killed last night and you're here to question me today?'

'Is it OK if I come in?'

'No, because I've got friends coming over to watch the Stanford game and these are people I've invited. It's kind of a party and they're going to be here soon.'

Stoltz didn't move to let Raveneau in. He felt flustered.

'Look, I was very angry when I went to prison, but that's a long time ago. I got over it. You've got to understand I lost a lot of my future to the incompetence of Bates and Whitacre. That was very hard to swallow at the time.'

'OK, you've got friends coming over so let's make this easy. Where were you last night?'

'I was in Carmel and I've got receipts. Do you want me to prove it?'

'You do that and I'll leave.'

'Wait here and I'll make copies of the hotel and restaurant bills.'

Stoltz was angry and scared as he went upstairs. He used the printer to make copies of his receipts and handed those to Raveneau.

'When did you drive to Carmel?'

'Yesterday afternoon. I took a ride with some cycling friends and then drove down. I think it was around four in the afternoon.'

'Can we verify that with your riding friends?'

'No, because that's my personal life and you guys don't get to fuck that up twice. What's the old saying, first time shame on you, second time shame on me. You don't get to mess with my life twice. I don't want my friends looking at me sideways because some half-ass homicide inspector can't even figure out how one of their own was killed.'

'What time did you get to Carmel?'

'Don't remember. Check with the hotel on that. I went there first.'

'Did you stop anywhere on the way down?'

'Not that comes to mind right now.'

Raveneau scrutinized the receipt showing Stoltz's hotel checkout time this morning. 7:00.

'On the way back, did you stop anywhere?'

'I bought gas but there's no receipt for it. I paid cash.'

'Where did you buy gas?'

'At a Shell station or maybe it was a Chevron. I don't remember.'

'Where?'

'Monterey or Sand City, someplace along the way.'

'In the Lexus out front?'

'Yes, and it was a Chevron. We're almost done here, Inspector.'

'Did your hotel room have a view looking out over the ocean?'

'Come, again?'

'I've stayed there before. I'm asking if you had an ocean view.'

'You know what, I didn't pay any attention and I probably drank too much at dinner.'

Inspector Raveneau made a show of pulling a piece of paper out of his coat now. He handed it over and asked, 'Do you recognize these license plate numbers?'

Stoltz stared at the numbers before saying, 'Those are mine.'

Stoltz felt his face flush. The inspector was an inch or two taller than him but looked at him almost eye to eye. This guy was much different than Bates or Whitacre.

Gravel crunched as a car drove up.

'My guests are arriving,' Stoltz said, and waved to his friends getting out of their cars now. 'Wait here, Inspector, I've got something for you.'

He found his wallet and then the card, and brought it out to Raveneau. 'If you have any more questions call this number.' The card read

Crofton, Jacobs, & Peters LLC. 'Ask for Lindsay Crofton. She's my lawyer. But by all means call me personally if Bates also dies unexpectedly. I'd like to hear that first hand.' He added, 'Can't say I'm sorry about Whitacre. The opposite, actually. See you later, Raveneau.'

TWELVE

Raveneau called Becker and asked for approval to make a trip to Carmel. After Becker gave him the nod, he called la Rosa.

'This is an out and back to Carmel. I won't be gone long, but if you catch a homicide while I'm in Carmel, Inspector Adler will go out with you.'

'When are you coming back?'

'Should be late tonight.'

'You're driving all the way down there and back and checking out his alibi at the same time?'

'Hotel, restaurant, and where he got gas.'

'And I'm supposed to go out with Adler if there's a call?'

She seemed uncomfortable with that which surprised him.

'We've got fifteen tips off the TV report,' she said.

'Yeah, I know, I've got the list with me.'

He split the list with her and made a series of calls as he drove south on 101. Then he just drove, and looking west at the foothills remembered a summer afternoon twenty-five years ago when he picked up his ex-wife Angie at the San Francisco apartment in the Marina that she shared with two friends. That day they drove from summer bay fog into the heat of the Central Valley and in the dry foothills swam in Rollins Lake before continuing on to Lake Tahoe. He remembered the feel of the cold clean water of Tahoe, sitting on a granite slab at the water's edge talking and laughing as they dried in the mountain sunlight. He saw the blade-like blue of Tahoe and the radiance of Angie's face as if it were yesterday.

In Carmel he met with the hotel manager of the La Playa first and read the young man as wanting to assist and help the police. Raveneau showed him his gold homicide star and learned that Stoltz had reserved at the La Playa two and a half weeks ago. So it wasn't an impulse trip. He stayed in room twenty-one, checked in at six fifteen p.m., and more importantly, checked out the next morning at seven.

The one night he was in Carmel Stoltz ate at a French restaurant, Anton & Michel. A waitress had no trouble remembering him.

'He was weird. He asked if we could make scrambled eggs with truffles and I think he knew we wouldn't have any truffles right now and that the chef couldn't just do something off the menu. We were very busy that night. What was weird was he was so insistent. I went back to the chef twice.'

'What else did he do?'

'He ordered an expensive bottle of Pinot Noir and gave most of it to staff. He wanted me to sit and have a glass with him. Our management likes us to know all the wines, so I did, but I don't think he really cared about the wine.' She smiled a half-smile. 'Weird but good looking, I mean, he wasn't a bad guy, but it was like he really wanted to make a point.'

'What do you think his point was?'

She laughed. 'You know, I'm not sure. But what's going on, why are you here?'

'I want to make sure he was really here.'

'Oh, he was definitely here.'

Raveneau spent hours watching video at the Chevron in Sand City before spotting Stoltz standing outside his Lexus gassing up. The time on the tape read 7:42. Stoltz had left the station at 7:48 after using the bathroom and paying cash for gas and water just as he'd claimed. It was lucky the video hadn't already looped over itself, lucky the video system had been recently upgraded to carry more videotape capacity, the manager explaining earlier they had a problem with people gassing up with stolen credit cards.

Raveneau called la Rosa from Salinas as he got back to 101 and turned north. He worked through Stoltz's chronology on the drive home.

Checked in at La Playa at 6:15 p.m.

Dinner at Anton & Michel 7:30 p.m. reso, paid by Visa, first drink at bar 7:21, bill rung out at 8:50.

Checks out of La Playa at 7:00 a.m. next morning.

Gas at Sand City Chevron 7:42 a.m.

Maid cleans room at La Playa, 11:00 a.m. Remakes bed. Replaces shampoo and soap samples.

Two of the times mattered: when the dinner bill was closed out and when he checked out of

La Playa the next morning. The window between was a little under twelve hours, more than
enough time to leave the restaurant, drive three
hours north, murder Whitacre, and return to the
hotel to check out at 7:00 a.m. So the alibi was
valid, but not solid and digging deeper would
have to wait.

He drove home and didn't walk in the door
until two in the morning. He ate a sandwich and
drank a flat half bottle of beer sitting in the
refrigerator. He left his notes on a counter in the
kitchen. He showered. As he lay down he reached for his phone and sent a text to la Rosa, 'I'm
back.'

THIRTEEN

The next morning Raveneau and la Rosa put on the booties, spacesuits, caps, masks – the whole get-up – before going in to watch their Jane Doe autopsied. The medical examiner quietly catalogued female, five foot four, one hundred twenty-three pounds, of mixed race, likely Asian/Caucasian, black hair, brown eyes, significant large black-colored moles high on the right side of her back, a tattoo of a diamond on the heel of her left foot, two inch scar on her left knee, another small tatt low on her back and one on her scalp inside the hairline. Approximate age: thirty. A tiny stud piercing in her left nostril was removed. Wounds: ligature marks at neck, hemorrhaging at eyes and tongue, scalp wound at right temple, bruising at the back of the neck, another bruise, two inches by one inch, on the right thigh just above the knee. An abrasion on the right elbow that likely occurred shortly before death, possibly from a fall. There was more bruising where ankle and wrist restraints had been removed.

Raveneau listened to the medical examiner's quiet progress, heard him say 'no evidence of sexual assault'. He looked at the gray skin of her face and tried again to guess the reason she was

65

in the China Basin building. There weren't any
needle marks, nothing indicated drug use.
Prostitution or a sexual liaison was possible, and
his guess was still that she came in through the
gate with her assailant. One of them had a key.
He and la Rosa would need to interview Heilbron again, as well as the realtor.

As they cut her open he and la Rosa left the
room. They'd get the rest from the report. They
didn't need to watch her liver weighed.

'What do you make of the tattoo on her heel?'
he asked after they'd stripped off the suits and
were outside in the cool breeze of the corridor
leading back to the Hall.

'I don't make anything of it.'

'Maybe we can track down her name through
the tattoos.'

'That seems like another goose chase.'

'Another one?'

'Well, like one.'

Their Jane Doe's sketch had run in this morning's *San Francisco Chronicle*, but how many
people read the newspaper any more? Still, at
Homicide they had new calls, new tips. In the
late morning an email tip on a different case
arrived via the 'Contact Us' link on the SFPD
website. The tip named two kids who'd alleged-
ly witnessed a stabbing outside a club in the
Mission several weeks ago. Raveneau called the
high school and confirmed that both young men
were seniors and at school today. At noon they
drove over, met with a dean first, and then one of
the two young men, who immediately denied
having been at the club that night.

La Rosa took the lead with the second young man and impressed Raveneau. She was soft spoken and easy with the boy, a sixteen-year-old named Robert Fuentes. She was more relaxed and confident than with Heilbron. She'd also changed her look, cut her hair short this weekend, turning her proud face more handsome and mannish, something she told Raveneau on the drive here that she regretted. She told him something else this morning, that her roots were upper middle class. Her father was a knee surgeon, her mother in marketing, and both tried and failed to talk her out of police work, arguing that she could do better for herself.

Raveneau spoke decent Spanish but la Rosa was fluent and hip to the language the kid used. Forty minutes into the interview Fuentes gave up a name, H Man, Hector Jimenez, a gangbanger, and told them where to look for him.

They picked Jimenez up off the street in the mid afternoon and brought him in. He was a big man, coffee-colored, half-Puerto Rican, half-Mexican and muscled, wearing a canary-yellow shirt that came down to mid thigh. Jimenez knew to say nothing and lawyer up but inexplicably did the opposite: confessed to the shooting, saying he was high and the victim had come on to the girl he was with so he had no choice. They were hours with him in the small interview room and after he signed a confession they booked him.

Then they went to see Heilbron who was hostile and unwilling to talk to them at all. The thrill of confessing had passed and he made no attempt to answer Raveneau's questions. Instead, he said, 'I made up the whole thing, I didn't kill her. I got everything from one of the cops outside. He'll remember me. Ask him.'

Raveneau and la Rosa knew they'd have to kick him loose, but that didn't mean they weren't conflicted about it. Then, as they were leaving, Heilbron called to la Rosa. She glanced at Raveneau and then went back, demanding as she got close, 'What is it?'

'I know you're not married. I want to ask you out. I'd like to spend time with you.'

'Would you?'

'Last night I kept waking up thinking about you. We should get together.'

'Let's do that. Let's do it in an interview room tomorrow morning and we'll talk about San Jose. How does that sound?'

She didn't wait for his answer. Outside, Raveneau turned and said, 'Let's get a drink and celebrate our first week on-call together and you getting the Jimenez confession today.'

In the old days Raveneau drank Scotch and when somebody wanted to buy the homicide inspector a drink he usually accepted. He'd get warmed up and entertain a small crowd with stories as Angie waited at home. That was back when he thought it meant something to appear on TV answering questions about a homicide investigation at a press conference. It was also when he thought an eighteen-year-old Scotch meant the whiskey had been in a barrel for eighteen years, as opposed to the truth, which was that just a fraction of the barrel had. He hadn't known anything more about Scotch than he'd known about homicide investigations. Now he ordered a glass of wine, la Rosa a margarita.

'The homicide dick who drinks white wine,' la Rosa said after the waitress left.

'When I was the Great Inspector I drank Scotch. In those days I couldn't find a hat big enough to fit my head.'

'How do they fit nowadays? They must be tight still.'

'Not as tight.' He studied her a moment and said, 'I should have asked you this weeks ago. Everyone calls you Liz, but what do you prefer?'

'Oh, I don't care.'

'No, I'm asking, I mean it.'

'I like Elizabeth but no one uses my full name.' She smiled a warm smile. 'I'm OK if you just call me Inspector. I'm still getting used to it and I love the sound of it.'

'I'm going to call you Elizabeth.'

Raveneau finished his wine and as la Rosa downed her margarita they ordered another round. It felt like they got somewhere today and maybe also crossed a generational gap. Getting the Jimenez confession made it a lucky day, but that was before they knew what had happened across the bay in Oakland.

FOURTEEN

Charles Bates's wife, Jacie, routinely took an evening walk, mostly when there was still light and often with CD, the D for Charles's middle name, Douglas. Tonight she was walking alone. Not even their old dog, Chief, was with her. With his back legs Chief was too slow. She left the house a little after five, knowing it would get to dusk as she came through the end of the walk. Even so, she stopped to chat with a neighbor before starting for the dead-end street that turned into the park.

She picked up her pace. Jacie heard that she could lose weight at her hips by walking faster and she wanted to be down five pounds before she and CD went to Hawaii. They had a condo rented on Maui, same one they went to last year on their thirty-second anniversary. She looked forward to going there more than anything else right now.

Up ahead, joggers, hikers, mountain bikers, parked their cars in the rough dirt lot between the trees near where the park trails started. Lately, there were two small construction remodels in the neighborhood and those workers were still figuring out that the road didn't go through, so when a white pickup passed her going fast

70

toward the dead-end she figured it was another construction worker about to make the same mistake.

The man driving the pickup glanced at her as he passed. Where she was she wouldn't see him turn around, but she knew it wouldn't be long. It wasn't. She heard his truck rattling back down the narrow road, coming faster making up for the lost time, and she moved over to the side, close to the edge but not in the mud. When he got closer she might step off, but because he had come by her slow on the way in she wasn't much concerned.

Now the truck rattled around the corner, frame floating toward the crown of the road and Jacie frowning disapproval. She heard it accelerate. In the cool gray light of dusk she made out his white face and dark hair, but not his features. She raised a hand, meaning to say slow down, but not waiting, getting out of the way as he swerved, either losing control or coming on purpose. She was once a very good dancer and was on her back foot turning and two steps off the asphalt before the gap closed. She heard the sound when it hit her, but that was all.

She didn't know that afterward he wrestled the truck back on to the road, straightening the wheel to keep it from rolling, or that his bumper carried dry grass and dirt from where it gashed the hill. She didn't know that the old pickup's glove compartment had popped open or that he'd recovered from his near crash and backed up over her body, resting the truck with a foot on the brake as the wheel rose up on her chest.

The impact crumpled the right fender and broke the headlight. A chrome headlight ring was left up on the slope. Pieces of headlight glass were all over the road shoulder. Neighbors heard tires squeal. But the whole thing took less than ninety seconds from start to finish. What the driver worried most about was his right headlight. If traffic was bad it would be nearly dark when he got there. Last thing he wanted was getting pulled over for a blown light.

But, hey, no worries, everything went fine. He parked under the freeway among the empty warehouses in drug city and moved quickly, emptying five gallons of gas inside the truck cab, coughing blindly at the surge of fumes as he backed away. He was in the car, engine on, headlights off, when the flash of light came and the faint tinkling sound of windows breaking came from well down the street. Warehouse windows caught the light and made the fireball bigger. So big that as he drove away the street radiated a cheerful orange-yellow light.

FIFTEEN

'It was a hit-and-run. Bates is at home right now. Some neighbors are with him and his daughter is on her way,' Becker said. 'I want you and la Rosa to go to the scene. We can't ignore the possibility of connection.'

Raveneau stepped out into the street to wave la Rosa down before she drove away and asked, 'What do we know so far?'

'White pickup truck, male driver, and that Oakland PD is treating it as a hit-and-run.'

'We'll have to tell them why we're there, and level with them. That may put it out to the media.'

'I know, but ask them to hold tight.'

Jacie Bates's body lay on the street under a blanket. Raveneau saw Oakland PD collecting debris and it wasn't hard to spot the detectives. He and la Rosa introduced themselves to a detective named Hendricks, a tall, thin, taciturn man, and a second detective, Pete Stalos, who questioned them and took notes after Hendricks returned to the gash in the slope.

'Does this Stoltz drive a pickup?'

'If he does, we don't know about it. We know about a white Lexus and we know he's got other cars registered to the same corporation, but I've also got to say we don't have anything at all on him. This all comes from the inspector who died, Whitacre, believing that he was being tailed by Stoltz.'

'So you literally have nothing?'

'That's right.'

'Yet you're here, so I gather you're not telling me what you do have.'

'What we have is an improbable series of events.'

'What is an improbable series of events? What we have here is an apparent hit-and-run and I'm not sure what an improbable series of events is. Your inspector probably ate his gun because he was given a fatal diagnosis and was distraught and in pain. That's probable, right? What's improbable? Fill in the gaps for me.'

Raveneau understood where Stalos was coming from, but was unfazed.

'Nothing connects to anything yet, but it was Whitacre and Bates who took Stoltz down. Stoltz wrote a number of angry letters from prison and Whitacre believed Stoltz was following him in the days before he either shot himself or was murdered. That was last Thursday night. The victim here was the wife of Inspector Charles Bates.'

Stalos looked down the street at his partner and then back at Raveneau.

'What else?'

'I'm working on an alibi that Stoltz gave me.'

'So you believe he followed your inspector?'

'I'm not one way or the other yet.'

'You're here and you want cooperation, and so

74

do we. Where do we find this Stoltz so we can talk to him?'

'Why don't you let us help you with that?'

'Right, except that this is an Oakland investigation and whereas Stoltz may have stalked Whitacre, there's no proof. Isn't that what you're saying? Whitacre believed he was being followed, but it was never determined.'

'Something like that.'

'Whereas this, at a minimum, is manslaughter, that is to say, it's an active investigation and it doesn't sound like you have one, unless there is more you haven't told me.'

Raveneau glanced at la Rosa. He was going to leave her with Stalos, guessing she'd have better luck with him.

'Is it OK if I take a look first and then we can talk about how to work together on this?'

'Go ahead, but watch out for my partner. He doesn't like people and he hasn't had any good inter-departmental experiences.'

Raveneau walked up to the gash in the hillside where she was hit. Under the lights the grasses on the hill were brown and thin, and the road narrow, barely wide enough for two cars to pass, so maybe it was accidental and the driver fled. Driver figures out the road is a dead-end, turns around, and then races back making up for lost time. It could easily have been that. He walked up to the other detective, Hendricks.

'Can I look at her?'

'What?'

'I'd like a look at her body.'

'Did you know her?'

75

'Socially.'

'You work with her husband?'

'Yeah, but he stepped off the desk several years ago.'

'What do you know about the marriage?'

'They also struck me as close. Married a long time.'

'Follow me.'

Hendricks lifted the sheet and Raveneau registered that Jacie's neck was broken and that her right arm and side may have taken the impact. He saw something else he couldn't make sense of until he asked Hendricks to move the sheet just a little so he could see more. Then he could read the marks on her neck, collarbone, and across her sweatshirt. One of her running shoes was missing. He realized she faced the truck at an angle as it hit her. But that didn't fit with these other marks. Then he got it.

He stepped back and looked at Hendricks. 'The driver wanted to make sure or it was personal, or both.'

'You are good,' Hendricks said. 'Yeah, he drove over her again. He crushed her chest. I think he let the truck rest on top of her.' He added, 'I'm going to find this guy.'

Hendricks draped the sheet carefully. He didn't drop it. He watched Raveneau study the flattened grass and tire marks on the slope, then added, 'We got a decent casting of his tires. He lost control, bounced up on the slope and cut into grass. Those marks there are his tires. What we have so far is we may be looking for a late model white pickup and a male driver, possibly Cau-

76

casian. Could this Stoltz do that?'

'I don't know. Doesn't really fit. This guy is from a well-to-do family and a bright light in some computer coding circles.'

'You said he wrote threatening letters.'

'Threatening, yeah, but the kind of stuff meant to seem threatening without being overt. Cautious.'

'Have you been to see him?'

'I have.'

'Did you tell my partner that?'

'Not yet.'

'You got sent over here. Would you have come anyway?'

'Probably.'

Raveneau and la Rosa were still there when word came that a 2009 Ford 150 pickup was torched between warehouses just west of 880. They left the Oakland detectives and drove there. Fire vehicles and two police cruisers sat close to the burned chassis. Heat still radiated off the truck. The air stank of melted plastic, gasoline, and burning rubber, but they saw the crumpled right front fender and they left there with the name of the registered owner, a Thanh Nguyen with a Van Nuys address in southern California.

Later they'd learn that address didn't exist when Nguyen or someone using that name bought the vehicle. The house address had existed but was demolished for a road expansion project in 2008. What that meant Raveneau didn't know yet.

SIXTEEN

Before dawn the next day Raveneau drove to Lincoln Park Golf Course, paid the fee, and rented a cart. On the first tee three old boys cut the chill by spiking their coffee with brandy. Cigar smoke mingled with the smells of newly mown grass and alcohol. One gaffer pointed a glowing cigar tip at Raveneau.

'Tee off,' he said. 'Play through us; we're just marking time until the end.'

Raveneau had brought a handful of his old clubs, a three-wood and some rusted irons, but he wasn't here to play. A groundskeeper who worked here remained a prime suspect in one of his unsolved cases, one that pre-dated la Rosa. He hoped to find the man, Ray Bryce, cutting grass. Not that he had any new reason to interview Bryce. He was only here to let Bryce know he hadn't forgotten.

He teed off and as his first shot sliced into the trees the old boys hooted and offered to spike his coffee. The cigar smoker gave him some free advice as he got in the cart to leave.

'Don't count the first two shots and slow down.'

Bryce migrated west after serving six years in a Virginia prison for attempted rape. He'd

78

arrived in California fourteen years ago and found work as an electrician's apprentice. When Raveneau looked at him for the Angela Ruiz murder and started unpeeling his past, he discovered Bryce had been questioned in southern California in 1998 after the disappearance of a thirteen-year-old girl who'd lived down the block from him in El Cajon. Three weeks after the girl's body was found, Bryce moved north to San Francisco.

Raveneau found Bryce working on the tenth green. When Bryce saw who it was he got off his mower and said, 'You can't do this to me.'

'I'm not doing anything to you. I've got an open homicide that happened here and I'm going to work it until I solve it. You can understand me doing my job, can't you, Ray?'

Bryce's claim was he'd stopped his mower pre-dawn and gone up into trees between two fairways to urinate. He'd relieved himself no more than five feet from her body and claimed he hadn't noticed her until after he'd finished.

This morning his black work boots were speckled with wet grass clippings and his knees wet. He smelled like fertilizer and as Raveneau teed up a ball he was unsure for a moment what Bryce would do next. What he did was hop on his mower and drive down the path to the green Raveneau was playing toward. When Raveneau chipped on to the green Bryce stooped and picked the ball up. He put it in his pocket, flipped Raveneau off, and drove away.

With that, Raveneau turned around and took the cart back to the clubhouse. He took a call from la Rosa as he pulled away from Lincoln Park.

'Two San Jose detectives are with Heilbron right now. How far away are you?'

'Ten minutes.'

Raveneau missed most of their interview but got there in time to hear them tell Heilbron that the DNA had turned up and this was his last chance for a plea bargain.

'We'll have results tomorrow, so you're at the decision point, bud. Come clean and we'll go to the DA and make sure he understands you co-operated.'

Raveneau knew this wasn't going anywhere but he watched Heilbron closely, especially after la Rosa went into the interview box. Heilbron focused on her as she sat down. He answered the San Jose detectives' questions while looking at her. When she ignored him and left the room his face changed, became completely impassive, his dark eyes unreadable.

At two that afternoon they cut Heilbron loose and the crime lab released his van, though not before showing la Rosa and Raveneau the hole drilled for the camcorder mounted inside at the rear of the van and operated with switches mounted at the dash. Heilbron got in his van and, with Raveneau and la Rosa tailing him, drove straight to China Basin.

SEVENTEEN

Heilbron slowed as he reached China Basin then continued south to his former employer, Boyle's Auto Body. He pulled into an open bay, probably to pick up his last check or ask for his job back. Up the street, Raveneau eased the car over to the curb.

'Who is this guy?' la Rosa asked, and he understood what she meant. The San Jose detectives brought their file this morning. La Rosa read through it. So had he.

'Here's what I think,' Raveneau answered. 'When Heilbron walked into the homicide office and tossed out the San Jose rape after confessing to this killing, he was building his credibility. He knew the DNA was missing, probably wouldn't magically show up, and if it does Heilbron's probably been advised by a defense attorney that the amount of time it was lost will get it discredited as evidence. The district attorney won't go anywhere near a chain-of-custody problem.'

'OK, but he knew the San Jose detectives would come interview him again.'

Raveneau paused. He looked over at her.

'He wanted that. It was another chance to taunt them and that's probably what he's trying to do with us. I'm not seeing the evidence yet that he's our guy and I doubt we will. He was standing outside talking to the responding officers when we were upstairs. He got what he knows about the inside of the building from them.'

Taylor, the younger officer, had looked at a photo of Heilbron and IDed him.

'Then why are we following him?' she asked.

'Because the rape was probably him, and we aren't one hundred percent certain yet on China Basin.'

Heilbron's van backed out suddenly on to Third Street forcing a bus to veer around it. He accelerated away from the auto shop and Raveneau had to jump on the gas just to stay within two stoplights of him. Heilbron drove to the house he leased in South San Francisco and backed into the one-car garage. Inside, he pulled the shades in the bay window that faced the street.

'Let's go back to Boyle's,' Raveneau said. 'Let's find out what happened.'

In Boyle's Custom Auto Body an employee restoring a yellow Camaro pointed them toward a rear office with this warning: 'Boyle isn't here today, but the office manager Katrina is, but she's worse than the hurricane was so watch out.'

Katrina had a pinched nose, hair dyed a light red, and earrings that looked like car keys hanging from her ears. She took Raveneau's card and studied it as if she was with Homeland Security. Raveneau watched and then pulled his homicide star.

'Carl Heilbron just got fired,' she said. 'He

doesn't work here any more. Why is he walking around anyway? Why isn't he in jail? Seems like every time the police talk about a person of interest they're back on the street the next day. If he said he killed her, does he have to prove it to you before you keep him in jail?'

'He recanted his confession and we don't have anything to hold him on.'

'So hold him anyway. He's a creep. He delivered a car to the home of one of our customers last summer and the next night was caught looking in the windows of her house. He didn't get arrested and now she gets free engine care.'

Katrina stared at them as though he and la Rosa had let that happen.

'Boyle talked the customer out of calling the police.'

'That's your boss?' Raveneau asked.

'Yes.'

'Is he around?'

She rolled her eyes and said, 'Only if it rains.'

'Why is that?'

'Simple. When it rains he can't play golf, and since he doesn't like to be around his wife he comes to work. Boyle thinks Heilbron is the best auto body man here, so Boyle and the rest of the misogynist pricks look the other way when Heilbron goes into the bathroom for an hour with one of his magazines. He's disgusting.'

They listened but didn't learn much and drove back to the homicide office. Raveneau saw the TV vans from three blocks out. He counted five as they picked up coffees at Café Roma, and then watched a reporter warming up, practicing,

pulling her voice down lower, getting more bari-
tone into it as she asked, 'Is a killer targeting San
Francisco's homicide detail?'

'Shit,' he said, 'here we go.'

Upstairs Becker told them to stay completely
away from all media. The brass would handle
this one. They sorted new tip calls and emails,
and Raveneau left messages for several people
and made contact with two; the first was an older
woman who thought the sketch of the China
Basin victim she saw in the *Chronicle* was her
daughter stolen from her stroller in Iowa in
1949. The second was a young man who said he
didn't know her name but recognized her from
meeting her in a bar one night.

'You recognize her from the sketch?' Raveneau asked.

'Definitely. She was at Dorati's. I'm just having trouble with her name. It was something like
Alice or Alicia.'

'What about a last name?'

'I know, man, I'm trying.'

'We'll come see you. How do we find you?'

He got the young man's name and a phone
number and email. La Rosa struck out with her
calls, left nine messages and talked with two
men and a woman, people they'd go see but
didn't sound like leads.

At three, the door to the homicide detail got
locked and a general meeting held. Captain
Ramirez asked Raveneau to summarize events
from his Thursday morning meeting with Whitacre. He knew the feeling among the inspectors
was that Whitacre ate his gun and this meeting

was an unnecessary melodrama. He didn't have anything that would change that belief, but he did recount in detail what he and la Rosa learned in Oakland and what he knew of Whitacre's death.

When he finished, Captain Ramirez stood and said, 'Across the street they think they're on to a big story and they may end up feeding the ego of the killer if there is a connection, so I want all of you to be more careful.'

No one made any cracks as he said that. No one wanted to get bit by Ramirez. As the meeting ended he motioned for Raveneau to follow him into his office.

'What were you doing at Lincoln Park this morning?'

'Checking on a suspect.'

'Does that mean you have new evidence, a new lead, or what does it mean? I'm asking because Mr Bryce filed with the Office of Citizen Complaints and then called here to let us know. They'll want to know why you went by there. He's claiming you're harassing him.'

'Someday I'll arrest him for murder.'

'Well, you haven't arrested anybody for that lately. You inspectors think you're immune, but I'll tell you right now, you're not. You're out chasing this guy around a golf course and I'm taking the blowback. I don't like that. We need investigative results, not harassment complaints. You can take that message back out with you.'

'I'll let you deliver it, sir; you're better at it.'

Late in the afternoon Lieutenant Becker took Raveneau aside and asked, 'What did you say to

Ramirez?'

'That I've got a stack of General Orders on my desk and three memos about the next shooting qualification day, and that if we got rid of those we'd have more time for golf.'

Becker looked perturbed, then annoyed.

'You don't want to alienate Ramirez. It's not worth it, and you of all people know that. So I don't know what's gotten into you, but if you push too hard right now you're going to wake up one morning in Idaho, living in a little one-room cabin next door to your old partner, Kidd.

'Every morning the two of you can chop wood together in the bitter cold before the sun comes up, and then warm up in the town café eating eggs, bacon, and a stack of pancakes, eating your way to a heart attack before you spend your afternoon on a little boat on some wind-fucking-driven mountain lake with your war stories and your fishing poles. I hear it gets to fifty below where Kidd is, so you'll have ice fishing to look forward to as well. And you'll have your satellite dish. You've got to have that.

'They're pushing hard from above. They're pushing so hard I don't know if it wasn't someone in the brass who called the press today, and I can guarantee this: If the solve rate doesn't go up around here, a sea change is coming and seniority isn't going to mean—'

They never finished their conversation and that was fine with Raveneau, and for that matter he was glad he got under Bryce's skin. La Rosa waved him over. She was on the phone to the crime lab and covered the mouthpiece.

'They've got a copy for us of the video off the camcorder in Heilbron's van. They think there's footage shot in China Basin. Do we want to pick it up this afternoon?'

Raveneau nodded. 'Tell them we'll come get it right now.'

They've got a copy for us of the video of the conversation to Halliday's suite. The thing it does, and in a funny little way, but we want a back-up in – it never

ndewed – find it ever

EIGHTEEN

After the ride Stoltz drank a beer with the two patent attorneys he regularly cycled with. They had pushed it this afternoon. It was good ride, just under two hours. The bikes were loaded and they'd taken over one of the picnic tables outside Guthrie's, a local haunt where they always parked before riding the loop. Not that he saw these guys that often, maybe once a month. Usually, he rode alone. It felt good now though to lose the helmet and kick back together in the last sunlight with a beer.

Both Jonathan and Steve were in tight physical shape, same as he was, middle-aged guys but eating up much younger riders and having fun with that. But among the three of them, Stoltz easily dominated. He was just stronger.

Stoltz saw their expressions change as he said, 'I've never talked about this with you guys because I've wanted to bury it and forget it ever happened to me, but now I'm going to ask your advice.'

Neither responded, wariness entering as he fucked everything up by bringing personal problems to the after-ride beer. Stoltz started with Steve who at least looked curious and was also the softest so easiest to get to.

'You guys know I went to prison. Obviously, you know that. I had this good friend named John Reinert, a software engineer, a great one. You both would have liked him. He married a woman named Erin he'd only known for about three months.'

'Bad news,' Jonathan said.

'You got that right, and I was best man at the wedding. She moved into his apartment in San Francisco and the three of us hung out a lot together. Then sometime in the spring she fell in love with me, only I didn't really know it. I mean, I knew she was attracted, but hey, all women are attracted to me.'

Jonathan and Steve chuckled.

'The night John got killed we'd gone back to their apartment, and I don't know how well you guys know San Francisco—'

'I read about it,' Jonathan said. 'We both googled you before we started riding with you.'

'Right, you didn't want to fuck up your careers, but now that I'm back there's a pretty good chance I'm going to come up with some stuff that makes you some money. So you talked it over with your wives. Yeah, I've got you guys figured out.'

This time they giggled like little girls. Stoltz smiled.

'Want me to shut up?'

'No, keep going,' Jonathan said.

'OK, well, everything you read was wrong, or almost all of it, and I had a real hard time dealing with that. It took me a long time to get my head on straight.'

89

'But you took a plea bargain,' Steve said.

'I did, but the way they set it up you don't really have much choice. The DA's office isn't there for justice. They're just about putting points on the board. Anyway, back to that night. I'd just broken off a long relationship and wasn't seeing anybody, and that was probably part of the problem with Erin the night John got killed. She thought I was available.'

'But she was married,' Steve said, and got a little prim look on his face.

'Young man, it happens even when they're married.'

Jonathan laughed hard at that and Steve looked away. But Stoltz needed both of them.

'She was awesome,' Stoltz said, 'but she was married to my best friend so I avoided ever being alone with her. That night we went back to their apartment after dinner. Erin had some great tequila she'd bought in Mexico and some good dope.'

As soon as he said dope, he knew he'd made a slight miscalculation. He saw a little twitch under Jonathan's right eye and remembered Jonathan had a problem with marijuana.

'She and John liked to get high, but I don't do any drugs, so I went down to my car to get something after they lit up. I had a BMW in those days, an M5—'

'What color?'

With the car he had Jonathan back, nodding at him, ready to cut in with his own car story.

'Dark blue.'

'I bet you thought you were some hot shit.'

90

'I did, and I wasn't.'

'I had one of those too.'

'Did you?'

'Same car.'

'No wonder we're riding together. Anyway, I was a geek with new money.'

They both smiled. They saw a lot of guys get self-important when they hit it big.

'If I hadn't gone to my car, none of it would have happened.' He stopped there and took a drink of beer. 'That night we were talking about going up the coast in two cars. John had a Porsche and the weather for the weekend coming up was supposed to be good, so we thought we'd race each other up to Mendocino. I went down to get a map.'

'Hold on,' Jonathan said, 'I'm getting lost here.'

'The night it happened I was at their apartment. We'd gone to dinner and then come back to their apartment. I went down to the parking lot to get a map out of my car.'

'How far down?'

'One flight. The cars were in this tiny lot in back, and I don't know what it's like there now, but then it was pretty quiet except that you had this kind of slopover from the Haight-Ashbury area. Some drug dealing went on close by and that night I'd done something stupid. I'd left my car unlocked after getting the map and had a gun in my car because John and I had been going out to a range and learning how to target shoot. There'd been a couple of carjackings in recent months in the area where I was living, so I'd bought a gun and was learning how to use it.'

He caught a second reproving nod from Jonathan and without giving any sign of having seen it, held up his hand and said, 'I had decided no one was going to take my car from me. But it was a stupid idea to keep a gun in the car.'

'Was it registered?' Jonathan asked.

'Of course, and I was learning to shoot at a range.'

They gave him blank stares because a few carjackings doesn't mean you start packing a gun, unless, of course, something was always wrong with you anyway. Stoltz understood. He got it. He had a plan for that.

'We'd also gotten into skeet shooting. We'd gone out and bought expensive shotguns. We were pretty competitive.'

'Why does that not surprise me?' Jonathan said, suddenly switching back and trying to lighten it up, trying to help him out a little. Stoltz nodded at him. How these two reacted would tell him a lot about how everybody else would react and he needed to know where he stood. Boy Scout Steve still looked suspicious and Stoltz drew a deep breath.

'Anyway, I got the map out of my car and went back up, and when we started talking about the trip, somehow we got in an argument about which way to go, I mean, a really stupid drunk and high argument. I suggested Erin ride with me because that way she wouldn't have to sit in a car as long, meaning John was going to get lost.'

'I thought you were avoiding being alone with

92

her,' Steve said, 'and how does anyone get lost driving up the coast?'

'Hey, I was never alone with her, not once. Look, I knew John was jealous and I was kind of pissed off that night. I didn't like his paranoia. He had a coke problem. But it's true, I suggested she ride with me just to piss him off. Anyway, I decided it was time to go. I left and when I got to my car there was some grungy fuck sitting in it. I didn't even realize John had followed me down and all of a sudden the guy's holding my gun and pointing it at us. He told us to lie down on the pavement and that's when John charged him.'

Stoltz took a deep breath and looked away before speaking again, his voice flat and quieter now.

'The guy shot him through the head, dropped the gun, and ran. I knew John was dead so I chased him.'

Stoltz bowed his head.

'In a way it was all my fault. I left the car unlocked. I fucked up and then worse when I didn't go back. I didn't know what to do. I was in shock. Then a cop picked me up. My prints were all over my gun and obviously it fired the bullet that killed him. That's how I ended up with voluntary manslaughter. I made all the wrong moves. That's why I'm restarting my career.'

'Never too late to invent,' Steve said.

'Hey, I watched the boom from prison. I watched all my friends get rich, even people that were totally incompetent, but I'm not telling you this so I can bitch about it. Maybe you've heard some news about a San Francisco homicide inspector who either shot himself or was murdered, and then yesterday or the day before the wife of a former homicide inspector was killed in a hit-and-run. Turns out these are the two inspectors who took me down, so because they don't have any other suspects they're hassling me.'

Stoltz held his hand up like he was going to swear on a Bible.

'No, that's not quite full disclosure. I wrote letters from prison. I was angry. I didn't write threatening letters or anything like that. I was just trying to get them to reopen the case.'

'You seem like you're doing OK,' Jonathan said, like he was coaching.

'I'm doing fine.' Stoltz broke eye contact with Jonathan, glanced at Steve, and then back at Jonathan. 'I trust you both. I'm thinking of suing them, like bang, overnight a lawsuit if they harass me in any way. What do you think? Is that a stupid idea or should I give it right back to them?'

'My advice is not going to be what you want to hear,' Jonathan said, and for a patent attorney he looked pretty pumped up.

'Mine either,' Steve threw in but left it to Jonathan.

'OK, tell me because I trust you guys.'

'Forget about suing. It's long, complicated, and you'd probably lose. It's the job of the police to talk to everybody who might have a grudge against this dead inspector or the wife. Even though it's hard, the best thing you can do right now is cooperate.'

'I'm trying but I feel like I should get a lawyer and hit back.'

'Are you kidding? Always have a lawyer.' Jonathan smiled, reached over and patted him. 'How else are we going to make money? Hang in there, they're just doing what they do, but by all means have a lawyer present. Right, Steve?'

'I agree with everything he said.' Steve stood up and said, 'What do you say we hit the road?'

They all stood and then clicked across the asphalt in their bike shoes.

'Sorry to put you guys through that,' Stoltz said before they broke up. He shook hands with both. He knew they'd find reasons never to ride with him again. They wouldn't hear from him again either, and when he looked in the rear-view mirror as he drove away they were still standing in the lot talking about him. That was all he needed to know.

NINETEEN

Late Tuesday night, a radio unit responding to a report of a robbery and shooting followed a dark blue '78 Chevrolet Impala with two male occupants down Broderick Street into the Western Addition. When they hit their lights and the Impala didn't pull over, they went to siren and the car stopped in the middle of the street. That's where the officer and witness accounts began to differ.

Inside the Impala the man in the passenger seat shielded his eyes from the police spotlight and raised his right hand with an object in it. He didn't know it but twenty minutes earlier a German tourist was beaten and robbed by a young black male jumping out of the passenger side of an older American car.

Raveneau read the officer's account of the shooting on Wednesday morning. The men in the Impala were father and son. The father was stable after taking a bullet in the shoulder. His son died on the scene of injuries sustained by two gunshot wounds. Neither was armed and an angry crowd soon gathered. According to the father, his son used a paint brush to block the glare of the spotlight.

After interviewing the young man who claimed he'd met their China Basin victim at a bar, Raveneau and la Rosa drove to the Western Addition and looked at where the shooting had occurred. Most of the city homicides happened in the Mission, Bayview, Tenderloin, or here. Many of the killings stemmed from drug and gang related violence and those living in the affected areas of San Francisco were increasingly disturbed by the inability of the police to stop them. Worse, many believed the police didn't care much about the residents in these areas and though one of the officers involved last night was black, race would loom large in the debate over what had happened.

Raveneau talked and continued driving after they left the Western Addition. His hands moved as he described parts of the city, the southwest corner, the Richmond where the Asian populations were higher and homicide investigations tended to be complicated by language and often revolved around gambling, loan sharking, and the influence of gangs, some as far away as Shanghai.

'In some of these Asian hits,' Raveneau said as they were driving again, 'they'll just sit on a car. They don't try to hunt the victim down. They'll watch his Honda or Mercedes because they know sooner or later he'll come for it. And there's a lot more weaponry than when I started. That's everywhere. You can buy an AK47 or a 223 assault rifle made in China or Mexico cheap and get it from a van in a liquor store parking lot. But you know this, you saw all this at Vice.'

'No, keep talking, I want to hear it.'

'OK, since we're close I'm going to take you by Lincoln Park.'

'Do you really want to go back there today?'

'We'll go in quietly. Bryce is gone by noon anyway.'

They went up the steps and into the white-painted clubhouse and stood at the clubhouse bar and ordered coffees. Then they went out the French doors and around the eighteenth green.

'Her name was Angela Ruiz. She was out walking her dog. She had a roommate who worked at a pub near here and she'd sometimes go down there at night with the dog, and other times she'd walk the dog up here.'

They came down the cart path under the tall pines and cedars that bordered the fairway. To their right California Street dead-ended into steps as wide as the street that climbed up to Lincoln Park. Raveneau pointed down California at a building.

'Those windows up on the upper floor there, the second ones in, that's where she lived. With her dog she'd routinely come up these steps and into the park at night. Her roommate told me that Ruiz had said that if her dog did its business in the trees along the golf course fairways, then there was no need for a doggy bag. So she'd bring the dog up here regularly right around sunset.

'My prime suspect is a groundskeeper who hates dogs. He told me that if he catches a dog on the golf course he'll take its collar off and drive it to a pound in another city. That way it's just another stray with the clock ticking down as soon as it gets to the pound. The dog's owner puts up posters on the telephone poles with the dog's picture, but Bryce has turned the missing dog in at a pound fifty miles away.'

'Don't they have chips they put in pets now?'

'Sure, but not all dogs.' Raveneau pointed. 'She was in those trees. Bryce told us he found her by chasing her dog. Later he changed that to stopping his mower there because he needed to go up into the trees and urinate.'

He showed her the spot under the tree where Ruiz had been. There were weeds but still the bare spot.

'That spot had pebbles arranged as numbers. Her dog had pawed part of it, so we could only read a few of the numbers. Maybe if we could have read the rest we'd know more, but that's where the "Numbers Man" case name comes from.'

They left Lincoln Park then drove the Embarcadero, following the waterfront as Raveneau talked about Hunter's Point and the expanse of navy property the city didn't patrol, which gangs out of the projects used routinely. Ironically, the crime lab was located there in a rehabbed area near the water. New development was slated for Hunter's Point. But beyond the enclave with the crime lab were big abandoned structures, rotting wharfs, and dry docks. As they drove through, Raveneau pointed out the crane that had once loaded the Hiroshima bomb.

'When there's a killing in the projects we try to get there fast and get to the children who were witnesses. The kids have no problem saying it was a man in a bright green coat on a little bicycle who stopped and shot the other man, then rode off. Then we're looking for a guy with a lime-green parka and a little bike in an area with the worst poverty in the city, with empty rooms, no phone or electric service, rock bottom nothing. We can usually find him, but bringing a case against him, that's a different deal. That's why we take anonymous tips.'

'Bringing the case is what we've got to do more of.'

She said that with such fervor he glanced over at her.

'It is. But out here they're not going to testify if they're going to get killed for it later. Who would?' He turned to her. 'Ready to head back?'

Later that afternoon they watched the copy of the Heilbron tape again. Images were date and time marked. In one thirty-five minute period Heilbron covered several square miles of the city, filming lone women, most of them walking along city sidewalks. His set-up had a zoom feature so after the camera was on them he often zoomed in. Some of the women must have become aware of the van from the way they reacted. Others seemed oblivious. He filmed eight different women before driving into China Basin and to the building where their victim was killed. Resolution was poor. The lighting was poor. But it was definitely the building, and the next shots were of Boyle's Auto Body.

What followed was a sort of manic period of moving around with the camera running. He sat outside two clubs south of Market. He backtracked several times between Seventeenth and Twenty-first on Valencia Street. At one point a woman approached the passenger side of the van, but disappeared from camera range.

Then he returned to China Basin and Raveneau saw it as he watched this time. Heilbron came back to the building. He was fixated on it and Raveneau got the feeling that Heilbron wanted the street clear. The lens followed the few pedestrians in the area until they were gone. He wanted them gone. Was he waiting for a chance to bring their victim inside?

'Let's back it up,' la Rosa said.

The camera pointed once more at the chain link fence where two individuals or what looked like people showed inside the fence. The time was 11:17 p.m., the night of the murder. Raveneau froze the frame. Neither individual fit the profile of Deschutes. The gate was shut. They were away from the front door and heading around to the back. Heilbron's camcorder had high quality light enhancement features, but even so Raveneau couldn't tell. Neither could la Rosa. If he had to guess, one was female, possibly the other as well.

'We'd better turn this over to the lab rats in the morning,' he said. Computer enhancement might get them there. 'I'm going to play it once more,' he said. He hit 'Play' and the figures moved away from the reflective face of the building and down the dark south side. In seconds they were gone.

'What do you get from that?' la Rosa asked.

'That they both might be women.'

'No way.'

Raveneau replayed it again and after a moment of quiet la Rosa allowed, 'It's possible. Yeah, you might be right.'

TWENTY

Everyone on the homicide detail attended the service for Whitacre at a Catholic church in Burlingame. When it ended and Raveneau and la Rosa were outside talking in the church lot, Bates approached, wanting to talk alone with Raveneau. Bates's face was dusty, ashen. He looked as if he hadn't slept in days. He's truly hurting, Raveneau thought, and then walked far enough away to talk alone with him.

'I lied to you and Ted. I told you I sat on Stoltz and watched him, but I didn't. I lied and I can't stop thinking about it. Ted kept calling me. He called almost every night. I just figured he was breaking down, coming apart, and imagining things.'

'You already told me that and I understand.'

Raveneau said that slowly. He didn't want to dismiss the apology, but there was also nothing gained in Bates rationalizing it.

'I caused everything that's happened. It all could have been prevented. Ted, my sweet Jacie, my God, I got Jacie killed.'

'No, you didn't.'

'You don't know what I'm saying, Raveneau. I got my Jace killed when I lied to Ted and you. Most nights we'd make that walk together. I was supposed to be there. I told her I'd be there and I wasn't because I was with a friend having a drink. If I'd been there, it wouldn't have happened. Same way I lied to Ted and you. Came easy and now Jacie is gone.'

Raveneau had known cops with strong marriages but few like the Bateses who seemed to just naturally belong together. Anyone watching them knew they didn't have to work at it.

'I don't know if I can make it without her. I don't know if I want to, and I'm going to tell you that if Stoltz killed her, I'm going to take him out.'

'We don't have anything that ties Stoltz to this, not a single thing.'

'I heard you came up with a twelve hour window from when he finished dinner to when he checked out of the hotel in Carmel. Tell me if that's true.'

Raveneau felt shocked as he realized that was why Bates wanted to talk, and he took a step closer to him.

'Charles, listen to me, you're hurting but you're going too far too fast here. I don't have anything on Stoltz. Yes, there's a window of time he could have acted in, but that's it. You've been through a terrible thing, but you've got to step back.'

Bates couldn't be convinced. His grief blocked his view of the outside world. He turned from Raveneau and walked to his car. La Rosa was waiting as Raveneau returned.

'Still want to stop at Heilbron's?' she asked.

'I think so.'

'What are you hoping to get out of it?'

'We make our presence felt.'

'Like the guy who works at the golf course?'

Raveneau was still thinking about Bates but he was listening. La Rosa didn't want to hitch on to a potential harassment claim and he didn't see it that way at all. He saw Heilbron as confessing to a rape he almost certainly did and a murder he wished he'd done, and might have.

'We want to keep the conversation going with him. We want to keep an element of the unexpected in our presence.'

'OK, but I'm going to throw this out there. I don't think this is smart. We've been to a memorial service. I think we should head back to the Hall and go home.'

Heilbron's van was out front of the house in South San Francisco. He didn't open the door until Raveneau knocked a second and a third time. When the door opened Heilbron looked like he'd just awakened.

'We've been looking over the video you took,' Raveneau said. 'OK if we come in and talk about it?'

Heilbron didn't answer and for a moment the only noise was the TV in the background. He wore gray sweat pants, a long-sleeved T-shirt and sandals. His breath was terrible, and it didn't look like he'd shaved or bathed since they'd released him.

'We're not here to take you back in. We looked at what you caught with your camera. You film-ed two people outside the building the night of the murder. We're trying to figure out if our victim was one of the people.'

Heilbron stepped back and waved them in. Raveneau sat down on a couch. La Rosa took a chair, and Heilbron turned off the TV. This time he didn't turn and stare at la Rosa. He looked at something behind them and said, 'I hate police.'

Raveneau nodded as if that was normal and asked, 'Didn't we treat you fairly? We went down to the building with you. We took you seriously about the San Jose rape and called the detectives who handled the case. If we could have charged you after you confessed to the murder, we would have. We just didn't have the evidence and then you recanted. You made our job even tougher when you recanted. Now we need your help.'

La Rosa shot him a look of disbelief, but Raveneau was determined to try this.

'You were there when two people went through the gate.'

'They were already through.'

'When you drove up?'

'No, I was already parked down the street when they got there and I didn't want to follow them in. One of them was hurt, probably her. She was walking funny and he was helping her.'

'It was a man helping her?'

'Yes.'

'Could you tell anything about him?'

'He was too far away. They were around the corner by the time I got up to the gate.' He turned toward la Rosa and made eye contact as he added, 'They moved into the darkness before I reached the gate.'

'What about a car?' Raveneau asked.

'I saw a white Camry or maybe it was a Ford pickup truck with a crushed right front fender.'

Raveneau knew the type of truck that struck Jacie Bates was public knowledge. Heilbron no doubt got it from the TV. He didn't react, didn't show Heilbron anything, and neither did la Rosa.

'You saw a Camry?'

'Might have been a Honda Civic.'

'Did you see the man leave the building?'

'I left after twenty minutes.'

'Do you feel pretty sure it was around twenty minutes?'

'Might have been twenty-one and a half or twenty-two minutes. Let me think about it and get back to you.'

Raveneau nodded and said, 'So twenty-two minutes and you don't know what kind of car. But here's the part I don't understand, you say they were going around the corner when you got up to the gate. Is that right?'

'Did I say that?'

He smiled at them and Raveneau said, 'Yes, that's what you said but your film shows them right at the corner and you're not in the film, so I guess like the car you've got it a little screwed up.'

'They were already around the corner.'

'There's a way that could work and you tell me if I'm wrong. You were in the van when they went around the corner. You didn't get out like you said. You filmed from the van.'

'Now you're getting it.'

'And there were no lights on the building so

you didn't have much of a view.'

Heilbron smiled. 'You'll never catch him. He'll do another one and another and another and another and you'll never catch him.'

'We might with your help. Can you describe the man at all?'

'Did I say I saw a man?'

'You did earlier.'

'Do you really think I would help you?'

He laughed. He turned and looked at la Rosa.

'Elizabeth, I don't know how you got stuck with Inspector Clouseau, but I would still like to go out with you. I know we could have a lot of fun. Why don't you ditch him and stay here tonight?'

La Rosa got to her feet. She spoke only to Raveneau, 'See you outside.'

TWENTY-ONE

La Rosa was quiet as they drove away. Her fingers drummed on the seat and she squinted as they passed through some of the last of the day's sunlight. She stared at a couple holding hands standing talking on a corner as they waited for the light to change.

'There are a lot of things one can do with one's life,' she said. 'There are people like Heilbron in the world, but the world isn't about them. They're the abnormals. Don't you ever get sick of just being in the same room as someone like him? Do you ever wonder at your decision to spend your best years chasing the worst of humanity?'

'It's about justice and protecting people. It's about speaking for the dead.'

'Yeah, sure, all that, but we just came from Heilbron's house. Do you know what it smelled like to me in there? It smelled like someone took a quart of vomit and heated it slowly on a stove for an hour in a tight space. I can barely stand to be around him, let alone sit in his living room. You wanted to go there and he took you up on your challenge. He pushed the taunting up a notch because we showed weakness by asking for his help. Or ostensibly asking for it, and that makes him feel stronger and it may make him more dangerous.'

'He witnessed something.'

'And he's going to hold it over us forever. He'll never tell us. He was there in his Stalker-mobile and saw them go in, and later put two and two together. Now he's got information and he's in control.'

'He wants the dialogue. He wants to tell us.'

'I don't think so. I think he lives to fuck with us. I think I could waste my life talking to people like him, but I have another idea also, which is he did kill her and you're right, he's feeding us information gradually. He knew a search of his house and van would turn up nothing except for the video and the video would bring us back. But what's your real feeling? What's your gut? Are you after what he videotaped or after him?'

'I think he's still riding a thrill but with some regrets. If he had it to do over again, he probably wouldn't come in and confess. He got all lit up the night of the murder and chatted up the responding officers, but it's probably vicarious. He wishes it were him and has fantasized about killing a woman in that way, and when this live action came along he couldn't resist claiming it.'

'That's what you said before, but now you're working him for what he saw. Are you hoping he'll make a mistake? And what about the fact his key worked in the padlock?'

'Looks like a lot of people can get into the building.'

La Rosa didn't believe that. Her fingers returned to drumming on the seat.

110

Early the next morning Raveneau fielded a call from a woman who said she was calling because she'd just seen the sketch of their China Basin victim and recognized her as someone she used to work with at a pottery wholesaler in Hollister. She gave a name, Alex Jurika. Raveneau got the caller's name, phone number, and place of work. He thanked her and said he'd try to come see her today.

Then he ran Alex Jurika's name through the Department of Motor Vehicles database. He learned there were twelve Alex Jurika's with driver's licenses in the state. Three were local, one was in San Francisco. The SF Jurika had an address in the Hayes Valley.

When the DMV faxed a photo Raveneau caught it as it fed into the tray. He knew the second he saw the photo and walked it over, laid it in front of la Rosa alongside the sketch of their victim. 'Here she is. DMV shows a Hayes Street address. Want to take a ride?'

The apartment manager's annoyed look vanished when they told him they were homicide inspectors. Raveneau showed him the DMV photo.

'Do you know her?'

He did. He went to get a key for her apartment and then explained that he didn't know anything about her whereabouts. She often went on short business trips. He knew Phoenix was one place she traveled to regularly.

'What about a boyfriend or relatives?'

'She had friends but I don't know any of them. I asked her out once and she turned me down,

TWENTY-TWO

As soon as the front door unlocked, Raveneau turned to the apartment manager and said, 'We'll take it from here. We'll bring the key back to you.'

Inside it smelled heavily of used cat litter and a small red cat appeared and meowed as it rubbed against Raveneau's leg. He leaned over and picked it up. Raveneau found some dry food in a kitchen cabinet and fed the cat, and then got on the phone to CSI as la Rosa went back to the car for latex gloves. Raveneau looked around as he waited. One bedroom, one bath, and a lot nicer interior than the dirty exterior of the building.

On a shelf they found several photo albums. She had a Facebook page and a Twitter account. They'd get on to the Facebook page when they got back to the office and made the call. They read through her Twitter feeds, her emails, and la Rosa called AT&T for phone records. She banked online. Either he or la Rosa would call the bank when they got back to the office.

He walked into the bathroom, looking but touching little as la Rosa was on the phone with AT&T getting Jurika's voice mail password. He went through her photos on the computer and emailed several of those and her email address book to both his address and la Rosa's. Then he printed off the emails she'd sent and those received in the last month. As the printer clacked along CSI arrived, and he walked out to lead them in. La Rosa was on the computer when he came back.

'Did you read these?' she asked. 'This must be a friend of hers.'

Raveneau read, 'u going?'

'yes. u?'

'We need all of her friends.'

In an hour they had gone from knowing nothing about Alex Jurika to sorting through information. Raveneau watched la Rosa's hands move over the keyboard. She was three or four times faster than him. She clicked through emails, pausing on one reading, 'You're going to love this.'

CSI pulled prints and latents off counters, the table and door knobs. They had prints from two different people. One was likely Jurika; the other they guessed was also a woman. Nothing Raveneau found suggested Jurika intended to travel; no packed bags, passport, itinerary, plane tickets, or email records of flight confirmations. From the cat pictures and the rest, Raveneau couldn't see her abandoning her pet, leaving it here to starve. So good chance she was abducted.

AT&T called back and promised to fax a record of her incoming and outgoing phone numbers for the cell and landline. After the CSI pair left and Raveneau couldn't think of anything more to do here, they locked the door and

Raveneau told the manager, 'We'll be back later today. We'd like to keep the key, if that's OK.' Then he asked, 'Do you have a way to take care of the cat?'

The manager wrinkled his nose. 'They're not even allowed here.'

Now they crossed the Bay Bridge on their way to a print shop in Emeryville, where the woman who had recognized Jurika and called in this morning worked. Her name was Sally Cheung and she turned out to be seasoned, tough, and no nonsense. She nodded as Raveneau showed her a photo.

'That's her, and she wasn't the most honest employee, but she was always fun.' After a pause she added, 'She got fired for stealing.'

Fired for stealing credit card numbers, but never arrested and prosecuted according to the former boss they talked to that afternoon. 'Hiring her was like catching a bad cold on a plane. In the end it didn't hurt us much, but it was shitty while it lasted.'

They read about her all afternoon and finally got on her Facebook page, then started contacting her Facebook friends, none of whom had contacted the police on their own. Late in the afternoon they went back to the apartment building and made another search for the green Toyota Camry registered to her. At seven that night Raveneau said, 'Why don't you come over? I'll cook dinner and we'll keep working.'

When la Rosa arrived she spotted the cat exploring the roof.

'Isn't that Jurika's cat?'

'Yeah, I couldn't leave it there.' When the cat ran back over he picked it up and showed her the name tag, Visa. La Rosa smiled, shook her head.

He fired up the barbecue as la Rosa checked out how he lived. At 10:30, just as they called it a night, Raveneau's landline rang. He saw Celeste's name on the screen and remembered they were going to try to see each other tonight if it all worked out. With everything happening today he forgot to call her late this afternoon.

'Celeste, I'm sorry, I saw the message light blinking when I got home, but we caught a break in a case today and I've been caught up in that.'

'Are you still working on it?'

'Just finishing.'

In the background la Rosa laughed at something the cat did.

'Who's that?'

'My partner. She came over for dinner so we could keep working. We got an ID on that woman in China Basin I told you about. We know who she is now.'

'I didn't know you had a woman as a partner.'

La Rosa laughed again and when he looked over the cat was jumping up two to three feet straight up off the deck.

'She sounds young.'

'You've got a good ear if you can tell that, but you're right.'

'What's her name?'

'Elizabeth.'

'Pretty name.'

He looked at la Rosa as he answered, knew she was tracking the conversation and said, 'Yes, it

116

is a pretty name. Too bad her personality doesn't match it.'

La Rosa smiled and Celeste said, 'Have fun, I'll talk to you later.'

A moment later she hung up.

TWENTY-THREE

The first words of the older sister of the victim, Gloria Jurika, were, 'I'm not surprised.'

But she was surprised and shocked and had trouble talking. She declined Raveneau's offer to pick her up at the airport and didn't call his cell until she reached the Hall of Justice. He found her downstairs standing alone twenty feet from the elevators, the black hair, wide forehead and thin nose unmistakably similar to her sister's. People walked past her and around her; she seemed in a space all her own until he touched her shoulder.

'Gloria, I'm Inspector Raveneau.'

'Will you take me to see her?'

'Let's go upstairs first.'

In the office Gloria Jurika said the last communication from her sister was an email asking to borrow fifty thousand dollars. A moment later she added, 'Fifty thousand is all of my savings. The last time I loaned her money she didn't pay it back. Do you think she was killed over money?'

'We don't have any idea yet. We're hoping you can help us.'

'She also tried to borrow from mom. She flew down, went to the nursing home, and got mom to sign a check. One of the employees at the nursing home called me and I put a stop on it. That was about a week and a half ago. Before that, Alex hadn't visited mom in two and a half years.'

'What did she do for work here? Tell us about her.'

'I don't know what she did for work. She wouldn't tell me.' After a pause she added, 'Alex never finished high school.'

'We've got some email addresses we'd like you to look at. These are out of her computer, people we haven't contacted yet, but maybe you'll recognize somebody. We've also run her name through some of our systems and haven't come up with any criminal record. Do you know of any criminal arrests in her past?'

'There was one before she left home. That was about drug dealing but it was pretty minor, though in our family we've never known how she earns her money.'

'She's had various jobs.'

'We know about the jobs but they don't explain her clothes and jewelry. What would you think if you had a sister like that?'

He'd think what Gloria was thinking and reluctant to say, that the money came from somewhere. They had run Alex Jurika through the local, state, and national systems, and hadn't come up with anything more than a minor possession of marijuana charge eleven years ago at eighteen, which was likely the arrest Gloria referred to.

He listened as Gloria continued to criticize her

119

sister. It made him think of parents flying into San Francisco to reclaim the body of a runaway child. Sometimes, initially, they displayed anger toward the child, or spoke as though the child had gotten what they deserved. They had already imagined all the worst things. They had expected something bad to happen. But that's still not the same as having it actually happen. He thought Gloria was in that space right now.

They showed her the emails and watched her sift through and then touch an email address. 'That's her cousin, another thief.' Her voice broke. 'My sister was a thief.' She covered her eyes. 'I don't know why I didn't just say it a half hour ago. I'm sorry.'

'You don't need to be sorry. What kind of thief?'

'Credit cards.'

'And this cousin is an accomplice?'

'Yes.'

'Did she tell you that?'

She shook her head.

'But you figured it out?'

'Yes.'

The cousin's name was Julie Candiff. Gloria gave them a Phoenix address and phone number for her, and then the phone number of Julie's parents, Gloria's aunt and uncle, in case Julie had moved or didn't respond.

'Her parents will know how to get a hold of her and she's afraid of her dad, so if she lies to you or won't talk to you, mention him. She and Alex were terrible influences on each other when they were younger. They were the same age and my parents flew Julie out when she was twelve so they could get to know each other, because we have a very strong extended family. But the first thing they did together was start shoplifting. It was like Bonnie meeting Clyde.'

A tear leaked from her left eye and she swatted at her face as though a mosquito had landed there.

'I'm sorry to be like this, I'm really sorry. I guess I'm just really angry she got herself killed. She was so sweet when she was a little girl and then everything went wrong.'

Raveneau opened one of the photo albums they pulled from Jurika's apartment. Gloria flipped through them with a pained expression, and then slid them away, unable to find a photo of the cousin, Julie Candiff. She wasn't one of Alex's Facebook friends either.

They took her down to see her sister's body and unlike those who need to touch the cold skin to know it's really final she just stared and then stepped back. She said nothing about the marks on her sister's neck, wrists, and ankles, and stared blankly when la Rosa asked if she wanted to ride with them to her sister's apartment. She finally shook her head and said, 'I'll drive myself.'

In the apartment she walked quietly through, touching nothing but pointing to a white horse carved out of ivory.

'I gave that to her when she was eight.'

'And she kept it right there where she could see it every day,' la Rosa said. 'Do you want to claim the things here?'

'No.'

'At some point the apartment manager will clean out everything.'

'I don't want anything.'

'She had a cat,' Raveneau said. 'Do you know anybody who'd like her cat? I've got it, right now.'

'I don't know anybody.'

After Gloria left and they were still in the apartment, la Rosa summed up her opinion.

'That's one cold fish.'

But Raveneau didn't see her that way at all. He thought she was deeply sad and close to breaking down.

'Why don't I call the cousin before we leave here,' la Rosa said. 'I'll make a run at her woman to woman. I think I've gotten a feel of her from the emails.'

'Sure, but from the way Gloria was talking I wouldn't count on the cousin knowing she's dead. It's not clear to me that Gloria has told her own parents yet.'

Raveneau overheard Julie Candiff answer the phone and after la Rosa explained, the words, 'Oh, no, oh, no.'

La Rosa was on the phone with her forty minutes or more, finally pulling something out of Julie that sent her to the bedroom closet. With the phone still in her left hand she reached up on a shelf and pulled down three empty purses they'd previously checked. In a burgundy-colored leather purse she followed Julie's directions and found a seam near the bottom bound by Velcro. When she pulled the Velcro apart it

122

exposed a pocket sewed behind the lining. In it were six driver's licenses, all with Alex's face but none with her name or true driver's license number. For each license there was a credit card. When she hung up with the cousin she looked at Raveneau and said, 'Looks like Gloria was right about credit fraud. So is that what got her killed?'

TWENTY-FOUR

Not long after Stoltz started his five year prison sentence, his new cellmate, a pug-faced guy who went by the name of Chulie, suggested with a good-natured grin that since they were trapped with each other and without women, they should service each other sexually. When Stoltz declined, Chulie turned sullen.

Then came the night Stoltz was lying on his back trying to go to sleep, trying not to obsess about what had happened, and breathing the rank prison air while listening to the animal howls of some crazy asshole down the cell block, when something inside him snapped. The lights, noise, loss of reputation, the narrowing of his existence down to this locked building full of losers caused a tightening in his chest that felt like a hand crushing his heart. He could barely breathe and croaked Chulie's name.

But Chulie thought he was calling for a different reason and when he'd realized it was medical help he'd wanted, decided to watch rather than yell for a guard. In seconds Stoltz became drenched in sweat and overwhelmed by fear. Four hours later a disdainful prison doctor told him his heart was fine and that his head was the problem. An anxiety attack was not uncommon for those just starting their sentence.

'Let me give you some advice,' he said. 'Your life has changed irrevocably. Nothing will ever be the same. People will never accept you in the same way, and those who tell you later that the fact you went to prison doesn't matter to them will all be liars. You'll be an ex-con for the rest of your life and that means you'll always be a lesser human being. It does mean you'll never again have the life you had before. Accept that and acknowledge you took another man's life, and then you can move on. There's a price for what you've done. Fight it and it's going to eat you from the inside out. The claw marks in your chest today came from your head. Think about that.'

He didn't take that advice and got through five years of prison by vowing to get his old life back. Now, he almost had it. Not quite, but almost. In prison he had part-time access to a computer and gave away his best ideas to those that could help him get back on his feet later. Some of that paid off. He was ready to fight and win again, and a hatred of Raveneau was growing in him. The hatred he nurtured for Whitacre and Bates was for all of them now, but he needed to keep that in balance. Still, he was sure Raveneau would be back. Raveneau would be the one. Raveneau was the locus, the center, the eye, the one to watch.

TWENTY-FIVE

'Let's play a little basketball,' la Rosa said as they got back from Jurika's apartment near dusk. 'I keep thinking about Heilbron and need to clean the smell of him out of my pores.'

'You and me, one on one?'

'Sure, why not, unless I'm too intimidating.'

'You're not.'

'You sure?'

'Where would we play?'

'I belong to a club. They've got pretty good indoor courts and there's usually one open. It's in South San Francisco but you could go down Third and avoid the traffic.' She touched his arm. 'But honestly, not if it scares you, and it's only fair to tell you I played point guard at San Jose State for two years. Most of that was on the bench, but I'm sure I can still embarrass an old man. Come out and play with me.'

'I haven't played in years.'

'I believe you but you're all that's available and we can keep talking about the case on the court.'

At his last physical Raveneau's doctor told him, 'Buy a blood pressure monitor. Go to Longs or Walgreens, plenty of places sell them, and start taking your blood pressure in the first

126

hour after waking in the morning because that's when it's highest. Keep a log. You're borderline and I want to see if we can bring it down with exercise before we get into a prescription.'

Raveneau bought the blood pressure monitor and used it twice before rolling the rubber hose tightly around the cuff and putting it in a drawer. The readings he had gotten weren't great but they weren't terrible and he already had enough other things to worry about. He did buy a new pair of running shoes and started aiming for three to four runs a week. He averaged one or two.

He met la Rosa outside the club and she insisted on paying his guest fee. It was a nice club, clean, a lot of modern weight and aerobic equipment, a spin room, rows of racquetball courts, a whole world of people living a way he didn't have much connection with but probably ought to. He followed her on to the court and shot a dozen baskets before she said, 'OK, let's do this.'

La Rosa went around him and scored as soon as she got the ball. She took the first game of one on one without working hard at all and he learned that she had a pretty good jump shot, but that she favored the left side of the key, which was also her go-to side for lay-ups. She had a third shot, a fall-away hook that she bounced off the iron twice, and made only one of three of in the first game.

No one was going to be shooting any free throw fouls and she bumped hard as she worked in, pushing him back with her ass and shoulder, telling him something more about her and her style. She wasn't shy with her elbows either and rode a hand on him, pushing back whenever he dribbled across the key and in. He spun, came up, and bounced one off the glass and the rim as she pushed him and he landed hard.

'Is that how they played in your league?' he asked, and got a grim smile as she dribbled at the top of the key and broke around him again.

'There need to be more women on the homicide detail,' she said as her shot dropped, and then added, 'Three isn't enough. The change is too slow. It needs to happen faster.'

'That would mean a bigger department and they're not hiring right now. They're talking but not hiring.'

'Maybe some people need to retire.'

'Yeah, who do you have in mind?'

'It's about old boy networks and prejudices. It's time to change.'

'I don't know about any network.'

'It's men looking out for men. Time for change.'

Raveneau was one of these guys who once he got warmed up, stayed that way. He'd always been like that and was down about ten pounds since the blood pressure scare with the doctor. He wasn't carrying much fat but he wasn't fit the way he should be either. A crease of sweat formed center of his chest, then his back, and she didn't shy away from his sweat-soaked back either. Her hand was right there, pushing hard against him, tips of her fingers digging in and nothing sexual in it; la Rosa fighting him as he worked his way in and got two points.

She checked the ball. He shot from the top of the key and swished it. She checked the ball back to him and he scored twice, before she picked up a rebound and he got to meet the real Elizabeth la Rosa.

She didn't back into him this time. She dropped a shoulder and drove past on his left, and when he fouled her as she went up and said, 'Sorry,' because he'd caught her pretty good and hadn't meant to, she said, 'My ball,' took it to the top of the key and started in, faked the same move, spun, went around him, her knees grazing his belly as she put it in.

When they started out they said, five games, and when she won four in a row and lost the last one, she wouldn't quit until they'd played another. His T-shirt was sweat-soaked and her cheeks and forehead were shiny, and sweat ran down from the damp hair at her temples. She wasn't big or tall, five nine, maybe one forty-five, but she was agile and quick and graceful, until fatigue caught her in the last game.

Raveneau dropped four shots in a row and took an early lead. That just made her angry. She got angry and he got faster. She wanted the last game, wanted to show him up, show him what basketball training and an eighteen year advantage in age was worth, but if Raveneau was anything he was tough when it mattered and now he wanted the game. Maybe his hair was salt and pepper, but he wasn't an old man and he wasn't moving out or away just at the age when he was finally getting good at his job.

He fell behind. For five games in a row she ran the same move and now finally he smoked the ball out of her hands as she went up. Next play he got the ball back and she was in his face saying, 'Nice play, but now you're going to have to get around me and score, or take another chance with that goofy-foot jumper of yours.'

Raveneau didn't answer, knew she was just waiting for a chance to steal the ball back, and she slapped at it now and almost knocked it loose, and then he was on the move. When she cut off the inside lane he tried a hook shot, some throwback to an era before la Rosa had been born. It hit the backboard and went in.

A couple of people had come over to watch and playing to them, Raveneau dropped a three pointer. He scored again and then had her. He was only one shot away and after she scored twice he got a rebound, worked it in and took it home for the win.

'One more game,' she said the second the ball dropped through, and he shook his head.

'That was it,' he said. 'I'm done.'

'No, come on, one more.'

'I'm beat.'

'You've got one more in you.'

'I've always got one more in me.'

He played another just to get to know his new partner better. His knees ached, his breath came harder, and he didn't have the drive he carried through the game before. He was ready for a beer when she beat him by one shot. Sweat had formed droplets on his forearms and soaked through his hair and clothes. He was spent but it felt good and they had a beer at the club bar before leaving.

'That was fun,' she said. 'We'll have to do that again. For an old guy you've got some staying power.'

'You're beating this age thing to death. Maybe you're missing all the talk about fifty being the new forty.'

'I'll be chief of police by the time I'm fifty and the homicide detail will be half female.'

He didn't answer that. He smiled and put his glass down.

'Let's go back at Heilbron tomorrow. See you in the morning.'

TWENTY-SIX

Raveneau woke to a hollow banging noise that died away within moments. When the sound woke him a second time he came to wakefulness with the memory of a corrupt police officer in Guatemala tip-tapping the barrel of his gun against the driver's window of a rented car, waiting for Raveneau to roll down the window. He listened to the noise another thirty seconds, realized it was three in the morning and got out of bed quietly and fumbled for his clothes. Once outside he walked across the big roof toward the noise, carrying a flashlight he hadn't turned on yet. He figured it was someone trying to break into the warehouse underneath him. He looked over the parapet and then clicked on the light.

Almost directly below was a metal access door to his landlord's business. When his flashlight beam caught the top of a billed cap, the would-be burglar dropped the iron bar he was using to get through the metal door and zigzagged into the darkness. He ran back toward the street and that was fine with Raveneau. Let the guy run. The last thing he wanted to do was deal with him inside the building. But a few seconds later, as he swept the asphalt lot below with the light, he heard the buzz of a bullet passing and the popping of another round going off. He ducked down behind the parapet, swore, and killed the light. Down the street a car with its headlights on accelerated away, and without a make on the car Raveneau walked to his phone. But he was plenty angry the guy had taken a shot at him.

Two officers arrived ten minutes later. They wrote it up as Raveneau limped around on the street. One of the officers looked at him and asked, 'You twist your ankle when he took a shot at you?'

'No, I'm just sore because I got a little exercise. I'm not used to it.'

The cops laughed.

'Anything else you want us to do?'

'No, I'm good.'

'Then we'll take a drive around. And you think it was a Honda?'

'Oh, hell, I don't know, I could barely make out the shape. But it looked like a Honda, probably late model.'

After studying the damage to the door, Raveneau wrote a note for the owner. He'd give him a call in the morning. Around the deadbolt the door was badly dented and the lock had been all but hammered off. Han would need to replace it all tomorrow. When he got back up to the apartment it was 4:30 and he was too wired up to go back to sleep. He showered, dressed, made coffee and drove into work.

There, he found a note from CSI. They'd gotten a hit on the second set of prints taken from Jurika's apartment and came up with a Deborah Lafaye, who'd been pulled over on Green Street three years ago and pled guilty to driving under the influence. Through the DUI arrest they had a Fulton Street address in San Francisco. He stared at her name, repeating it silently to himself because there was something familiar. Then he googled her and got it. He clicked on to the website of her charity foundation. The foundation's stated mission was to bring modern medical techniques and supplies to the world's poor. He skimmed that, read her bio, looked at photos, and tried to imagine a reason she'd be in Jurika's apartment. He couldn't come up with one and continued to click around on the website as he mulled it over.

Then he called la Rosa and woke her up.

'It's Saturday,' she said. 'What are you doing in there?'

'I shot baskets for a couple of hours earlier this morning and then I figured I'd just come in and work.' Now he told her what happened last night. Then he picked up the CSI note and read it to her. 'CSI got a hit on the second set of prints, a Deborah Lafaye.'

'The world health foundation, the woman with the fingernails.'

'You got it right away. I had to google her.'

'It must be a mistake.'

'They double-checked it.'

Now she was quiet as she did what he had done, trying to picture this minor celebrity in Jurika's kitchen. He remembered the fingernail story. Lafaye had most of her nails ripped out in a torture session and she wore the misshapen result like a badge of honor. He'd seen her on a talk show holding her hands up to the cameras, though none of that was on the website.

La Rosa did what he did, took another angle, asking, 'When was the DUI?'

'Three years ago as she was driving away from a restaurant. The note says they ran the prints twice, but I'll check with them again. Then I'm going to call her.'

'Call me first.'

The prints still came back as Deborah Lafaye's and la Rosa came into the office. She watched him cross the room and said, 'The way you're walking reminds me of my dog when he got so old he could barely stand in the morning. I finally had to have him put to sleep. He was blind by then and he couldn't hear either. You have reading glasses, don't you?'

'Yeah.'

'Did I hurt you?'

'Listen, I've been reading more about Lafaye. She's a pretty big deal and she's got some friends with throw weight.'

'Throw weight?'

'Yeah, like a missile. It's a word out of the Cold War, another event you missed. Check out the web page, you'll see a picture of her with Clinton. Seems like I remember when she started out and it hasn't been that many years. She's brought that foundation a long way.'

Like a true cop, la Rosa read the arrest article first, and he made coffee. Though it was Saturday and the office empty but for one interview underway, la Rosa had dressed in a coffee-colored suit and shoes to match. Maybe that was for an anticipated meeting with Lafaye, but who knew whether Lafaye was even in town. He got the impression from the website and everything else that popped up on Google that Lafaye traveled a lot. Seeing her nice clothes reminded him of a period of several years when he'd worn nice suits every day and told people that it was out of respect for the dead.

But that respect for the dead had also coincided with when he was most full of himself. Looking back now, he figured he'd known a few very good inspectors and some very bad ones and the clothing hadn't made anyone better or worse. Some of the bad inspectors had dressed immaculately yet couldn't find a soldier on an army base.

The good ones connected to some pulse running through everyone. One of the very best had taken him aside at a retirement party and walked him out into a warm May night on a patio to tell him, 'Dump the expensive suits, you don't need them. I've been watching you and you're the real deal, but you're missing details because you're spending too much time trying to keep coffee off your tie.'

At some point after trying to live larger than he was, Raveneau had figured it out. He sipped the coffee now and waited for his new partner to agree. When she did he punched in the first of two numbers they had for Deborah Lafaye and got an answer on the third ring.

'This is Inspector Ben Raveneau with the San Francisco Police. My partner and I are investigating a homicide – a killing in China Basin a week ago Thursday. Maybe you read about it?'

'I haven't.'

'Or saw the sketch that ran on TV when we went out to the public.'

'Inspector, I've been out of town so I'm not sure how I can help you. Why did you call me?'

'We believe you knew our victim and we'd like to meet and talk with you about her. Her name was Alex Jurika.'

'Oh, my God.'

'Did you know her?'

'Yes. Yes, oh, really, my God, Alex is dead? She once worked for me. I can't believe she's dead. When did this happen? She was murdered? Alex was murdered? That's terrible news.'

'Yes, she was and I'm sorry. It sounds like you knew her well.'

Lafaye immediately qualified that.

'I haven't seen much of her in the last five years. This makes me so sad. What happened?'

'We're investigating. We don't really know what happened yet. We found her body in a building in China Basin.'

Raveneau paused one beat and said, 'We'd like to talk with you in person today.'

There was a gap as she debated that, but he knew what the answer would be. His guess was that right now she was spinning different scenarios about how they connected her name to Jurika. She hadn't volunteered that she'd been in Jurika's apartment.

'I'll have to ask you to give me a few minutes. I don't even know my own schedule. I need to call my secretary and then I'll call you back.

What number shall I use?'

When she called back she said, 'A driver is going to take me to a meeting in Napa. Would it inconvenience you, Inspector, if we met in the parking lot at the Larkspur Ferry in Marin? I realize that's probably not what you had in mind, but there are people I'm supposed to rendezvous with there, and we could meet ahead of that. I can give you my cell number, or if you give me yours I'll call you as I get there. Will that be OK?' After a moment, she added, 'I'm just so shocked.'

Thirty minutes later Raveneau was at the ferry landing and on his cell phone to Lafaye. He watched a big ferry gliding out and then churning a heavy white wake as it turned toward San Francisco, and Lafaye guided him to where she was waiting.

She was a lean woman, silver-haired, blue or almost violet-eyed, taller than average and eye-catching, though she must be his age. He couldn't help but look at her fingers. The man who'd done it to her had done a very thorough job.

She caught his secret glance and said, 'Don't worry about it. Everybody looks at my hands. I knew as soon as you told me she was dead why you'd called me. I just wanted to talk to my lawyer before meeting you. You're wondering what my fingerprints were doing in Alex's apartment.'

'That's right.'

'I hope you're not wondering if I killed her.'

'Why would we wonder that?'

'You're in the suspicion business.'

'I've always thought of it in a different way.'

'And you wanted to meet face to face.'

'It's better that way.'

'Then why don't we get coffee and talk?'

Something about her eyes was arresting, the color maybe. 'Let's do that,' he said, and then added, 'We're just hoping you can help us.'

She smiled at that and said, 'I use that line all the time myself when we're fund raising.'

TWENTY-SEVEN

They took an outdoor table at the coffee house in the mall across from the ferry landing. The table was in sunlight, the fall morning pleasant. When the coffees came Lafaye didn't touch hers.

'Alex worked for me in 1997 after I started the foundation. She was very good at getting people to pledge money, and I don't mean the rich or the corporate, but the average person. She had that touch. She could get a guy who couldn't make his rent to give a hundred dollars. I would sit in a chair sometimes and just listen to her on the phone trying to figure out why she was so successful at it.'

She watched Raveneau now as she added, 'I still see her about once a year.' She touched her face. 'Or I did. I really am in shock over this.'

'I understand.'

'I hope you do. I saw her a week ago, Tuesday or Wednesday. She wanted to pitch an idea to me so I went over to her apartment to have a glass of wine and listen.'

'Was it a good idea?'

'Oh, yes, and many of her ideas were great ideas, but I would never consider bringing Alex back into the foundation.' She reached across the table and touched his arm. 'I don't want to say anything bad about Alex.' She looked up suddenly. 'You haven't told me how she died.'

'She was strangled in an empty building in China Basin. What did she pitch you?'

'Strangled. What was she doing there?'

'We don't know yet.'

'She said she was moving to Phoenix. She proposed setting up a facility there for my foundation. Her idea was to consolidate all the monthly pledges made all over the world via credit cards. She wanted me to hire her to oversee that aspect and run it from Arizona.'

'Was she qualified?'

'Well, it's funny you ask that because she was the farthest thing from the type you'd expect to run something like that, but I'd say she was way above the level of your basic MBA. She was remarkable with numbers. She could have organized anything numerical.'

'But you were reluctant to pursue the idea with her.'

'Is that what we're here to talk about?'

'No, but we have questions about how she earned a living, so anything you can tell me helps.'

'She only talked about this idea of a consolidated credit facility. We had our yearly glass of wine and I left town the next day. I didn't get home until yesterday so maybe that's how I missed hearing that she'd been killed.'

'Where did you go?'

'Washington. Do you want the names of the senators I met with?'

He thought about that a moment. 'Sure.' He

141

wrote down their names.

'Why wouldn't you rehire her?'

'I'd rather not discuss that.'

'Then let me say this, we believe she may have been involved in a credit card theft ring.'

Lafaye shook her head. She looked dismayed. She looked past him.

'When she left us the foundation received complaints regarding credit card charges. Obviously, if it had tied to Alex I wouldn't have been drinking wine with her a week ago, but it was a factor in not talking her out of resigning. A private investigator suspected her. I decided to keep the friendship but never mix it with business again.'

La Rosa walked up now, took her sunglasses off, introduced herself and handed Lafaye a card. Lafaye looked surprised, even nervous that a second inspector had showed up.

'I'm pleased to meet you,' Lafaye said to la Rosa, 'but I'm afraid I'm out of time. I wish I knew more about Alex's life. I'm truly sick at heart that she was killed and I'd like to do anything I can to help you catch her murderer, but I have no idea how to help. But please call me if you think I can.'

'Before you go I want to say I'm a great admirer of your foundation,' la Rosa said. 'You've really made a difference.'

'I hope to continue to. I appreciate you saying that.'

She stood and picked up her purse but left la Rosa's card on the table. The inspectors stood as well and Raveneau said, 'I need to take a couple of notes.' He opened his notebook with la Rosa alongside him now as a witness. 'Did you say it was a week ago Wednesday that you were with Alex Jurika in her apartment?'

'I believe it was Wednesday but it may have been Tuesday. You can double-check my memory of it being Wednesday by finding the tenant in her apartment complex that just had back surgery. I rode up the elevator with him and we chatted about his surgery. You might try him.'

'Did you call her before coming by?'

'We had set it up a month or so before. She was in touch with my secretary. I can ask him. What am I missing here, Inspector? Why does it matter how we organized a glass of wine?'

'So far you're the only person we know of who was in communication with her just before she was murdered.'

'And, again, I'll do everything I can to help, but please reassure me you aren't even vaguely imagining that I know something about her murder.'

'I thought we had covered that.'

'Well, it's the way you're asking things, and this business of opening your notebook as we're getting ready to say goodbye.'

'I'm a great admirer,' la Rosa said. 'Honestly, I just wanted to meet you.'

Lafaye's cell rang and as she retrieved it she said, 'You've heard my phone ring while we've been here. Hasn't it rung at least ten times?'

It probably had.

'That's what my life is like,' she said as she looked at the screen but didn't answer.

'You must be so organized,' la Rosa said.

'No, I'm the opposite but I have people around me who are very efficient.' She turned her attention back to Raveneau. 'It was Wednesday because Thursday I was on a plane to London. If I had to guess, I'd say I left her apartment at around seven thirty. I'll try to remember more before we speak again.'

This time as her phone rang she answered it and waved goodbye as she walked off.

'Now what?' la Rosa asked.

'We go back and regroup. She's hiding something.'

They went back to the homicide office and Raveneau got a call from Lieutenant Becker.

'There are a couple of Oakland detectives who'd like to talk to you today,' Becker said. 'Are you available?'

'Are they named Hendricks and Stalos?'

'Yes.'

'Tell them to come to the office. I'm here with Elizabeth following up on a new lead on the China Basin killing.'

'Stay there. I'll be coming in too. The Oakland detectives have new questions about Bates. They want your opinion. They're wondering why he doubled the life insurance payout on his wife three months ago.'

'Is that right?'

'That's what they claim.'

Forty minutes later Becker arrived. The Oakland inspectors were right behind him. They were all charged up and it was written large on their faces. They had it all figured out.

TWENTY-EIGHT

'We understand Ted Whitacre asked you for help. Is that correct?'

Raveneau nodded.

'When you met with him what did he ask you to do?'

'Knock on Stoltz's door and let him know we knew he was following Ted.'

'Warn him off?'

'Yes.'

'Did you?'

'Ted died before I got to Stoltz. I was on-call that week. I had planned to go see him as soon as I was off.'

'Did you tell Charles Bates that you were going to visit Cody Stoltz?'

'Sure. The day I met with Whitacre I called Charles on my way back to the Hall.'

'How did he respond?'

'He was skeptical Whitacre had been followed by Stoltz. He said he was getting regular calls from Ted at night about old cases and guessed it had something to do with the cocktail of cancer drugs, Ted wanting to clean up the unsolved cases before dying. I'm sure you've asked Bates – what's he told you?'

Stalos checked it with his partner before

answering. Hendricks gave the faintest nod.

'Basically, he told us what you just said.'

'Whitacre was a pretty reliable guy. I took him at his word that he'd seen Stoltz.'

'After Ted Whitacre's body was found did you ask Mr Bates to drive with you to Los Altos where Stoltz lives?'

'No, I went alone.'

'What was the point?'

'I wasn't convinced Ted's death was suicide.'

'What do you think now?'

'I think he was murdered.'

Hendricks spoke for the first time, saying, 'We agree with you,' and Stalos added, 'The Burlingame detective, I can never remember his name—'

'Choy.'

'Yeah, Ed Choy said you came in the door calling it a murder.'

'That's not quite right, but I was upset at how fast he was moving and I was upset anyway. I'd worked with Ted for twenty years.'

'We hear you. We understand.'

Stalos leaned forward a little more, setting up to confide. Raveneau had done this many times himself.

'Detective Choy gave us a look at what he's got so far. Seems to us he just made an assumption about suicide. I've got a copy of his report. Do you want to take a look at it?'

'Not right now. Why don't you tell me why you're here? I understand that Bates doubled the life insurance on his wife three months ago, or you think he did. So start there.'

Hendricks stepped in on that one, saying emphatically, 'He did double it.'

'Here's what we have,' Stalos said. 'We've got a significant bump in the life insurance coverage on both Charles and Jacie Bates that was done six months ago, not three months. That's unusual for a man with heart and prostate problems and a police pension to pay for it. It ramped their payments way up. Jacie had her own medical troubles, and then there's the girlfriend thing. Bates has been seeing a younger woman who works for the Alameda DA. We got a tip about that and it checked out. So now we're wondering what we've got.'

'Who bumped the insurance coverage?'

'Jacie Bates did, but it doesn't mean he didn't talk her into it.'

'Go on.'

'He missed the walk that night and neighbors say he was pretty good about making the walks with her. He didn't miss many of them.'

'But he missed some or did you find a neighbor keeping track on a calendar?'

'We know they mostly walked together.'

'He was home when the pickup burned. How do you explain that?'

'He had her hit. Hired somebody to run her down and burn the truck. It has started to look like a different investigation. So we're here to talk to you. Did he have a girl on the side when he worked the detail here?'

'Not that I ever heard about.'

'Did he ever talk about problems with his marriage?'

'Not to me and I always had the impression that he and Jacie were very close. My wife and I divorced years ago. I used to look at Bates and think he had a really strong, good thing with Jacie.'

'Do you want to hear the whole wild ass theory?'

'Go ahead.'

'OK, Bates killed his former partner so that he could then kill his wife and make it look like Stoltz did it. He knew Whitacre would talk to other people about being followed and he saw an opportunity. Stoltz wouldn't know where the key was under the flagstone in Whitacre's backyard, but Bates did. He told us he did. His old partner was starting to have Stoltz sightings, and was dying anyway, so he starts thinking about a way to free Whitacre from his cancer and deal Jacie out of the game so he can be with his girlfriend.'

Hendricks held up his left hand, the fingers long and thin as a pianist's. 'How many days has it been since Jacie was killed?' He counted them off on his fingers. 'Damn if I can't almost count them on one hand. He was with the girlfriend last night. What's that say about his grief?'

He waved his hand as if erasing everything said.

'But we admit we don't know much yet and obviously we don't want our theory to be right.'

'I can tell how.'

'No, I mean it, Raveneau. We'd like to be wrong on this. That's why we're looking to you. We want you to prove we've got our heads up our asses.'

'Maybe I can help you with that part either way.'

That got a smile from Hendricks.

'You say he never mentioned this girlfriend to you and you don't know him as a man with girls on the side.'

'That's true.'

'What do you think about him spending the night with the girlfriend this close to Jacie's death? We haven't even released the body.'

'It surprises me, but I don't know what he's feeling and having a girlfriend doesn't mean he killed his wife.'

He felt both watching him and then it was Hendricks who put the question to him.

'If we need it, would you be willing to wear a wire?'

'No.'

'What if we have solid proof?'

'If you've got that kind of proof, arrest him.'

They didn't like that and it kind of quietened the room. Raveneau figured they must have been counting on selling the wire idea.

'We've got some questions we want you to ask him. We think you're the one to talk to him since you're the one with the Whitacre murder investigation, and you and your partner are looking at this Cody Stoltz. We think Bates will want to know what you learn and monitor your progress.'

Raveneau didn't answer.

TWENTY-NINE

Raveneau didn't inform the Oakland detectives, nor had Becker, but for the past two days an undercover team from San Francisco's Special Investigation Division, SID, had covered Stoltz. Right now, a black limo was in the driveway with the trunk up. Four pieces of high quality black plastic luggage, neither masculine nor feminine looking, that could belong to either Stoltz or his mother, had just been loaded into the trunk. Somebody was taking a trip.

Yesterday they learned that Stoltz had a route where he came through the garden, alongside the guest house, past the tennis courts and pool, and in through the doors of a sunroom at the rear of mom's place. Stoltz alternated his daily routes and Mike Malloy, the Special Investigations Division officer watching, wondered as he had several times in the last forty-eight hours whether Stoltz knew he was under surveillance.

They had learned a fair amount about him in the last two days and Malloy was somewhat impressed. Stoltz had a gift and reputation for pattern recognition. Yesterday afternoon they watched him knock out a book of Sudoku puzzles over a latte at a Starbucks. Among his friends, and this guy did have friends – he wasn't isolated even if he lived on the estate with mom – he was known as 'The Engineer'. Ordinary enough nickname and otherwise corny, but not so much since it came from guys who also spent their lives in front of a computer. Stoltz probably could have gone somewhere much bigger with his life if he hadn't fucked up. He had a few strange habits but nothing too out of the ordinary, and definitely nothing like some of the people they watched.

Outside of what they'd gotten from Homicide, the SID team had questioned a number of people on their own, including a goofball named Chulie who'd been Stoltz's cellmate. Chulie remembered Stoltz wanting to even the score with SF Homicide, but he also wanted something in return for remembering.

Malloy knew the mother lived with only a housekeeper who served as cook and caretaker. The mother was seventy-five but looked and sounded like a hardened sixty. Cosmetic surgeries had turned her face into a tanned ping-pong ball. Malloy watched her get in the car. Then Stoltz walked out of the house. He strode across the stone porch and down the steps with a light linen sport coat draped over one arm. He got in behind the driver, the whole move over in less than ten seconds.

'Suspect is in the vehicle and the vehicle is moving.'

SID leapfrogged the limo as it drove to SFO. When it pulled up to the domestic terminal they'd already had two officers stationed inside, who then watched them check into first class at the United counter. Malloy went through special security with another officer and saw them board. He'd bet a beer on Hawaii, based on the way Stoltz was dressed. He'd hoped for Hawaii. If it had been, he'd be getting on the same plane or the one after it.

But it wasn't Hawaii. It was LA, and LAPD would catch them on the other side, as Malloy and another officer followed on a later plane. The United supervisor they talked to was hesitant before divulging Mrs Stoltz's itinerary. She showed an Irene and Cody Stoltz flying first class to LAX, and Irene Stoltz continuing on to Cabo San Lucas four days from now.

'Do you show Cody Stoltz on the Cabo leg?'

'No, sir, and I don't show any return flights with him.' She pivoted the screen so he could read, adding, 'He must have other plans.'

THIRTY

Late in the afternoon, as he drove away from the homicide office, Raveneau called Celeste and said he was on his way, but running fifteen minutes late. He stopped to buy green papaya salad, stuffed crêpes, and two appetizers, one that was prawns in a hot sauce and the other a chicken deal tied up in rice paper. Then he drove up to Twin Peaks and met Celeste at her car. They walked up the trail with the food, a bottle of wine, and a blanket. The early evening carried a November chill, but sitting on the blanket and next to each other kept them warm. With the clear air the lights of the city below were very bright as dark came.

'Sorry about the other night,' Celeste said. 'I guess I got jealous. I don't know what I was thinking.'

'Forget about it. How was Napa?'

'Very beautiful. There was a low fog over the grapes that burned off with the first sunlight and the grass on the hills is the color of a lion now. What was your day like?'

'Like sitting in a small room with fluorescent lights that flicker too much.'

She laughed at that and at him. He liked that about her. There were good days and bad days and she didn't walk around expecting them all to be good.

'I heard something just before I came here that I can't really talk about,' he said. 'But it's got me disturbed.'

'Great.'

He took her hand and her fingers were cold now. It was just about time to fold the blanket up and get off the hill. Still, it was lucky to have this and better than sitting in a restaurant somewhere tonight. Celeste had her hair pulled back and a blue fleece coat zipped up under her neck. She was flying very early in the morning to a wine convention in Las Vegas and had to get home and pack tonight, so they left it that they'd try to get together as soon as she returned. He kissed her and when they parted they were like kids on a date or tourists winging a picnic in the city.

The guy Celeste lived with for ten years and expected to marry had left her reeling. The hurt ran deep and made her a little insecure. It didn't surprise him that she called him minutes after they said goodbye and asked, 'Should I call you from Vegas?'

'Or I'll call you.'

'Be safe. I just heard another news report.'

Meaning she heard something about the homicide detail. The media was working it. He turned on the radio after hanging up, but didn't hear anything new. When he got home Bates's car was parked out front.

'I would have called but I'm afraid they're tapping my phones.'

And this is how things can change; he let Bates

154

walk into the warehouse in front of him. He didn't want him behind him. Upstairs, he found a couple of beers in the refrigerator and made Bates dinner because he said he hadn't eaten since yesterday morning. Raveneau chopped an onion and broke a couple of eggs into a skillet and made a frittata.

'Did they come talk to you today about me and Jacie and our life insurance?'

'They did.'

'Changing the policies was Jacie's idea, not mine. She pestered me for a year but I wouldn't call the broker, so she did it herself.'

'They wouldn't be doing their job if they didn't look at everything.'

Clearly, Bates didn't believe that. He was quiet and then said, 'These guys are after me. They're building a case.'

'They are looking at you.'

'Did they say that?'

'You already know it.'

'What did they say to you?'

Raveneau looked Bates in the eye. Whatever they'd told him, they'd already asked Bates, but he still wanted Bates to volunteer it.

'You tell me.'

'My girlfriend.'

'How long have you had a girlfriend?'

'It doesn't matter. What matters is they're adding it up wrong. I went to LA and got them information. I put them on to guys who deal stolen vehicles long distance and sell them online. Now they're setting me up with what I gave them. I figured out where the truck came from that was used to kill Jacie. I gave what I learned to those detectives and they're trying to turn it against me. Setting me up for my sweet Jacie, that's what they're doing.'

Sweat started on Bates's forehead, a sheen wiped away with his hand. He stood. He moved to the slider and opened it so the cold air was on him, then sighed and said, 'Jacie couldn't have sex any more. She wasn't physically able to. She had a woman problem that got worse and it just built up in me. I needed somebody to hold, but you know Jacie was my life, man. She was everything.'

'What's the name of the girl?'

'Shaye Baylor.'

'What's she telling them?'

'Do you hear what I'm telling you?'

'I'm listening.'

Raveneau flipped the frittata and slid it on to a plate. He got out a bottle of balsamic vinegar and popped the bread out of the toaster.

'Eat. Pour a little of that vinegar over the eggs. It'll make them taste better. How long have you been with Shaye?'

The way Raveneau figured things, if this came back a lie it mattered. He watched Bates spill balsamic over the eggs.

'It's been going on about a year. I saw her last night but I could feel Jacie's ghost in the room. I couldn't see her but I could feel her, and I couldn't make it happen with Shaye. Losing Jacie ... it's just a big hole in my heart that isn't ever going to fill.

'These detectives are asking around about me

and Shaye. There's a bar we go to. They've been in there asking questions about me so they're following me. They're going to sweat her for whatever they want her to say.'

'And you're telling her to give them the truth.'

'Of course, I am. Look, man, I haven't been building a life with her. It's both of us needing the same thing right now. She knew I'd never leave Jacie. She was cool with that and she doesn't want an old man with health problems. But they're going to read in it what they want. They're like two bloodhounds on a scent. You know how it goes.'

'Have you ever told this girlfriend that you're going to be together with her, marry her, and take care of her, that you love her and someday you're going to be together?'

'Did they tell you that?'

'I'm asking you.'

'No, what I told you is what is, and I broke it off with her last night.'

'Then as long as she's straight with them, I don't think you'll have a problem there.'

'Bullshit. I've got an insurance problem. They think I put Jacie up to doubling the policy.'

Bates had eaten most of the eggs and finished the beer, but got up abruptly, went to the bathroom and threw up. Raveneau heard the toilet flush several times and slid the slider open as the smell of vomit spread into the room. When Bates came out, Raveneau handed him a glass of water and Bates asked, 'Who killed her? Did Stoltz kill my Jacie?'

'We had this conversation already, but now

I'm going to give you some advice. Call the detectives and tell them you want to meet and bring a lawyer, but keep the lawyer quiet. Anything you've lied to them about, clear it up, and get it off the table. If you told them there was no girlfriend and they found out on their own, come clean.'

Bates wasn't here for advice. He was here for information and ready to leave now.

'You've got to slow it down,' Raveneau said as they rode the elevator down. 'You need to sit down with them.'

'Bullshit, I do. All they want to do is charge me.'

Raveneau watched him get in his car. He was sure Bates had lied to the Oakland detectives about the girlfriend, and Bates was right, he didn't have much time. The detectives were just days away from charging him.

THIRTY-ONE

When Raveneau met up with the China Basin realtor the braggadocio was gone, and listening to him, he got the feeling the owners of the building had come down hard on him. The Great Recession was yet to let up on real estate and Raveneau doubted the owners thought a homicide in their building was a selling point.

'We've cleaned it up,' the realtor said as if talking to a potential client. 'Let me show you.' Once inside, he toured Raveneau. 'Look at this now. Imagine working here with that view of the bay. We've lowered the price, you know. Or maybe you don't know that.'

Raveneau didn't know. He looked across the water at Yerba Buena/Treasure Island. Plans had floated to build a new community, put up skyscrapers, casinos, build a mini-Hong Kong, or alternately a green community. But you heard little of that any more. The architects he knew were all looking for work or getting by on a lot less, and that's what it looked like ahead, and what he figured we'd all do. Do more with less.

They had painted, re-carpeted, cleaned the windows, put in a new gate and exterior doors, added a video surveillance system, and gotten the power turned back on. The new video

159

camera caught something last night the realtor thought they would want to see, so la Rosa was also on her way here.

Raveneau looked through a window at the video camera sitting up on the edge of the roof parapet like a sea gull. He guessed that somehow it was cheaper to put it up there. It was and the realtor explained how.

'There's an unused vent pipe on the roof that they ran the wire down. When the building sells we'll take the equipment with us. The monitor is in a broom closet down the hall here.' As they reached the room where Jurika was killed, Raveneau stopped and looked in at the newly painted walls, beige carpet, and a ceiling light fixture with a price tag dangling off it.

'We got it all,' the realtor said. 'You can't tell anything happened here, can you?'

He couldn't. Raveneau followed him to the broom closet and watched the video. The system was a cheap one and the camera angle on the roof wasn't good, but the van was Heilbron's. He watched Heilbron walk up and try several keys in the gate lock.

'Recognize him?' the realtor asked.

'Yeah, he's someone we've questioned.'

'What's he want to get in here for?'

'We'll ask him.'

'Who is he?'

'I'd like to get a copy of that tape if I can.'

They watched as Heilbron walked back to his van and opened the rear doors. Getting to his toolboxes, Raveneau thought. Heilbron returned to the gate a few minutes later and the realtor exhaled loudly and said, 'This city is nuts. I've got to get out of here.'

Raveneau watched Heilbron open the gate. A few minutes later he was through the main door. A small side camera caught that.

'Was your lock damaged?'

'No. Can't you arrest him anyway?'

'We'd need better footage to prove it's who I'm sure it is. Did he take anything?'

'Not as far as I know. At least tell me why he wants to get in here. You must at least have an idea?'

Raveneau turned to him. He saw the disbelief on the man's face.

'I don't know why. I'm wondering the same thing myself.'

THIRTY-TWO

Stoltz walked slowly through the Getty Museum with his mother gripping his elbow and her perfume enveloping them. He hated the smell of it and this controlling act of hers.

'I like this painting,' she said, 'but I'm sure you don't.'

She couldn't be more right.

'You're upset, Cody. You're worried about the police, aren't you?'

'The police have no one else, so in their knee-jerk way they're focused on me. What am I supposed to do with that?'

'You don't have to do anything with it. Just let it be. The police aren't stupid. They're not the brightest men in the world, but they work through things eventually. All you have to do is wait until they figure out their mistake. They will.'

She smiled her little girl smile, senility's breathless first dance. Then she surprised him.

'But I am disturbed by how quickly the police came to talk to you after that police inspector was killed. Why did they come to you so fast? Did you write more letters?'

'No.'

'Have you had any contact with any of them?'

'None.'

They looked at more paintings then ate lunch at the museum. At the table she reached across and took his hand.

'I want you to come to Mexico with me. If you're out of the country and something happens again, they won't look your way any more. That'll end it. I'll have Rosalie make you a plane reservation and you can continue on with me tomorrow.'

'Because of work I can't do that.'

'What do you have to do that can't wait?'

'Without me, the project I'm on stalls.'

'I really believe you should change your plans.'

'I wish I could.'

'I'm afraid I don't believe that, and I'm going to say it again, I want you to come to Mexico.'

'Like I said, I wish I could.'

She stared and he looked for the waiter. Then he pulled out his phone and checked his email. He glanced up, smiled and said, 'Next time, we'll go together.'

THIRTY-THREE

By dawn the next morning Stoltz was two hundred miles north of Los Angeles sitting in a red plastic booth at a chain restaurant along I-5, waiting for the waitress to bring the crap he'd ordered. When she did, he took one look and shoved the plate away.

'Sir, is there something wrong?'

'Just with the food, but it's not your fault. I should have known better. I'm ready for my check.'

She huffed away and instead of his check she returned with a pimply little guy in a checkered shirt who looked like an unemployed jockey. He turned out to be the manager. The manager also wanted to know if there was a problem and Stoltz said, 'The problem is you're serving food out of your dumpster.'

He started to get into a debate with the manager but ended it asking, 'Didn't they teach you the customer is always right?' He slid out of the booth and dropped ten bucks on the table. When the manager started to say something more, Stoltz said, 'Take my word for it, I'm the type to write a letter. So why don't you just shut up?'

When he got in the car he was shaking and unsure why he'd lost it in there. Three hours later and after two more stops, one for gas and one for a nap that he'd hoped would clear his head but left him feeling like he was jet-lagged, he deviated from his plan and took the cut-off for a state park, following a road rising toward dry hills and a reservoir. In this rural country a little state park wasn't going to be crowded, and he needed to be somewhere he could sit and think because he was screwing up.

He pulled in and parked next to a brown and white trailhead sign. Fifty yards to his left was a cinder block toilet structure for hiking types. Two other cars were in the lot, an old Subaru with a bike rack and a Chevy pickup. It felt safe enough and he locked his car and walked up a trail to a stand of pines, hoping the cool air and sunlight would help him calm down inside. He found a place to sit where he could still see his car, and then tried deep breathing. He lay on his back for a while thinking about everything that had happened in the last week and a half.

Then, as he was close to leaving, another car drove into the lot, a late model, white four-door Buick with a trim gray-haired man getting out, a guy in his early sixties, who immediately looked through the windows of Stoltz's rented Nissan. He got something out of his car, laid down on the pavement and reached under the Nissan. Stoltz moved around the back of a pine tree and watched the man dust himself off as he stood up, nothing in his hands any more. He got back in his car and pulled out. Like in a movie, like something you wouldn't believe had happened unless you saw it.

Stoltz drove back to the freeway and then north thirty miles before taking an exit that led to a shopping mall. He needed a place to park and look under the car. He drove through the mall and had a crazy idea as he saw two California Highway Patrol cars parked side by side, with an open space between one cruiser and a mammoth Ford Expedition blocking the officers' view, where they sat at a table in a Fresh Mex.

He pulled into the parking space, walked around, opened his passenger door, leaned over, then sank down and slid under the Nissan. He scanned the dark underbody until he found it, like a blister of metal attached to the chassis. He wrenched it free. Nothing but magnets had held the GPS tracking device in place, so he figured he could do the same with the CHP car. He slid out and then underneath the CHP chassis. The magnets snapped against metal as the device grabbed, and Stoltz was on his feet, locking the Nissan before going into the Mex Fresh to buy food to-go. He was still waiting for his food as the CHP officers left. He watched them drive away.

Then he did a lot of driving and doubling back. He didn't turn in the rental until after dark and took a cab to the warehouse. At the warehouse he rethought everything and changed his plan yet again.

THIRTY-FOUR

Raveneau waited for a call from an old friend, Bob Moore, who'd built a consulting business doing credit card fraud work. A decade ago Raveneau tried to help him learn the truth after his daughter died illegally bungee jumping off a railroad bridge in northern California. Moore couldn't accept the conclusions of the local sheriff's department and his anguish over it was so intense that Raveneau had done his own investigation. He concluded what the sheriff had, that her death was accidental but needless, and that recklessness by the more experienced bungee jumpers she was with had contributed but wasn't malicious. He did that investigative work at his own expense and would never have considered asking for money.

But yesterday he'd called Moore asking for a favor. Moore was an industry expert. He booked months in advance and Raveneau asked him to jump Alex Jurika to the front of the line. When the phone rang it was Moore calling back about the cards they'd found in Jurika's apartment.

'One of those cards had fifteen thousand four hundred forty-two dollars charged to it from January sixth to July one this year. So that's more or less twenty-five hundred dollars a month. Alex Jurika or whoever used the card also made regular payments and not all of those were the minimum payment. She paid down a thousand dollars in April and made another sizeable payment later, could have been in June. I've got the date here, hold on a second.'

Papers rustled.

'Sorry about that, it was in June—'

'This past June?'

'Yes, and eleven hundred and twelve dollars, enough so it doesn't look like your typical fraudulent usage. The card belongs to an elderly woman in San Rafael. She didn't even know she was missing her card. Her daughter figured it out. She told me her mom has twenty cards and hardly ever uses any of them.'

'What's the cardholder's name?'

'Miriam Shapiro. Do you want her address and the daughter's phone numbers? I can email them to you. Here, I'll do that now. Let me know when you get them.'

'I got 'em.'

'Where was I?'

'Miriam Shapiro's daughter.'

'That's right. OK, so I know what the daughter believes, but I don't really know what the San Rafael Police concluded. It probably makes more sense for you to talk directly with them.'

'I'll call them.'

'Good, and here's the story. Last summer, old Miriam broke her hip and needed home care. After the home care started, a Visa disappeared from a bundle of a dozen credit cards Miriam had sitting in a desk drawer with a rubber band around them. The credit card company was then contacted with a change of billing address. Whoever made contact had all the requisite info on Miriam Shapiro, so they gathered up more than just a Visa at the house. Bills started mailing to a UPS Store outlet mailbox in San Francisco.'

Raveneau copied down the address.

'Identity thieves will rent a mailbox or an apartment and pay the rent out of cash advances on cards. They'll make significant buys, pay the bill in full and then get new credit card offers and a higher line of credit. When it gets high enough they borrow the whole amount and disappear. It takes a certain amount of risk management and patience.'

It was a common enough credit fraud scheme, but Raveneau didn't comment. He didn't want to derail Moore's momentum.

'The daughter for reasons of her own – she told me she was just curious because her mother never lets her open mail or pay bills – went online and checked her mom's credit score. When she printed off a credit report she saw all the cards paid except for this Visa with the fifteen grand run up and a new address. She called the credit card company and the police.

'But here's where it gets more interesting. An arrest was made of a Latino woman at the UPS Store in San Francisco as she picked up mail, which in this case included eleven other credit card bills, Miriam Shapiro's and ten others that were also fraudulently obtained. Your department made the arrests but it was a San Rafael Police operation. I have the case file number.

I'm emailing it to you, right now.

'It turned out the Latino woman didn't speak English and could prove she'd only been in the country for three months. She was actually here legally and there were lots of tears and weeping because she claimed she'd never broken a law in her life and couldn't understand why anyone would do this to her. All she did was answer an ad in a Hispanic newspaper and get a part- time job to collect mail from a few spots, and that may have been the truth.' He paused a beat. 'I believe it was.

'She met with the woman who hired her one time only. The interview was in Spanish and she got laid out on her mail collection duties and told how she'd be paid – in cash and dropped once a month where she's living. Because she was only getting three hundred bucks a month, getting paid in cash didn't seem like a big deal to her.'

'I'd like to get a printout of what was bought with the cards.'

'The most significant purchases were for com- puters, printers, phones, a shredder – equipment as though someone was setting up an office.'

'Shipped or bought in stores?'

'Shipped, bought online, and I'll give you the address they went to. That's about it. That's all I've got.'

'That's a lot and thank you.'

'You call me anytime you need any help. I'll talk to you later.'

Raveneau called the San Rafael Police and a Lieutenant Cordova got on the line and suggest- ed he drive over.

'I'll copy everything before you get here,' Cordova said.

San Rafael's police station was beneath the city offices on Fifth Street, down a handful of brick-lined steps off the sidewalk. Lieutenant Cordova handled credit fraud and business was booming.

'In the Shapiro case the credit card didn't walk out of the house on its own,' Cordova said, 'so I started with the people taking care of Mrs Shapiro. That led to a firm that provides skilled home care help, which led to a woman named Brittany Rodriquez who worked at the Shapiro residence. I think it's likely this Rodriquez took the card and handed it off to someone else. The name of the home care firm is GoodHands. It ought to be StickyHands. They have offices in Los Angeles, San Francisco, and Seattle, and there have been other similar complaints in each of those cities about them.

'The business is owned by a woman named Faith Silliman and she may be legit. She provided employment records on Brittany Rodriquez, gave me a way to find her, and was very cooperative.'

'What about this Brittany Rodriquez, where would I find her? If you think she might have stolen the card we've got and handed it off, I need to find her.'

'She disappeared and I haven't been able to find her. GoodHands, the company, got its ass generally fired around Marin County as word got out. With Rodriquez we never had anything to hold her with.'

171

'OK, what about the owner, Faith Silliman?'

'We could probably get her on the phone. Do you want me to call her? She told me her business depends on her credibility and integrity and that for me she'd be available twenty-four seven.' He looked up and grinned. 'Let's find out.'

Cordova called, got her, and then explained he was with a homicide inspector from SFPD. He handed the phone to Raveneau.

'Does the name Alex Jurika mean anything to you?' Raveneau asked.

'It sure does. Alex was with me on and off for two years before I fired her. I flew in from Seattle to do it myself.'

'Why did you fire her?'

'She was stealing credit card numbers. There was no proof, but no question either. I paid out nine thousand dollars to take care of it.'

'Was she a friend of Brittany Rodriquez?'

'I think she was and they colluded. She said no.'

'Alex Jurika is our victim. We found a credit card and a driver's license in Miriam Shapiro's name in Jurika's apartment.'

'Alex was murdered?'

'Yes.'

When she spoke again her tone had changed. She sounded far less judgmental. Raveneau looked at Cordova as he answered Silliman's questions about the murder. The case was going somewhere now and he felt the difference.

'Can I ask you to email me records of when she worked for you?' Raveneau asked.

'I'll do it right now.'

Raveneau opened the email on his phone and read through the records before driving away. Some hard things had been written in Jurika's termination record. He thought of her sister Gloria's comments about Alex's character and how different she'd been as a child. He spoke to Alex now as he drove.

'I don't know where you went wrong,' he said, 'but your sister is right. You did go wrong. And Deborah Lafaye is probably right, you had a lot going your way that you didn't make good use of. But we're going to find who did this to you. We're getting closer and we will figure it out. We will get there.'

THIRTY-FIVE

A second warrant to search Heilbron's house was denied, the judge stern with Raveneau after inviting him in and offering him coffee.

'You searched his house once and found nothing tying him to the China Basin murder or a rape in the San Jose area. You never charged him for the murder. You didn't have any evidence and still don't. You had a confession of sorts but it didn't stand up. By your own account it wasn't credible and you knew that after you and your partner took him to the China Basin building. Am I correct in saying you didn't believe his initial confession was credible? That there were inconsistencies with the murder scene?'

The judge waited and when Raveneau delayed, he asked, 'Do you want milk in your coffee?'

'No thanks, and yes there were inconsistencies. We hoped to hold him on the rape charge. That one—'

'I agree that one is eerie but the victim was unable to identify him. The San Jose police showed her photos, did they not? She couldn't identify him and if I'm not mistaken she told them that she never got a very good look at his face, even when he was working on the tire. She

174

didn't completely trust him. She didn't stand too close to him. She was on her cell phone.' He handed Raveneau his coffee. 'And there's no DNA evidence.'

'That's why he confessed to it, and I'm sure that's him in the video. I know his look, I know his walk.'

'That's not good enough, Inspector. You arrested and held him once already for five or six days, and you've already searched his house. I can understand why he worries you and why you're focused on him, but you haven't given me enough.'

'We have reasons to focus on him.'

'I'm sure you do, but good reasons or not, you don't have enough for another warrant. This camcorder or videotape arrangement attached to his van is very disturbing, as is the tape he shot, but you've got to bring me something closer to probable cause.'

Raveneau picked up the coffee. He didn't want coffee but he did want to buy time.

'Let me try again. Maybe I didn't write it up well. I thought he was off-balanced and possibly thrill-seeking when he first came in and confessed. Now I realize the first confession may be part of some larger plan or fantasy. Whether he was our killer in China Basin or not, I think the killing was a catalyst for him. It happened in an area he considers his own. Possibly it's a way of killing he had fantasized about. A little over a day later he came in to confess—'

The judge was exasperated.

'I know all of this. You can't re-churn the same

stuff you got the last warrant with.'

'We need to get in front of him before he acts again. We need to get back in his house and in his van and be more thorough.'

The judge jumped on that. 'The law doesn't protect you from lack of thoroughness.'

'We need another chance to search, your honor.'

'I'm sorry. I just can't sign it with what you've got. Get me something concrete.'

'What if I rewrite it?'

The judge shook his head. Raveneau took a sip of the coffee, and then set it down near the kitchen sink. At the door before leaving he said, 'I've been at this more than twenty years and I've never really seen a guy quite like this one.'

'There's always somebody worse.'

Raveneau nodded. He shut the judge's front door and went down the steps to his car.

THIRTY-SIX

Raveneau drove through the Tenderloin before going into work. The morning sky was particularly clear and the sunlight bright, high on the buildings ahead. He cruised slowly down Eddy Street, looking for Deschutes, knowing he used to hang here. He was close to giving up when he spotted him sitting on a bench in the park outside City Hall. Deschutes picked up on him as soon as he slowed. He started to leave, then stayed on the bench and watched as Raveneau approached.

'Man nearly killed the brother of a police officer last night.'

And that's how Raveneau came to it. Deschutes heard it in a restaurant on Van Ness Street where he'd gone in to get warm and use a bathroom. They had a TV there. He had watched a report of the shooting but fumbled for the name he'd heard. 'Backer, Beckurt, like that.'

'Becker?'

'That's the one. His brother got shot.'

Raveneau didn't believe it, but didn't disbelieve it either. He pulled a five dollar bill from his wallet.

'Get yourself some breakfast, Jimmy. Where can I find you later?'

'I'm around.'

177

'Where are you going to be?'

'I'm not going far.'

Outside the gray-faced Hall of Justice five lanes of Bryant Street ran one-way. Many commuters treated the street as a freeway on-ramp, hammering through the yellow lights as they accelerated toward the Bay Bridge ramp a block away. When the light changed, pedestrians jay-walking across the five lanes on their way to the Hall entrance steps sometimes had to run for it. But not today.

Today they wouldn't have any problem because the TV vans were two lanes deep, blocking traffic as well as access to the alley and the entrances to the bail bond shops and other businesses opposite the Hall. Rubberneckers slowed traffic to a crawl and Raveneau avoided his usual parking spot. He parked six blocks away and walked in.

La Rosa was in conversation with a deputy-chief out in the corridor when Raveneau got off at the fifth floor. From the way they stopped talking as he neared he guessed the deputy-chief was la Rosa's angel in the brass. Inside Homicide a meeting was underway at the conference table outside the captain's office.

Becker's brother, Alan Becker, an attorney in Walnut Creek, was shot and badly wounded by an unidentified assailant as he unloaded groceries last night at his suburban Walnut Creek home. Those were the bare facts and Raveneau gathered not much more was known yet. Possibly it was an attempted carjacking, or an interrupted burglary, but the probability that some

178

connection existed between Whitacre, Jacie Bates, and this could not be ignored. What had seemed improbable now seemed possible.

Raveneau took in the scene and then walked to his desk. That didn't buy him much time, but he did get more details on the Becker shooting before Captain Ramirez came to get him.

Now he was at the conference table, and they were telling him a task force was forming and that he and la Rosa were expected to participate. Raveneau nodded, though in his view task forces were largely for people who enjoyed meetings. He hoped that whoever headed this one didn't need a phone call every four hours.

At noon a general meeting of all homicide inspectors was called and more brass sat in. One of the inspectors, Sanchez, interrupted Ramirez and asked, 'Where's this Cody Stoltz and why is he walking around without us knowing where he is?'

Ramirez turned to Raveneau, asked, 'Do you want to take that?'

'Sure.' He glanced at Sanchez who almost certainly already knew the answer, and then addressed the room. 'An SID team was on him but he took a trip to LA with his mother and LAPD picked him up. With his mother he was staying at the Beverly Hilton. Then it appeared he was continuing on to Mexico, to Cabo with her, but she went and he didn't. Basically, he went to the airport with her, checked in, went through security, and then didn't board the plane.'

'What about the mother, has she been questioned?' someone asked.

'Yes. He gave her some last second explanation that he had too much work, too much depended on him. He left her as she was literally walking down the boarding ramp and LAPD missed him leaving the airport. We don't know where he is now, though he has checked in with the people he works for.'

'Then they know where he is.' Sanchez again.

'They say it's not unusual for him to hole up with his laptop and work on a problem.'

Raveneau gave more back story on Stoltz and when the conversation moved to Jacie Bates there was no way to avoid the Oakland detectives' interest in Bates. Everyone agreed more information was needed about the shooting of Becker's brother and grumbled as the meeting broke up that the brass formed the task force in a knee-jerk response to the media.

A few minutes later la Rosa tapped him on the shoulder. 'Captain Ramirez and Deputy-chief Grainer want me to go to lunch with them.'

She was gone an hour and a half. When she returned he guessed from her expression that they'd made her some sort of offer.

'They want me to act as spokesperson for the task force.'

'Are you good with that?'

'I said I'd do it. Am I good with it, I don't know. That's a lot of cameras across the street. I'm a little scared.'

She downplayed it, though sounding excited, and it was clear she'd been given a career pep talk and the point had gotten made that how she handled herself in the swirl of media attention would count for a lot later. Careers got made in crisis situations. Everything became larger than life. That's what drew the brass this morning.

Raveneau stayed at his desk that afternoon. He phoned a cop in Concord that he knew had friends on the Walnut Creek force. In 1988 an undercover San Francisco officer was killed in Walnut Creek and some strain remained ever since between the departments. He was hoping his friend in Concord had a route to the detectives assigned the Becker shooting. Turned out his friend didn't know the detectives personally, but knew someone who did and made the call. He called back an hour later.

'They're looking at an ex-boyfriend neighbor of Alan Becker's daughter because your lieutenant's brother and the boyfriend got in a shoving match over the daughter two months ago. Alan Becker called the police and threatened the kid with a restraining order. And Sunday night a neighbor saw a man on a bicycle around the time of the attempted murder. Evidently, this kid is an avid cyclist, so they've taken his bike and all the associated clothing, shoes, helmets, everything. They also found his recreational drug stash and they're holding him with that.'

'They've questioned him?'

'Sure. But he's watching the same news reports they're about a killer targeting SF homicide inspectors and their families. He's keeping his mouth shut. What's it like where you are?'

'We're trying to connect the dots.'

'Well, hang in there. I'll call you if I hear anything more.'

THIRTY-SEVEN

The Stoltz family owned a small house in wooded hills west of the Napa Valley. The house sat well back from the road hidden from passing cars by a stand of oaks. Stoltz liked the house. He felt comfortable here. For hours he worked at the kitchen table with his laptop in front of him, and gave only occasional thought to the homicide inspectors. He was good at compartmentalizing things.

When he turned the TV on and Raveneau's partner, Elizabeth la Rosa, was saying they'd just like to talk to him, it was for a moment as if she was speaking about another person, not him. She looked poised in front of the camera. She looked like a natural and spoke as though personally to him, asking that he just come in and talk with them. After that, she took questions, and answered with the usual police evasiveness.

'Do the San Francisco police believe he should be questioned regarding the Walnut Creek shooting?' she was asked.

'We'd like to talk to him about a number of things.'

'Do you have proof the Walnut Creek shooting is connected to the two murders?'

'We haven't connected the murder of Jacie

Bates to Inspector Whitacre's death. We have ongoing investigations and many open questions. We need the public's help in locating Mr Stoltz and convincing him to talk with us.'

'Are you aware the Walnut Creek police arrested a suspect an hour ago?'

'Yes, we're aware they have a person of interest.'

'Do you have any comment about that arrest?'

'No.'

The press conference ended and then his face was on the screen with the announcer saying, 'Police are looking for help finding this man. Anyone who has seen him is urged to call—'

He left the TV and walked to the window. He looked through the trees to the driveway, wondering if they knew he was here. This wasn't exactly a secret site. His mother paid property taxes. The house was in her name.

When he returned to the TV the report was over. They'd moved on to sports. Stoltz sat down and closed his eyes. So he was their prime suspect just as he'd known he would be, and they were trying him in the press because that's the way the system works. Later, he'd sue them and win, and wasn't that what he'd wanted? It had to end the way it was supposed to, which had nothing to do with the San Francisco police.

He listened to a branch scraping the roof and tried to think it through. The growing media presence was a factor that he needed to adjust to. If the media stayed with this story she might become aware. She might figure it out. She might know he was coming for her.

THIRTY-EIGHT

The next morning a partial toxicology report on Alex Jurika came in. Full screen would take another four to six weeks. Raveneau read through it and then handed the report to la Rosa. Jurika had a common date-rape drug, a horse tranquilizer, Ketamine, in her system. That was the most significant finding.

La Rosa read and stated flatly, 'Heilbron,' and Raveneau didn't respond. Ketamine was in her system but she wasn't raped. Was a sexual assault interrupted? Did she asphyxiate too soon and Heilbron lost interest in sex as he'd described, or was it a mistake to connect Ketamine to its usual companion, rape?

'Here's a different angle,' Raveneau said. 'Let's say there's no sexual element and the Ketamine was for a different purpose entirely.'

'For what, then?'

'To loosen her up and get her to talk about the credit fraud and identity theft businesses. Suppose someone wanted to gain control over her and in a drugged state get her to answer questions. So they brought her there, drugged her, and questioned her before killing her. Money as a motive.'

'There are all kinds of other places easier than

184

that building.'

'True, but what if whoever wanted the information also planned to kill her afterwards? Then the building works well, or well enough. A filthy mattress used by junkies and whores puts a different spin on it.'

'I like Heilbron,' she answered. 'I see him masturbating rather than raping her, and not leaving DNA evidence behind. He's a voyeur. We know that about him already. It's not hard to picture him getting aroused watching, same as he probably does driving around and filming. And he's weirdly fixated on that building. I'm back to believing it could be him and he purposely misled us with the wrong room and wire instead of rope. He's played us.'

They continued the debate on the drive over to Jurika's apartment. Gloria was out front when they arrived. Her sister's body was released to her this morning and she had asked to meet at the apartment. Raveneau wasn't sure what that was about, but once they got inside she confessed, 'I knew more than I told you last time. The cousin I told you about, Julie, she told me that she and Alex have used other people's credit cards for years. She bragged about it when I confronted her in Phoenix. She said she didn't think it was wrong since the cardholder doesn't get stuck with the bill. She thought it was OK to cheat the credit card company.'

'You more or less did tell us that,' Raveneau said, 'and we figured out the rest.'

'Last January, Julie showed up in Los Angeles in a new full length leather coat, and I mean a really nice coat, light, high quality leather, a really pretty black – a five thousand dollar coat. I threatened her with all kinds of things and that's when she told me her part was to keep an apartment rented where the credit card bills came and to pay them online under an account opened in a false name. She also told me the cards all came from older people with money. They had some way of getting them. If you want me to, I'll call her right now.'

Now she had their attention. Raveneau was quiet waiting for more when la Rosa said, 'Why don't I call her? I've talked to her already. She knows me.'

She pulled her phone out and sat down on a kitchen chair. Raveneau watched her punch the numbers in, heard a faint ringing and la Rosa asked, 'Is this Julie? It is, good, because this is Inspector la Rosa in San Francisco.'

La Rosa caught Raveneau's eye and speaking to Julie Candiff said, 'You remember me. That's wonderful. What's your day like tomorrow, Julie? We need you to fly out here tomorrow unless you want to come here this afternoon. We're standing here with Gloria and she's just told us what you told her and that means you lied to me, which really makes me angry. We're trying to solve the murder of your cousin and you're obstructing justice. We can contact the Phoenix police and ask them to help us, or you can book a flight and call me back and tell me what time you're going to get in. What do you want to do?'

Raveneau didn't have to overhear much conversation to realize Julie wasn't going for the idea of flying here.

'OK, then should I ask the Phoenix police to pick you up and hold you for us?' la Rosa asked. She was still on the phone with her when Raveneau moved into Alex's bedroom with Gloria, who sat down on the bed and started to cry.

'I always thought it would be OK in the end. I thought she would eventually come home and somehow she'd turn back into the sweet little sister I used to have. I really don't understand what happened to her.'

She pulled hair back from her face. She wiped her eyes.

'There's something else. I told you she email-ed me and asked to borrow money, but I didn't tell you that she also called me. That was two days before she died. She called me at work and I wouldn't take her call.'

Now she wept, her face in her hands, and Raveneau sat down on the bed alongside her. For several minutes he didn't say anything. He just sat with her. Then as she got a hold of herself he spoke.

'I had an older brother named Donny and we went everywhere together as kids. He was two and a half years older and I was always trying to keep up and compete with him. Donny got draft-ed and sent to Vietnam when he was nineteen. Before he went to boot camp he was this happy go lucky, handsome young kid the girls fell all over because he could also play the guitar like nothing else and was in a band. When he came back from Nam he was completely changed and had a heroin habit. He'd become an addict, or was well on his way to becoming one. That was right about when I decided I was going to travel around the world alone. I'd saved my money and took off. I left and traveled for three years, working some places and getting along. I lost touch with him, probably because I wanted to.

'When I got home in 1979 Donny was strung out on dope, skinny as a rail, filthy and wearing dirty rags. He didn't have a job or money, and our dad wouldn't let him in the house any more, which killed my mother, and I mean, I think it really did kill her. I was still talking to Donny, though he called me Officer Pig by then. I'd signed up with the San Francisco Police Department. He'd tell me it was an affectionate term but there was nothing affectionate in it, and the brother I'd grown up so close to, I could hardly stand to be around any more.

'Then over a period of about three weeks, I got five or six desperate calls from him. I was working graveyard at the time, just trying to figure out how to be a police officer and where I fit in. My hours were messed up, so I used that as a reason why I didn't get around to calling him back. Besides, it wasn't the first time he'd been desperate. Most of the time what he was desperate for was money so he could buy a fix. And it's not like I hadn't tried hard to get him into a program where he could break his addiction. Either way, I didn't return his calls.

'It was his last call that haunted me for years. I had an answering machine and saved the tape with Donny's call and I'd get drunk and replay it over and over, trying to hear what I should have heard. He made that call one night before driving out to the Golden Gate Bridge and parking on the Marin side. Then he walked out just past the north tower and jumped from a spot where he and I once saw a businessman from Cleveland jump off when we were kids. There were witnesses, and I know he did that to communicate with me that he hadn't lost his mind and that he still remembered everything. He parked his car in the same slot that guy had so long ago. That was his message to me.

'Donny's body washed up on the Marin side and I was the one to identify it. It tore me apart for a long time, so I know something of what you're feeling.'

When she lowered a hand he took it in his, something he never would have done a decade ago. Her body shook and Raveneau sat next to her as she wept for the way things had turned out, for the sister she'd lost, for everything that hadn't been the way she had dreamed it would be.

THIRTY-NINE

When they left Gloria Jurika, la Rosa and Raveneau were talking. They were getting somewhere. A theft ring inside an elderly care business, Alex Jurika with a history of credit theft and a sudden need for substantial money from her sister – more things were going together if not fitting together. It felt like they were brushing along the edge of solving this case.

As they got back to the Hall, Raveneau fielded a call from Deborah Lafaye, the woman with the charity foundation. She wanted to go to lunch with him and him alone, pointedly saying, 'Without your partner.'

He talked that over with la Rosa; then he met Lafaye at Slanted Door in the Ferry Building. She had already sat down at a booth. He slid in on the other side. From the booth they could look out across the bay. With the clouds the water was a gray-green and then bright again where the sun broke through.

'I wanted to have lunch with you because I didn't get the impression you understand how much information is out there and how easily it moves around now.'

'Will that help us solve Alex Jurika's murder?'

'It might. She was very tuned into the online

190

world, and I don't mean to offend you but I got the impression when we met that you might not realize how easily information about other people can be gathered now. So to make a point I've learned some things about you. I spent half an hour alone on a computer to do this. Do you want to hear what I learned?'

'Go ahead.'

'Your ex-wife lives in New York and has severe osteoporosis. I know some of the drugs she's taking, and you do as well. You've paid over twenty thousand in the last eighteen months for drugs for her. I found that out searching medical resources we're dialed into at the foundation.

'I know you like wine. You belong to two local wine clubs. It turns out certain types of wine drinkers tend to donate to foundations like mine so we track the club lists. We pay a fee and get their lists.'

The waiter arrived and after they ordered she started on the interconnectivity of the Internet again. She was accustomed to having people listen to her, but Raveneau wasn't that interested in a lecture today. He glanced out of the windows and followed the gray suspension span of the Bay Bridge.

'I'm boring you.'

'There's a lot going on today.'

'And you think I'm full of myself. You don't know why I'm going on about Internet connectivity. You think I suggested lunch to make sure you don't suspect me.'

'I think you're smarter than that.'

Raveneau ate Vietnamese rice cakes with rock shrimp and mung beans. Other than a glass of a Sauvignon blanc, Lafaye had ordered next to nothing.

'I invited you to lunch because I've known Alex longer and better than the impression I left you with. When she worked for me she was on the computer looking for that connectivity I was boring you with. I didn't know it at the time but Alex was already looking for that same connectivity in the market for identity theft.'

'How did you find out?'

'Actually, it came up in a joking way one night when I said that I needed another identity, including a passport for traveling in countries where my real name could put me in danger. I've been very active trying to shut down illegal trade in human organs and other things like aid dollars that end up buying Mercedes instead of medicine for poor children. Things that could get me killed. My name is known some places and combined with the foundation website and the growth of the Internet I wasn't as anonymous traveling as I used to be. Some areas became dangerous to go to with the reputation I'd started to get.'

'So Alex got you a false identity.'

'Yes. She knew someone who wanted to shed their current identity. I bought that identity so I could use it when I traveled in certain countries, and I only did it after there'd been an attempt to kill me. Mind you, this was quite a few years ago.'

Lafaye held her hands up, showed her fingertips, the scarring and deformation.

'I did a lot of things that seem crazy now, but one thing I knew was I didn't want this to happen again because I got recognized in the wrong locale. If you want to travel with me I'll introduce you to a man named Huarang. He did the manicure work on my hands, though we're on speaking terms now.

'Huarang deals in organs, mostly kidneys, but he'll get you a young healthy heart if you need a transplant. He's very computer literate, or the people who work for him are, and they're adept at locating potential donors by scouring hospital records. They match donors to recipients via databases they've built up during the years he's been collecting UN money to inoculate and do blood tests at his clinic. He also gets grants from the Red Cross. In fact, his clinics do many good things. With me, he's happy to provide the names of competitors.'

'Now you can lecture me; how does it work with a kidney?'

'When he gets an order for a kidney he searches his database and then front guys go out and locate the donor. If the donor is poor and the police are bribed, and it's easily proved that the donor was paid well for his kidney, then often there's nothing the unwilling donor can do later. He may have been drugged when he signed papers or had no idea what the papers said because he doesn't read, and of course he had no idea that any of this connects to Huarang's charity work, or that Huarang is connected to it in any way. He wakes up with stitches in his back and a check for the equivalent of five thousand dollars, which in the areas where Huarang works is a fortune.

'Usually, the donor is a young man with a match to the recipient that has been verified by the doctors who will do the transplant. The donor is always healthy and will recover; meanwhile his kidney will move along a well-traveled chain where everyone steps on the price until it gets to the hospital and goes into a rich American or Saudi, or someone who can afford it but cannot afford to wait.'

'Come on, you're not telling me it's this well known and he's out there today operating like this, and at the same time collecting aid money for his clinics.'

'He absolutely is and I became part of his Indonesia operation for a few months during the nineties. That's when he did my nails for me. I offered my services to get inside his operation. I had medical training and I told him I didn't have many scruples. That's the magic combination. I was in the operating room at the compound at least a dozen times as a surgical nurse, assisting as a young man's healthy kidney was removed. I watched the liver removed from a very fit young man I'd been joking with an hour before, a young man who thought he was just selling one kidney so that his mother could get a needed operation. They sewed him up, helicoptered him to a remote area of the jungle and shoved him out.'

'Were you in the helicopter when the kid got pushed out?'

'I was. I watched him fall. Without a liver he was dead anyway.'

'So it didn't matter.'

'Of course, it mattered.'

She stared hard at him.

'Huarang is just one dealer in one country. There are many people who need organ transplants. There are Americans routinely getting transplants outside the United States for the simple reason that it's more affordable elsewhere and, guess what, sometimes organs are more abundant and cheaper. Who knew?

'Huarang was probably trying to sell my organs when I escaped. When he destroyed my fingernails he did it because one of his men had found a video camera among my things and I was on tape talking about what I'd witnessed. I'd shot the operating room and the helicopter taking off from the pad in the jungle clearing on its way to make a delivery.

'Huarang said, "You beautiful woman, so I give you a choice." He pointed at one of the two goons who'd brought me in and said, "Either he'll dig your right eye out of its socket and fill the hole with gauze or we take your fingernails." They tied me to a chair and he tore my nails off one by one with pliers, the first one fast, I think to shock my system, and then more slowly. He said he would stop after I told him the truth about why I was there, and when I did, he didn't stop, and at some point I passed out. When I came to they were washing my hands with alcohol and he was washing his in a sink. They say you don't remember severe pain, but they're wrong.'

'Did you go to the police?'

'No, you go to the US embassy and try through them. Huarang pays off the local police and ultimately it was a local matter. The police chief went out and questioned Huarang. I heard he stayed for dinner and I was advised later by the State Department not to pursue it further.'

She told Raveneau other stories, and created the impression that she wanted to convey her bravery and foolish boldness and undaunted willingness to take risks for her fellow human beings.

'I often dream of that boy falling from the helicopter. Sometimes I see myself jumping after him. Maybe it's guilt that I didn't save him. I remember looking down and he was just above the canopy of the trees, and then he vanished. I remember thinking that the animals would eat him, and as he went through that canopy of forest he just vanished from earth as though he'd never existed.'

She rested one of her hands on the tablecloth, turned the misshapen nails of her right hand so they couldn't be ignored.

'I could have plastic surgery, but I keep them this way so I don't forget. I had a lot of anger, depression, sleeplessness, I couldn't focus for a long time, and then I saw where I could make a difference.'

She had told this story many times before. That was obvious.

'How did you know the identity you got from Alex wasn't stolen?'

'I knew her well enough.'

'Everyone we talk to says she was a thief and a liar, including her sister.'

'She was complex.'

'And I think you're pretty thorough and careful. I'm betting you looked into the history of the identity you were about to buy. You didn't buy another woman's identity blind.'

'I checked only to make sure she didn't have a criminal history. She did have one but she was smarter than me. She hid that history before putting her identity on the market. She'd already come some distance in trying to erase herself.'

'And why was she doing that?'

'She was afraid a man was going to get out of prison and then come after her.'

'And this was all here in San Francisco?'

'Yes.'

Sometimes things click together. Sometimes people contact you again and say they want to meet and talk more because they're one step ahead of you and are afraid you're going to catch up to them.

'Can I guess the woman's name?'

'That would be very impressive, Inspector. I'd be quite impressed. But first I want you to understand that I've never used that identity in the United States. I only used it in a few countries and I don't do that any more either.'

'OK, if you don't use it any more, where is it?'

'I don't keep it in the US. After 9/11 they started checking more and I don't want to be caught with my regular passport and that one as well. That would get ugly. I keep it in a safe

197

deposit box in Mexico City. It's sitting there right now. If I need it somewhere else they send it to me by courier.'

'Where did you use it before putting it away in the safe deposit box?'

'African countries, Latin America, and places in Asia where I knew they wouldn't be cross-checking my face with other photos.'

'And how about the woman whose identity you bought, do you know where she lives now?'

'No.'

'Do you know what name she lives under?'

'I have no idea.'

'Do you know if she's still alive?'

'Alex might have known. Maybe you'll find it in her computer.'

'What else are we going to find?'

'Hopefully what you need to solve the murder.'

The waiter returned now with the check. She waited until he left before saying, 'Now it's time for your guess.'

Raveneau put down his water glass. He made sure he had eye contact and he saw the tiny flinch at the corner of her eyes as he said, 'Her name is Erin Quinn. She returned to her maiden name after the murder of her husband. The man she's afraid of is Cody Stoltz and you're seeing his name in the news so much it's making you nervous.'

Now she looked like she'd been slapped, but she covered it well, smiling, her eyes lighting up, grabbing the check, laughing as she said, 'Wow, I insist on buying. How did you do that?'

'I've got a feeling you have more to tell me. Now would be a good time. Why don't you come to our office?'

'Not today, Inspector, and I think I've told you everything now.' She smiled at him. 'I am impressed.'

From the car Raveneau called la Rosa.

'How was lunch with Ms Goodworks?'

'She wanted to tell me about the name and identity she sometimes uses in other countries where it's not safe to use her own name. She must have felt like she had to get a jump on us.'

'Let me guess, Florence Nightingale.'

'No, the former Mrs Reinert, Stoltz's lover, Erin Quinn. See you in a few minutes.'

FORTY

The private investigator was an ex-Riverside cop named Blake Fame that Stoltz's mother had hired ahead of the trip to Los Angeles. She told him cost was always an issue, but keeping track of Cody came first. So obviously, mom was worried. No one at the table said anything to Fame about not coming to them before now, although Fame took a moment to try to cover his ass.

'She had her lawyer fax me a stack of papers to sign before she hired me and she'll sue me into the grave if she finds out I've come to you. I got sued once before. I don't want to go through that again. I'm violating client confidentiality by talking to you, and I'm going to ask one favor.'

'What's that?' Raveneau asked.

'That you get my GPS unit back for me. He stuck it on the bottom of a CHP car.'

Everyone laughed. No one at table would ever try to recover his GPS for him, except maybe Raveneau, but only so he could get him alone and tell him what he thought about him not coming forward sooner.

'He made a couple of stops for gas and food and then stopped at a state park. I've got a map; I'll show you where he stopped.'

He unfolded the map and tapped on the park's location.

'I thought maybe he had something hidden there.'

'In the park?'

'Sure, he walked up a trail. Tell me why he'd be doing that on a drive north from LA? He'd disappeared so I got under his vehicle and attached a GPS unit. He must have seen me. He stopped at a shopping mall, detached it, and put it on a CHP cruiser. I didn't figure that out until I started tailing the highway patrol officer. He was out on Highway Five jumping up to speeds of one hundred and then down to zero when he pulled somebody over. It took me twenty miles to figure out what was going on. By then I'd lost Stoltz.'

No one laughed this time, but Raveneau asked, 'Why didn't you ask for the GPS when you were right there?'

'He would have been suspicious and I would have lost more time. I got the car number.'

'Show us the park,' Raveneau said, 'and where you last saw him.'

Raveneau looked at the park location on the map and then asked him the name of the shopping center. La Rosa googled Valley Meadows Center and then its distance from the park, 29.7 miles, about one hour from Walnut Creek.

'Look, I may sound like an idiot for what happened with the GPS, but he didn't get past me when he left LAX and I heard on the news LAPD lost him. I'm just here to tell you that I know he came north in a Nissan he rented at

Hertz. I've got the plates.'

He gave them those and la Rosa left the interview box. Captain Ramirez stood as well but didn't leave the room.

'Let's go back to Mrs Stoltz. What else did she tell you about her son?'

'That he owns a dozen or more vehicles, though I can't find them and she doesn't know where he stores them. That he has money, he's not dependent on her. He has an inheritance from his father and got some sort of signing bonus where he's working right now. She said he's afraid of you. He thinks you're lazy and incompetent and will frame him.'

'So, corrupt as well.'

'I guess so.'

'What else?'

'He's into property and now that there are so many foreclosures and short sales he often travels to look at property.'

Or that's what he tells her, Raveneau thought. Fame didn't know much more. He left them six ways to get hold of him and asked who he should call about his GPS. Raveneau handed him a card.

'Call me.'

In the late afternoon the Oakland detectives stopped by.

'It's confirmed that the pickup that burned was the vehicle that struck her,' Stalos said. 'And we've interviewed the girlfriend again and she told us Bates said his marriage was over. He promised they'd be together in about a year. He'd ask for a divorce soon and she just had to

202

ride it out.'

They glanced at each other and predictably it was Hendricks who stepped in to ask the harder question.

'We interviewed you and then he came to see you. Did you call him when you left us?'

'No. He was there when I got home, but if you know he came to see me you must have had a tail on him, so you already knew that.'

'Why did he visit you?'

'Because he knew you two had been to our office. He put it together.'

'What did you tell him?'

'Nothing that compromises what you're doing.'

They went back and forth like this and the whole thing left a bad taste. At some point la Rosa tapped him on the shoulder and he stepped out to talk to her.

'I'll see you tomorrow,' she said. 'I'm beat. Deborah Lafaye trips me out. Walnut Creek is about ready to charge a kid with the Becker shooting that the media insists Stoltz did, and these Oakland detectives are trying to lean on us. I've got to clear my head; I'm going to go take a run.'

When la Rosa got home she changed into running clothes and walked downstairs and out into the cool twilight. She debated going to her gym but that meant driving and traffic, and the air was so nice tonight it didn't seem worth being inside. Better to run out toward Golden Gate Park than pound away on a gym treadmill.

She started jogging. She was tired, distracted, and her mind on the Bates conversation and this new connection with Erin Quinn and Deborah Lafaye. She toyed with the idea of Lafaye wanting Jurika dead because of what she knew about her past.

She picked up her pace a little as she came through the intersection at Lincoln and then was into Golden Gate Park, running on a path dark now in the dusk. She left the path and ran down a street barricaded to vehicle traffic. When she didn't work out she tended to pick up weight on her upper thighs and rear, and now she thought she could feel fat breaking up as the muscles stretched. She wanted to get into her best shape. Not only did she like the way it felt, but her thinking was also clearest when she was fit. She had more stamina, needed less sleep, and didn't crave sweets the same way.

As she left the park she cut west of the panhandle and on to Haight Street, figured she'd bear right and do some hills before walking home. She crossed Haight-Ashbury thinking of Raveneau and his stories about the city during the Sixties, and talking about how the department had changed in the years he'd been there; the little bar with the American flag behind it that used to open at five in the afternoon each day, and that the chiefs would sometimes stop by. She couldn't picture Grainer doing that or any of the brass she'd met, but Raveneau also said it was better now. She thought of Grainer's last advice.

'There's a danger in working too long in any

one aspect of the department. We've all seen the sergeant who's been sitting too long at a desk. Alliances get made, favors done, and a status quo settles in. In Inspector Raveneau's case, and this is not for outside this room, he's used to doing things his way. But, unfortunately, the city has changed. That's why his solve rate is down. That's why you two are together, his broad experience and knowledge and your innovation and a more scientific approach.'

She slowed now to a steady jog and wondered what Grainer really knew about solving homicides. What could you know if you'd never worked a murder case? La Rosa's face was flushed, her spine wet with sweat when she dropped to a walk. She figured to walk at least a mile to cool down. She liked this part of her workout. She could think better walking than running.

After several blocks she turned up a steep hill to loosen a cramp in her right calf. She lengthened her stride to try to stretch the muscle out and as she reached down to massage it saw a dark blue Volvo wagon slowing on the street behind her, probably looking for an address. At the top of the hill she figured to jog the last blocks home. She was ready for a shower. She didn't feel good about the way she'd ducked out earlier and needed to call Raveneau.

At the corner the Volvo was still there coming up the hill slowly and the cramp in her calf was actually worse. Bad enough to where she limped and didn't run as she turned right and started across the hill and toward home. Then the same

Volvo came around the corner behind her, now with its high beams on but still moving slower than her, which wasn't easy, which she didn't like. What registered now was that she'd seen the same car earlier, an older model she associated with being a teenager, riding to soccer games and getting told how to play by somebody's dad who'd never played himself.

She stopped and knelt, pretending to retie her shoelace, and saw the car had stopped, the driver's face unreadable behind the glare of the headlights. But she couldn't stay down. The cramp hurt too much and she stood and started limping forward, deciding to cross the street if the car moved again and didn't pass her.

What it did was pull out and speed up quickly, and when she turned the car braked hard alongside her, the passenger window was down, a man's arm rising and then a flash of light, a blow to her head. Her legs crumpled.

A witness later described the sharp, hard pop of the gun discharging and the woman, the runner, falling in a way that convinced them she was dead. The car sped away. The witness called 911 and ran to her.

FORTY-ONE

Raveneau got a call from communications command and drove straight to the hospital. He badged the officer guarding the door and walked in carrying his laptop.

'Elizabeth?' He took her hand and she opened her eyes.

'You,' she said.

'Yeah.'

'Man, my head and neck hurt.' She touched her forehead then the pillow. 'I hit the sidewalk.' Her voice was slowed, groggy. She could hear herself. 'I'm fine. I'm lucky, right?'

'Very lucky.'

'I know, I screwed up.'

'You didn't screw up.'

'I've got some stitches.'

'I heard.'

'It grazed me, my skull.'

She closed her eyes again. She'd been unable to get to her feet afterwards. She felt blood streaming from her head, heard a man talking to her and faraway sirens as she lay on the sidewalk. She knew the man with her was trying to help, but she couldn't quite understand what he was saying. She remembered the ride here and the doctor telling her how lucky she was as he

207

stitched her up. She opened her eyes again, stared at Raveneau.

'What do we do now?' she asked.

The coverage had gone national. Raveneau listened to local radio on the way here. KCBS reported, 'Police are looking for a male assailant who shot and wounded a San Francisco homicide inspector tonight. The suspect is believed to have fled in a blue Volvo station wagon with license plates beginning with the letters T and F. He is armed and dangerous and anyone spotting the vehicle should keep their distance and call this number...'

'Elizabeth?'

'Uh-huh.'

'I want to ask you a couple of questions.'

'OK, sure, let's go.'

Her face was very pale. She needed to just rest here in the dark. He knew that.

'Are you sure the shooter was male?'

'Ninety percent.' She mustered. She opened her eyes and said, 'Wearing a dark-colored mask, like one of those they have now for extreme cold. It covered his head down to his collar bone. Bulky coat.'

'How do you know he was male?'

'I think he started to say something as he shot me. His arm, size of his head.'

'Stoltz?'

'Maybe.'

'Heilbron.'

She didn't answer. She faded on him, then said, 'Maybe Heilbron. Something about his build.'

'Or neither?'

'I don't know.'

She closed her eyes again. Raveneau waited several minutes.

'Ben?'

'I'm here.'

Her eyes still closed, she said, 'He roared up and hit the brakes hard.'

Which was probably why he missed.

'What about the gun?'

'You're telling me we haven't caught him.'

'That's right. It's gone statewide.' It went statewide and became a bad night locally for Volvo drivers. 'Remember anything more about the car? Cracked windshield, faded paint, a rack on top, anything.'

She kept her eyes closed but spoke more clearly.

'Definitely Volvo, wagon type I rode in as a kid, kind of square looking, a black bumper, chrome wheels.'

Raveneau booted up his laptop to find images of older model Volvo wagons. As the screen came up, la Rosa opened her eyes.

'Put the laptop on my stomach when you find something.'

He rested it on her and held it steady as she scrolled between two photos and then said, 'That's it, that's the car, a Volvo 240 with the bumper wrapping around in back.'

'One idea floating is that it's Stoltz and he went after you because you're the spokesperson for the task force. But that seems unlikely to me because the task force just happened and you've

209

only had one press conference. How often do you run that same route?'

Slower answering again and closing her eyes, saying, 'Vary the runs, but generally the same direction.'

'At about the same time of night?'

'Erratic since I started at homicide, but, yeah, I like that route.' She smiled with her eyes closed, adding, 'Or used to.'

She was religious about her exercise. Raveneau's guess was she ran the route often enough for someone to get a sense of her pattern. He didn't go there now. He didn't push her on it, except to ask, 'Have you run it since joining this cobbled together task force?'

'Excuse me,' a woman said from behind Raveneau. He turned. He'd missed Deputy-chief Grainer walking in.

'What did you just say?'

'We're talking about the shooter,' he said, but Grainer ignored him now. She took la Rosa's hand and said, 'I'm so relieved you're OK.'

Then she turned to Raveneau and asked, 'Is that your laptop, Inspector?'

'It is.'

'Please take it off Elizabeth.'

She touched la Rosa's face, withdrew her hand, and stood looking down at her as Raveneau turned the computer off.

'Have you got your phone, Elizabeth?' Raveneau asked.

'Yes.'

'I'll call you.'

In the hallway he ran into Captain Ramirez.

'How is she?'

'She's OK. I talked to the doctor who stitched her up and he said the bullet grazed her. It tapped the back of her skull as it passed by. He told me it made the faintest groove on the bone right here.'

Raveneau touched his skull where the stitches were.

'Did you learn any more from her?'

'Not really. She believes he was male and of fairly sturdy build.'

'Which fits Stoltz.'

'It could. Or someone else we've been questioning. Carl Heilbron.'

'I'm guessing it wasn't coincidence.'

Raveneau didn't respond to that. It was an inane statement. He left Ramirez and rode the elevator down. Several reporters hustled toward him as he walked out.

'Can you confirm the shooter was Cody Stoltz?'

Someone in TV who ought to know once told him that national news was purely an entertainment business driven by constant market research polling, and to complain about endless nights of repetitive coverage of whatever current story they were selling was just naïve. He'd bragged that most of the time his national network decided what was news. Celebrities with brand names were easy to market, so significant lasting stories got built around them. Raveneau knew there was a higher plane of cynicism he had only glimpsed at, but he was pretty sure how the media would play this one.

It would be a more immediately saleable story if the wounded homicide inspector had died here in the hospital with her last words being, find my killer. But that's the breaks of the story-making business. You've got to work with what you have. Still, the story-makers were hard at work shaping the expectation – SFPD homicide detail and family versus unknown but driven and capable assailant.

So now it was a chase and a hunt, a reality-based action show where more might get killed and the stakes and the ratings were driven higher. Who doesn't love a good task-force sized hunt? Talk about turning the tables on a stalker, the media would compete to join the hunt, and you know what, Raveneau was OK with that. They needed the media's help.

He saw some familiar faces among the reporters, but ignored their calls on the way to his car. But as he drove away he did take a call from a reporter he knew and answered the questions as honestly as he could.

'Is there any true evidence that points toward Cody Stoltz?'

'Not yet.'

'Then why hasn't he come in with a lawyer and challenged this?'

'You'll have to ask him.'

'OK, all right, but you're looking for him.'

'Yeah, we are.'

'And he's trying not to get found?'

Raveneau didn't see any need to answer that one. His mind drifted back to la Rosa, how close a call it was.

'Was Inspector la Rosa able to give a clear description?'

'No.'

'Will she recover more memory, more of a description?'

'Maybe, but I doubt it. The assailant had a mask on and it happened fast.'

'Does that mean that, other than it was a Volvo he was driving, you have little to go on?'

'Right now, that's accurate.'

'OK, one last question, if you were Stoltz and you hadn't killed anybody and didn't plan to, what would you do now?'

'I'd call a lawyer and have him arrange a surrender.'

'Does that mean you'd arrest and charge him?'

'I can't answer that.'

'Perfect. Thanks, Ben, talk to you later.'

FORTY-TWO

San Francisco homicide inspectors are expected to clock in, work an eight hour day, and get approval for any overtime. If approved, you filled out one of the little salmon-pink cards, but Raveneau often ignored that. He worked whatever it took.

He was standing at the windows drinking coffee and watching the dawn when he heard the office door open. A few minutes later Lieutenant Becker walked back.

'I'm not in today,' Becker said, voice flat, eyes bloodshot as Raveneau turned and looked at him. 'I was at the hospital all night. My brother isn't doing well.'

Raveneau put an arm around Becker's shoulders, knowing there was little he could say. He washed two mugs and brought Becker coffee. Then they stood at the windows as the sky turned pink with sunrise.

'My brother's daughter, my niece, Jolie, just turned seventeen. She and her dad are close but she's a troubled kid, problems with drugs, a new tattoo or piercing every three weeks, and a knack for hanging out with all the wrong people. In any group she'll figure out the one who's going to get arrested and gravitate toward them unconsciously. But underneath it, she's a good kid. It's looking like they're going to charge her former boyfriend and I don't know how Jolie's going to handle it. I don't know what to do.'

'Where's her mom?'

'In Minnesota with two young kids and a new family. She remarried after the divorce. She knows Alan was shot but we haven't heard a word from her about Jolie.'

'Can she live with you?'

'My wife doesn't like her and we don't really have enough room but she's going to have to move in with us, at least for the moment. Right now, she's staying with her best friend. I've got to keep her in high school. That's job one right now. Somehow I've got to keep her on track, but all I can think about is her ex-boyfriend.'

'Is there new evidence?'

'They're waiting for DNA results.'

'When are those?'

'Today. There was blood at the scene that wasn't Alan's. The ex-boyfriend had a cut on his right forearm he claims happened when he fell off his bike. He also told the investigators he hasn't been at the house in months. If they get a match today they'll charge him.'

Becker gripped the coffee cup with both hands. He hadn't touched any of it. His eyes were bloodshot as he turned and said, 'Oakland is moving forward with a case against Bates. They've got a signed statement from the girl-friend.'

Raveneau nodded. He was aware. He had talked to Stalos for half an hour yesterday.

Oakland wanted them to agree before they charged Bates. They didn't want any blowback from SF Homicide.

'Where are we at with Cody Stoltz?' Becker asked.

'I've asked the FBI to get a UFAP warrant on him.'

'How are they going to do that if we don't really have anything on him?'

'They can get a warrant on anybody they want nowadays. They'll get the warrant.'

'We'd still need a way to hold him.'

'Yeah, but we also need help finding him.'

Raveneau told him about the private investigator following Stoltz north after Stoltz left the hotel late at night, but Becker seemed to already know about that. The Feds would get the UFAP and then they'd be all over Stoltz's phone pen register. With phones, the FBI could track real time and that might be their best chance of locating him. But Becker was right, unlawful flight to avoid prosecution was a probable cause apprehension. If apprehended, they'd need evidence to hold him.

'There was a phone call made from LA last night,' Raveneau said. 'That phone seems to belong to a non-existent person but it may have been him calling here.'

'Made to where?'

'Here. Want to hear it?'

Raveneau put the message on speaker phone.

'I'm ready to go again. Are you?'

He pushed the volume up. With just Becker and him in the office he replayed it several

216

times, then said, 'The call came from LA. It's similar to another one I got a day or two after we caught the China Basin killing. That's something I can't put together.'

'What was that message?'

'Also short, one line with some vehicle noise in the background, a man saying, "So you found her." That call was made from one of these PCS one month phones where you try out the unlimited local service for forty bucks or whatever it is. The phone owner gave a false ID.'

'This recent call was from Los Angeles?'

'Yes.'

'Could be somebody playing with us.'

'Sure.'

Becker set the coffee down, still untouched. He squinted up at Raveneau.

'And la Rosa is fine?'

'A mild concussion and stitches where the bullet plowed a groove in her scalp, and that'll be tender this morning, but it wouldn't surprise me if she showed up here. She wants to strap her gun on and go Volvo hunting.'

'What does she remember?'

'Not enough. It happened fast, shooter wore a mask, and she didn't see much.'

Becker didn't respond to that, no doubt had heard that already. Raveneau watched him go back into his grief. Becker left the homicide office soon after and returned to the hospital where his brother died just before noon.

FORTY-THREE

That same morning Stoltz walked into a car dealership and test drove a BMW, an older 330i with a sport package, relatively low mileage, and new Michelins. The body was as clean as they had claimed. He handed over a Visa with the name Steven Pullman on it, telling the salesman, 'This way I get the airline mileage.'

Then he sensed that one of the women working on the paperwork behind a glass barrier was watching him. He turned his back to her, moved out into the showroom, and waited nervously outside on a bench with the feeling that everything was closing in around him. Time was compressing. He needed to move carefully but faster. Twenty minutes later, he signed the papers and the salesman handed him the keys, smiling as he asked, 'Where are you headed in that beautiful car?'

'Vegas.'

'Man, I wish that was me. How long are you going to be there?'

'Ten days. I just got a bonus that was a long time coming.'

'Have a great drive. This baby should really run for you.'

Instead of heading toward Vegas, Stoltz went

218

north on I-5, making the same drive he'd made last Sunday morning. For the next three hours he sat in a fast group of cars running at speeds way over the limit, as if somehow a pack mentality protected them from the highway patrol. After three hours he left the freeway to gas up. When he got back on he made a bad mistake, accelerating to catch a car in front of him and touching one hundred and five miles per hour as he passed it.

Seconds later he hit the brakes, but too late. A black and white CHP cruiser was getting off a ramp up ahead and immediately came for him, closing fast, and as he did Stoltz moved his gun into his lap. But rather than pull him over the officer hovered alongside him for several seconds then sped off. What he might have done left him shaken.

He drove another forty minutes under the white sky and flat land of the valley, before pulling the clip from the gun and calling his lawyer. North of the valley town of Patterson he merged into heavier traffic. He crossed over the brown hills past the slow-winding windmills of Altamont Pass, and headed for the warehouse in San Jose. There he showered and changed, and tried to calm down.

But he didn't feel like the director of the movie any more. He felt like an actor. He felt lightheaded. He switched cars and a mile from his mother's house he called SF Homicide and asked for Raveneau.

Raveneau asked, 'Are you coming in?'

'My lawyer has advised me not to talk to you,

but I'm willing to meet with you. I don't want to deal with the media.'

'We'll bring you in through the back, but I have to warn you that as of a few hours ago there's a warrant out for your—'

'I want to talk to you alone first. Then I'll give myself up.'

'OK, we'll do it that way.'

'But I'm not who you're looking for.'

'That's why we need to talk.'

'I didn't kill the lawyer in Walnut Creek. I don't even know who he is. I didn't shoot your partner.'

'We've got a lot to talk about. Where are you now?'

'Almost home.'

'Los Altos?'

'Yes.'

He was still talking to Raveneau when a SWAT team closed around him. Raveneau must have heard the squealing tires, the yelling, the order to get out of the vehicle, and Stoltz breathed into the phone as he looked at a gun aimed at his head, 'If they kill me, it's on you.'

'I don't know how they found you, but do exactly what they tell you.'

They batted the phone out of his hand and jerked him out of the car. Then he was face down on the asphalt. He felt pebbles grind into his cheek, heard the handcuffs click, and let his body go limp.

FORTY-FOUR

Stoltz's lawyer adjusted her glasses and made a prediction. 'They'll release him within two days and my client will sue and win.'

It took Raveneau an hour to string together how the SID team knew Stoltz was on his way to his mother's house. Turned out the FBI tracked him real-time through his cell phone, and Raveneau didn't say it to anyone except la Rosa, but he regretted the takedown. He believed Stoltz would have come in, whereas now he was refusing to talk. He sat and talked strategy with la Rosa and then called Jurika's cousin, Julie Candiff. Candiff's fingers clicked over a keyboard as she talked with him. She was flaky but cooperating, flying in from Phoenix tomorrow morning just before noon.

'We'll pick you up at the airport.'

'I rented a car.'

'OK, it'll take you about thirty-five minutes to get here. Do you want directions?'

'No, I have my phone.'

'We'll see you tomorrow.'

She didn't answer and a moment later hung up.

'Is she going to show?' la Rosa asked, and Raveneau shook his head, no.

He called the LA car dealership that sold the

BMW to Stoltz and talked with the salesman who closed the deal. Somewhere between the LA dealership and where they took him down, Stoltz switched from a BMW into a Toyota Prius and Raveneau was looking for the salesman's help. He wanted the mileage on the car as it left the lot. He got that, 39,334.

After thanking the salesman and hanging up he used Google Maps to get the distance from the dealership to Stoltz's mother's house. Stoltz was a mile short of there when he was taken down. Now he called the Department of Motor Vehicles and got a list of other vehicles, cars and boats in the name of Steven Pullman. He sat back, thought about it, and then made another call and got the answer he expected.

'If he's paying his bills as Steven Pullman no judge is going to hold him on an illegal social security number and an alias on a credit card. In this state, if we started locking up people with illegal social security numbers we'd have to build a jail every fifteen minutes.'

As he hung up, he thought more about Heilbron and the case they were building against him, and then what was already starting to click suddenly made even more sense. It fit. It was too much to be coincidence. If Lafaye was telling the truth about buying Erin Quinn's identity from Alex Jurika, and they had that clear link to Stoltz's past, what if the Steven Pullman identity was also bought through Jurika?

By late afternoon he had a full record of everywhere the Pullman Visa had ever been used. He wrote up a request for a search warrant for

Stoltz's residence and vehicles. As he finished la Rosa walked back in.

'You're not going there without me,' she said.

'I wouldn't want to. Let's see those stitches.' He wrapped an arm around her after looking at them, then said, 'OK, partner, let's go see the judge.'

Los Altos police assisted and taped the road off as Raveneau drank coffee and ate a tuna sandwich. Then he and la Rosa walked down the gravel drive toward the guest house. A string of low landscape lights marked the way. He looked at the dark hills beyond and the pool and tennis courts and the lawyer waiting for them in the light of the open front door. Raveneau introduced himself and la Rosa to the lawyer. She had a direct look and seemed to have a genuine interest in protecting her client. She read the warrant carefully as Raveneau shook open a pair of latex gloves and put them on slowly.

FORTY-FIVE

Last time Raveneau was in Phoenix was to interview a witness on a July afternoon when the temperature tagged one hundred and fifteen degrees and he made the mistake of leaving a printout of a photo on the passenger seat of the rental car. The photo curled and faded in the baking heat inside. Left in there long enough it probably would have caught fire. But this was November and the morning was clear and cool. A light wind blew off the desert. He'd slept on the plane and felt rested.

The search yesterday of Stoltz's house yielded a few papers and documents la Rosa would follow up on today from the office. But he doubted anything would come of what they had found. Stoltz was ready for a search. He'd anticipated it. That was Raveneau's take-away.

He called la Rosa and let her know he'd landed and was pulling into the shopping mall where Julie Candiff worked as an assistant manager in a boutique clothing store. He found Candiff soon after walking in and asked her, 'Do you have someone who can cover for you for a couple of hours?'

'I'll get fired if I leave the store.'

'The police are going to let us use an interview

224

room at a precinct near here. You can ride with me or drive yourself. That's up to you.'

She stood up to him now. She looked little like her cousin, blonde hair to her shoulders, a small turned up nose and carefully made-up eyes.

'You really don't care about what happens with my job, do you?'

'Maybe I'll care more when I get to know you better.'

She disappeared for several minutes, and then was in a hurry to get out of the store so others didn't find out who he was or where she was going. At the Squaw Peak Precinct she said, 'All I ever did was rent the apartment. I never handled any money or any credit cards, or opened any of the mail that came there.'

'The problem is we have hundreds of emails and text messages between you and Alex. In fifty of them you're talking about the things you bought.'

'Of course we talked about shopping. We loved to shop together.'

'There's a record of everything you charged. We've got videotape of you standing at a store counter showing a fake driver's license as you use a credit card with someone else's name. That's credit fraud and it's a done deal that it was you, so from my point of view you're being stubborn. Or maybe you didn't care that much about your cousin.'

'That's a mean thing to say. You don't know how sad I am about Alex.'

'You're right, I don't. You hide it well and I'm getting frustrated. We're trying to find the person who killed Alex, and it feels like you're trying to block us. You make promises you don't keep. You dodge contact and I'm getting the strong impression you don't care whether her killer is found or not. You keep denying the business you and your cousin had and I feel as though you'd like me to just go away.'

'It was her business, not mine. I didn't know what was going on. I never knew.'

'You and Alex stole a lot of money and ruined the credit of dozens of people along the way. I have zero doubt about that, OK, just so we're clear. I know you stole credit cards and identities.'

Raveneau paused. When she finally looked up he continued.

'But what I'm working on is a homicide investigation. I'm not working credit fraud. I'm trying to figure out who murdered Alex Jurika, your cousin, your best friend in crime. I'm looking to you to stand up for her. I think the killing was related to the fraud, or came from it. That same killer may come for you.'

'But I don't know anything, Alex ran everything.'

'Doesn't matter. They may not know that. So you've got to talk to me.'

At some point he left her alone in the room and made calls and picked up messages. When he went back in she said, 'Alex worked for some company where they cleaned old people's houses and stuff and she would steal credit cards from them.'

'Steal from the houses they worked in?'

'Yes.'

'GoodHands?'

'I don't remember the name, but Alex sometimes traded online the card info she stole, other times she'd use the numbers herself.'

'What was your role?'

'Do you promise I won't go to jail?'

'No, but what I said before is true. All I'm interested in is finding Alex's killer.'

'But this is all recorded.'

'Yes, it's all being taped.'

When he flew home late that afternoon Raveneau felt he had a much better idea of how it all evolved. He was pretty sure Candiff's role was limited.

'Well?' la Rosa asked as she picked him up at SFO.

'It was worth it. She wasn't going to fly out. She needed the shock of us coming to her and interrupting her life.'

He downloaded what he'd learned.

'She claims not to know Deborah Lafaye or recognize the name Erin Quinn. She was out of the loop. Alex gave her the job of the apartment because she knew she could keep her happy by buying clothes and jewelry.'

'Then what was her role?'

'Jurika gave some of the new credit identities Phoenix addresses. She put a few in Scottsdale and other places in the greater Phoenix area. Four of the names had the same address, a Phoenix apartment where Candiff picked up the mail.'

Raveneau opened his notebook and went

through it point by point with la Rosa before asking about Stoltz.

'He walks tomorrow,' she said, and that's what happened. Mid morning the next day Stoltz got cut loose without a bond, because as Stoltz's lawyer put it, 'It's still legal in America to work long hours and take business trips.'

Stoltz also made a public statement wishing the police luck, saying, 'I am very sorry for the families of the officers and as much as anyone I want this killer caught. I've been treated very unfairly by the police in the past, but I apologize for not coming forward sooner.'

Raveneau watched it live and then again on late night news. He couldn't quite get his head around how easily the identity theft was brushed off. Stoltz had admitted through his lawyer to purchasing online the identity of a Steven Pullman who had died with his parents in an auto accident in 1983. Asked about it by a reporter, he was close to indignant, saying he always paid the bills, and dismissed using the identity of a dead child as inconsequential, saying, 'It's just a name.' And maybe that's where things were headed, to a world where identity was just another commodity. If so, what would that say about us?

FORTY-SIX

Before leaving the house Stoltz spent an hour on his laptop reworking the TV and room lights schedule. He went out the back of the house a few minutes before the computer turned on the TV and lights in the kitchen. He had no illusions; the police had the whole house covered.

Still, he'd run a lot of his own tests on what you could see from the ridge and the back of the orchard, and left through a window in the basement laundry room that opened into a bush at the end of an old hedge, where the plants were big enough that he could belly crawl under them until he reached the trees. At the trees he crouched and waited fifteen minutes until a stairway light and an upstairs bathroom light came on. Faint strains of music leaked from the house. No doubt they thought he was inside gloating that he was out and the media was focusing on Bates.

He worked from tree to tree to reach the storm drainage easement where the manhole was. He waited before prying the heavy iron manhole cover off, and then slid it back into place after climbing part-way down the ladder. He didn't turn on his flashlight until he got to the bottom of the ladder.

It was much cooler in here, cold, really, a dank

cold, but somehow comforting because they couldn't watch him. They didn't know about this. The concrete pipe was large though not big enough to stand in and he hunched down, turned the flashlight beam on the backpack and the fresh rat droppings on it. He saw a hole had been chewed through it and brushed the droppings off, but didn't yet unclip the pack from the wire and carabiner it dangled from.

How were the rats getting to the pack? Was it possible they crawled down the wire or did they jump from the manhole ladder? He unzipped the pack and was relieved not to find a rat inside, though it looked like one had made a nest of his coat. But the laptop was OK. The pack was suspended from a wire attached to an eye hook he'd drilled into the center of the top of the culvert pipe and however they were doing it, they were doing it. It didn't matter. He'd kill them. He spread rat poison just above the moss and trickle of water at his feet. He put some of it on top of the pack and then pulled on a headlamp and started down the pipe.

The bigger pipe ended where the other feeder pipes coming off the hills fed in, and from there he had to squat and walk forward like a crab, headlight bobbing, rats moving, scraping and scratching as they ran up ahead. He smelled rat shit and the long uphill grade was a slow tiring climb. He'd slept too little and burned too much adrenaline. He knew he was becoming manic, the way he did sometimes, and taking risks he shouldn't. Yet he couldn't stop right now. He had to get control back.

After forty minutes he reached the second ladder, but instead of climbing out the usual way, continued on and had to belly crawl through the slime in a smaller pipe, and then struggled getting the grate off the storm drain, finally jerking his way free. In the trees he stripped down to his running shorts and sweats, and left the filthy coveralls in a black plastic bag that he hid in the brush. He put the keys in the pouch around his waist, walked back out to the road and started the two mile jog up and over the grade, then down a long-falling road to where he called for a cab to take him to San Jose. He had the cab drop him half a mile from the warehouse and once inside showered and changed before loading up a car and driving to San Francisco.

He entered China Basin on Third Street and then found a place to park and wait. The light was off in the apartment where Inspector Raveneau lived. Raveneau's car wasn't in the fenced lot. If Raveneau came home and if the opportunity showed itself, he'd do it, but for now he reclined his seat, plugged in his iPod, and waited.

FORTY-SEVEN

Heilbron watched the same weird late night press conference with Stoltz. He squatted in front of the TV looking for the inspectors, but the clip was short and it was only the Stoltz guy. What was with this? Trippy fucking dude and definitely up to something. Definitely in-your-face-type angry, but sounding like he was all rational and reasonable about what had gone on. The newscaster came and Heilbron waited for him to talk about the investigation and Inspector la Rosa. Instead, they skipped to weather and he reached for the remote and went through the other local news, but there was nothing.

Time to check out the night. He left the TV on low and killed the other lights in the house. He watched from a window for a while, then went out the back and to the van. He had a bike in the van, chained so that it stood up. For three days he'd been home and not seen the inspectors, though their cards were in the door. He only kept la Rosa's card. He had four of hers now and cleaned out an Altoids tin to store them in. Four of her in the little tin box. Four was his lucky number. Of course, if it was really her she would need a bigger box and he'd have to take the bike out of the van for the box to have room. Then he'd be chillin' with Inspector Elizabeth la Rosa. Driving around or maybe he would drive somewhere special with her that wouldn't get figured out for a very long time. He drove sort of dreaming of what that would feel like.

He liked the way it felt to think of it, but it was still crazy what he'd done going to the Hall of Justice that morning instead of going to work. He couldn't believe he did it. But this dude, Stoltz, he knows in his head what he's doing while he's doing it, talking to the press, getting filmed, knowing he's going to be on TV and be famous. He's got a plan, Heilbron thought. I read the man. Definitely has plans. That's what I have to do, plan every detail, every small thing just like working on the cars. It's in the really small details. You have to get everything just right. Plan it, dude. Plan it carefully. Get it right.

Heilbron turned at the next corner. If Stoltz was able to pull something off, then he'd have to also. He thought about that as he drove downtown.

FORTY-EIGHT

'Hey,' Celeste said, 'where are you?'

'Just getting home.'

'Want to go back out instead? I just finished this wine thing at the Four Seasons and I've got a room here tonight and an expense account for dinner.'

Tonight the elevator seemed louder than usual and he could barely hear her as he rode up. Even if he went back out he needed to feed the cat first. He got out of the elevator and climbed the stairs to the cool air of the roof. Horsetails of cirrus clouds fanned into moonlight.

'Let me feed the cat and then I'll meet you there. I'll probably be half an hour. Is that OK?'

'I'll be in the bar.'

He called for Visa and heard a meow, but it took a while to figure out where it was coming from. When he did, he wasn't sure how to get Visa out.

Soon after he'd moved here, the owner, Mr Han, had hired a contractor to install iron braces that connected the roof framing to the brick parapet, a city earthquake bracing requirement. In March it had rained almost every day and there were leaks in and around where the contractor had worked, so Han was up on the roof innumerable times arguing with the contractor, and finally the contractor built a temporary plywood contraption over one of the seismic braces that leaked the worst.

Somehow Visa had gotten inside that plywood box and Raveneau felt around in the darkness for the opening the cat crawled through. When he found it, Visa still wouldn't come out. But a can of food did the trick and he left Visa eating.

By the time he got downstairs again to his car he was running late to meet Celeste. To head toward the Four Seasons he needed to make a U-turn, but ahead of him a car a few blocks down pulled away in a manner that made him curious. He followed it intending to turn around soon, but closed in a little when it became obvious the driver didn't want him catching up.

So now the cop in him kicked in and he stayed with it, an old Ford Taurus, one of the SHO cars, the faster model. It swung left, the driver tapping his brakes as he rolled through a stop sign, and then picked up speed. He went right with his tires squealing. As Raveneau neared, he swung hard on to the 101 ramp and gunned it on to the southbound freeway, Raveneau following but not gaining. When the Taurus broke right at the 280 split Raveneau picked up his cell and called the SID team leader.

'How certain are you Stoltz is home?'

'We just watched a light go off upstairs.'

'I'm following a car that was parked down the street from where I live. The driver is on 280 and moving at ninety. He doesn't want me to catch him. The car is a Ford Taurus maybe ten years old and dark-colored. I've fallen way back from him now and he's slowed but is still moving fast. I'm not going to get close enough for plates.'

'We can call the CHP right now.'

So could Raveneau but he didn't want that. 'I want to know where he's going,' he said.

He felt the minutes go by, felt Celeste waiting for him as he chased the car down 280. When the car exited near Palo Alto, Raveneau lost him in the hills, but was able to give SID a partial plate before turning back to San Francisco.

'Plates start with the letters A and L and contain the number four.'

'We'll keep our eyes peeled but we think he's inside.'

'Call me when you find the car.'

The officer chuckled, said, 'You got it.'

He called Celeste, told her what happened, and apologized. 'I'm on my way to you now.'

When he got to the Four Seasons Celeste was at the bar and a little bit drunk. She was trying to be cheerful but couldn't understand why he didn't call her earlier.

'I was afraid you'd stood me up. Remember I said all you ever have to do is call and let me know.'

'I'm sorry, I was wrapped up in this guy I was following. How about we restart the night?'

But it didn't work out very well. They split a bottle of wine at dinner but after drinking whatever she had before he got there it was more than she could handle. Suddenly they were talking about her old boyfriend again, how he left her, how much it hurt her, and then back to now and how all she needed was a phone call as she waited at the bar. That was all fair.

After dinner they went up to her room and Celeste said, 'I'm really drunk,' and fell asleep on top of the bed with her clothes on. He thought about going home but instead undressed her and put her under the covers, and then moved a chair over to the window and sat thinking about la Rosa's close call, the car he'd chased, and Becker's face after his brother was shot.

He listened to Celeste's soft snore and wondered how much he really knew about her. She'd gone a long way over the edge worrying when he didn't show up on time and put away three martinis. Maybe her old boyfriend leaving her had left her damaged in a way he couldn't help.

Sometime later he got into bed with her, and very late in the night he woke to her whispered, 'I'm sorry for thinking you stood me up and sorry for getting so scared. I didn't used to be like that, and I'm sorry I talk about Gary too much. I know if I don't stop you're going to go away. Sometimes I feel like I've done everything wrong. Things that seemed right at the time, that look like bad decisions now.'

'I like being with you. That's why I'm here.'

'Being with a drunk.'

'You're not a drunk.'

His cell rang and Raveneau reached for it.

'Inspector, sorry to bother you but about fifteen minutes ago in the hills behind Stoltz's house we found a Taurus matching your description and with an A, an L, and a number four on the plates. It's on a street about a mile and a half

237

from here and registered to a David Williams.'

Raveneau shut his phone slowly. He reached over for Celeste and held her tight for several minutes. Then kissed her and got dressed. If that was Stoltz in China Basin, then Stoltz was out of control. Celeste spoke as he was dressing.

'I understand if you want to end it.'

'That's the last thing I want. I'll call you.'

FORTY-NINE

They came up the road and around the curve, with the SID officer saying, 'Right up here under these trees, does that look like your car?'

'Yeah, that's it.'

'He could be watching this so I'm going to keep driving, but earlier we got a Los Altos patrol officer to shine a light inside and try the door. It's locked and there's nothing on the seats. The hood was still warm.'

'He must get home from here.'

'That's what we figure too. He burned us. It must be that a computer controls the lights in the house or they're pre-programmed. We think he got out through the rear.'

Trying to understand Stoltz leaving the car here, Raveneau said, 'He got scared when I chased him. He dumped the car here and he's probably back in his house now.'

'We would have seen him go back in.'

With Raveneau's testimony they could probably get another search warrant tonight and go through his house again, but they wouldn't find anything and tomorrow Stoltz's lawyer would make more noise. Yesterday, in a press conference, the lawyer even threatened the press, citing Richard Jewell, who when he was cleared of the

Atlanta Olympics bombing settled with NBC for half a million. She claimed SFPD was intentionally destroying her client's reputation.

The brass was a little worried about that and Captain Ramirez called him, but Raveneau knew this was the car he'd followed. It wasn't registered to Stoltz, but it was the car and here it was parked within a mile and a half of Stoltz's house. He was waiting for you to come home and when you flushed him out and followed him, he got so scared he dumped the car on the side of the road and went down his rabbit hole.

'Stop for a minute, OK. I want to stand outside.'

Raveneau walked over to the car. He looked down at the hillside falling away and up ahead, where the road climbed into country grown over with trees, brush, and rye grass. Maybe he had another car or motorcycle, or some other way of getting out of here once he parked the Taurus. Or maybe he had a way to get back to his house.

At first light a K-9 unit and a second surveillance team arrived. When la Rosa got there, she and Raveneau hung back as the handlers worked the dogs. A bloodhound went down the road shoulder and half a mile below moved back and forth along a guard rail.

The dog seemed to want to get around the guard rail, poking its head underneath and barking. When the handler walked it around the railing the bloodhound picked up the scent again and went down the slope.

They watched and la Rosa asked, 'Do you get poison oak?'

Below were several large poison oak bushes, their leaves mostly gone and what was left dry and close to falling. There was greasewood and rye grass and oak, and the handler and dog were partially hidden by the trees and brush.

'I got it as a kid. I don't get it any more,' he said, and watched the handler come to the base of the steep slope.

'Looks like he's about to wave us down,' Raveneau said. 'The dog has found something.'

He thought of other times he'd seen the dogs circle a spot along a creek bed or in trees down a ravine.

'Your dad was a cop, wasn't he?' la Rosa asked.

'Yeah, he was a uniform cop, a beat cop. He got discharged from the navy after World War Two, met my mom, and then they stayed and settled here. In those days SFPD still had cops walking the beat. He thought all homicide inspectors were prima donnas. He only trusted uniform cops. He congratulated me when I got my homicide star, but he didn't think much of it.'

'That's too bad.'

'It was fine. We figured out a way to joke about it.'

'Were you close to him?'

'Closer in the end, but he was hard on my brother and I growing up.'

'So who do you have?'

'I got divorced a dozen years ago, and we had one child, a son who was killed in Iraq.'

'I'm sorry, Ben, no one told me that.'

'I don't talk about it much.'

'Were you close to your son?'

'Yes, very close.'

'It must have been very hard.'

It still is, he thought, and asked, 'What about you?'

'My grandfather was a cop and I adored him. Even when I was little he treated me like I was an equal riding along with him in a big car. He died when I was in college. He was on patrol driving alone at night on a rural road in Minnesota and had a heart attack and ran into a tree. No one found him until morning, but they think he was alive all night and couldn't reach the radio. He drank vodka, smoked Marlboros, and ate blood-red steaks he had to beat the black flies off of. He was my hero.'

Ten minutes later, the dog handler and the bloodhound were back on top and the handler had taken his hat off and was telling Raveneau, 'There's a manhole cover over a storm drainage line. He may have gone in there.'

They went down the steep slope and took a look. From the spot where the dog had stopped your eye followed a line of brush and grass where the scar left from the installation of drainage pipes still showed. Raveneau sighted where it ran down toward the valley and it all began to make sense. He hiked back up the steep slope, slick with dry grass, and got a tire iron and the crowbar he carried in his trunk, and used the crowbar to lift the iron cover. It was the kind of thing he and Donny would crawl into as kids.

After looking down the manhole they started

making calls, trying to get someone from the local Public Works or Sewer Department, whoever handled run-off. Turned out the sewer people handled storm drainage easements and an engineer walked them through a map, pointing out the easement line.

'It's a forty-eight inch culvert that drains these hills,' he said. 'There are branches that feed into it and there's an easement through the property you're speaking of.'

'Will I be able to walk down it?'

'No, in most of it you'd have to work your way along in a crouch. As you get lower the pipe will get bigger. Everything up in these hills feeds in. But most of it is not too steep. Slick in places, I'm sure. Do you really want to go in there?'

'No.'

They drove back up and SID reported that they still hadn't seen any sign of movement in the house. Raveneau turned to la Rosa after retrieving a Maglite.

'He could be in there and my phone isn't going to work, so give me forty minutes and then come find me.'

'That sounds brilliant.'

'I'm going to follow it until I find the access ladder that comes up in the easement crossing the Stoltz property, just like the Public Works guy described.'

In the concrete pipe the air was cold and smelled of mud and the algae. Where it got steeper he fell several times and his back ached from squatting and shuffling forward. His flashlight only reached so far and there was a possibility he'd encounter Stoltz, so he was ready for that and tense all the way along, a walking target with a light.

When he reached the ladder that should lead up to the Stoltz property he found a daypack suspended there. For several seconds he held the flashlight beam on it, and then took photos with his phone before unclipping it and looking inside. He climbed the access ladder, shouldered the lid off and looked out along a tall row of pines at the back of the guest house. With the manhole resting heavily on his shoulder he called la Rosa.

'I'm looking at the back of his house. I found a daypack suspended in here.'

'What's in—'

'A laptop. I'm on my way back with it.'

FIFTY

Raveneau lingered, standing on a rung of the manhole ladder, his head and shoulders above ground. He rested a hand on cold dry pine needles and studied the terrain. Overhead, the sky was white and cold. In the walnut orchard to his right, the soil looked damp and dark. Mom's house loomed off the side of the guest house and he could only guess at what the property was worth or why Stoltz, living in circumstances most could only dream of, would come after them. The easement for storm drainage ran alongside a tall row of pines planted long ago as a windbreak. Branches reached over him. They shadowed the easement and at the end of the trees he saw a hedge that ran all the way up to the back of the guest house alongside the beds of roses. That had to be how he did it. That was his route.

The iron lid scraped loud enough to be heard some distance and he dropped his flashlight as he climbed back down. Fortunately, it didn't break when it hit. Leaning against the wall of the big concrete pipe he studied the backpack again. Taking it meant playing their hand, but he only debated for a few minutes.

He worked his way back, first through the big

245

pipe, and then into the smaller branch, carrying the daypack like a football, and after a while slipping the pack straps over his shoulders and wearing it. Working up the incline he straddled the green slime along the pipe bottom, but slipped several times and cut his knee deep enough to start blood trickling down his calf.

At some point the pipe got claustrophobic. His progress was slow up the incline, flashlight cutting a darkness that just seemed to go on and on. The four foot pipe wore him out and made his knees ache. Then he saw sunlight and crab-walked the last hundred yards fast to that bright shaft of light. Now he stood in the sun letting the ache ease in his back and knees, blinking at the brightness as he slid the pack off and handed it to la Rosa.

'Have a good time down there?'

'Yeah, it's great. We ought to pack a picnic and come back. There are a lot of rats so it's not lonely, but I've got an idea for how the little fellas can help us. But right now, let's go see what CSI can pull off the laptop, and then get it booted up.'

They drove back to San Francisco, la Rosa at the wheel and Raveneau talking with Public Works in Los Altos. In the CSI office several fingerprints got pulled from the laptop, though all but three were smudged. One was a fourteen pointer that matched Stoltz and there were hairs and a piece of a small scab vacuumed out of the spaces between the keyboard keys.

Raveneau had to step away to talk to the Public Works guys again. He needed a truck and some uniforms, but they had a protocol. It took the chief of police in Los Altos and a number of calls.

'We want it to be credible,' Raveneau said. 'It's got to be an emergency response as though you'd just discovered these rats, a public health warning, an infestation you're acting on immediately.'

'That's just going to give us bad press. It could get someone here fired.'

'No one is going to care. They'll just be surprised you're acting so fast and then we'll explain it all later.'

'What is it you're going to explain?'

'I can't tell you yet.'

There was silence on the other end, but he hadn't said anything about the backpack and laptop. He'd told the Public Works guy, Corrigan, next to nothing and yet was asking him to provide a truck and uniforms and at least one employee who could play along.

'There actually are a lot of rats down there. You do have an infestation.'

'There are rats everywhere on earth.'

'OK, well, these are the ones that can help us.'

'When do you need all this by?'

'This afternoon.'

They booted up the laptop and ran into a firewall and after an hour of trying to get through called one of the contract techs the city used. As the techs huddled over the laptop Raveneau and la Rosa went down to Café Roma for coffee.

'The last thing I need is coffee,' la Rosa said as they crossed Bryant. 'I'm already too wired up.'

247

But she bought a piece of chocolate cake and a big coffee. He got a coffee and they took a table. It was hard waiting and there was no way of saying how long it would be. Behind him, on the other side of a glass wall, someone worked on the big coffee roaster.

'How's your scalp?' he asked, and la Rosa the college basketball player, the girl who'd torn her ACL playing soccer as a kid and carried a scar on her leg from that repair and another scar above her left eyebrow from a lacrosse stick, leaned over toward him and lifted her hair. She was proud of how it was healing. Healthy red pink healing tissue swelled around the black stitches.

'Looks good.'

'I heal fast.'

'What about inside?'

'Are you asking if I'm thinking about how close a call it was?'

'I am.'

'You're thinking a situation could come up with Stoltz.'

'It could.'

'I've been thinking about it, but you're not imagining you're going to leave me behind.'

'I'm asking how you feel.'

She picked up her coffee and then set it down again.

'I admit I didn't want to get in that culvert with you. I should have gotten in there with you because he could have been in there.'

'I'm not asking about that.'

'Nothing like this has ever happened to me, so

248

it's not easy to answer your question.'

'You're not answering it.'

Raveneau's phone rang and it was the computer tech, Meacham. At the counter, the two employees standing there watched his reaction. The city was waiting and watching. La Rosa watched him, as did the media pair at another table, but he didn't betray any of what he felt about what Meacham had just said. He leaned toward la Rosa, said quietly, 'He got through.'

FIFTY-ONE

On the other side of the firewall was a single document, a file named 'Erin'. In it were pieces of information about Erin Quinn's life, a Louisiana driver's license number, her social security and passport numbers, addresses dating back to childhood, the schools she'd attended, the location of a sister and two brothers and notes on questioning them. Using Excel, Stoltz had outlined his search. He'd emailed extensively with one of her brothers who lived in upper Michigan, misrepresenting himself to Norman Quinn as an old girlfriend of hers named Melanie Pace, and writing that they'd been buds when they were in college together at San Francisco State. As Melanie Pace he was trying to get back in touch with Erin.

All of his emails with Norman Quinn, both sent and received, as with his emails with everyone, were chronologically arranged and spread. They often had margin notes alongside them, referring to what action he'd taken, how he was chasing down the lead. Norman had provided names of other people who knew her and in some cases had written or called an introduction ahead of Stoltz contacting them.

Then he'd written a final email to Stoltz that seemed to capture it all.

My sister is gone and really I'm the only one in the family who hasn't accepted that. She disappeared when he was in prison but from things she said, we believe somehow Stoltz had a hand in it. Erin called our sister, Lily, on 22 March, 2002, and said she was scared, that she'd had several hang up calls and had seen two guys this morning that she'd seen at the beach yesterday. She told Lily that Cody Stoltz had warned her he'd reach her from prison, that she'd betrayed him.

This is hard for me to write but my family thinks Erin is dead. If you continue to search for her, I'll help you in any way I can, but I'm afraid I've already given you every bit of information on her that I have. Like you, I can't bear the idea that somebody killed her. I pray to God that she's going to turn up someday with amnesia. After her husband was shot she lost connection with everything for a little while, so I like to think she's living somewhere and doesn't remember who she is. I think about her every day. I wish you all the best and it's comforting to know there's some-one else out there still looking for her. For that, I love you. Norman

The file on Erin Quinn totaled one hundred and twenty-eight pages and they had to copy it and take it with them because it was time to hook up with the Public Works people in Los Altos. As they got in the car, la Rosa said, 'This is amazing. Who is this guy? He's got a whole story and bio for this Melanie Pace he became online.

251

Listen to this: Melanie Pace actually existed. She was a San Francisco State student killed in a freak car accident when a thunderstorm caused a flash flood that swept her car off the road in New Mexico. He's got the newspaper article right here.'

But on page one hundred and fourteen it was a different name that caught them. Raveneau was driving as la Rosa read aloud to him.

'I feel like we should be saying Eureka, not Jurika,' she said. 'He worked some pretty small threads back to Jurika. He figured out Quinn shed her identity and Jurika sold it. Ben, he just figured this out, like two weeks ago.'

'And went to Jurika to get answers and ended up killing her.'

'That's it, isn't it? That's what happened.'

In Los Altos they rendezvoused with the Public Works guys who'd knock on the door of Mrs Stoltz's house. Raveneau listened to the conversation via the wire the Public Works foreman wore. He watched through binoculars as the foreman turned and pointed at an exterminator van in the street.

'He's with us, ma'am, and we've got an emergency. With your permission we'd like to access our line through a manhole in our easement through your property.'

When she learned that a large rat infestation had been discovered yesterday in the storm drainage pipes running back into the hills, she gave immediate permission to get on to the property. She knew about the easement and manhole, but now came a trickier part.

'Is anyone living in the other house?' the foreman asked.

'My son is.'

'Is he home?'

'I don't know.'

'Would you mind calling him?'

'No, I don't mind at all, but his car is there. He must be home but that doesn't matter. I'm giving you permission to do whatever you need to do on the property.' She started down the gravel drive to the guest house and then turned on the foreman. 'Oh, come on now, you know who my son is. You must know. Everyone knows what they're doing to Cody. You don't have to pretend with me.'

'I'm not pretending about the rats, ma'am, and I'm just being polite about your son. I don't want to surprise him.'

Good line. They watched her knock on Stoltz's door with the big foreman standing to her side. If Stoltz answered, no question he'd object. Then he'd have to sneak out there and try to retrieve the daypack and they'd videotape that, maybe meet him coming back up the hole. But Stoltz didn't answer and the foreman and crew went out to the manhole and the SID team dressed as exterminators followed with a Public Works foreman.

They placed a groundhog camera near the manhole to try to capture Stoltz's discovery that Public Works had gone down and found the backpack. If he called and claimed it, and slim chance he'd do that, but if he did, they'd refer him to the exterminators. The exterminators would admit that yes, they had found it. They'd ask, is it your pack, sir? If he said yes, they'd get that on tape. They'd tape his explanation and let him know the daypack and laptop were safe and that they'd return them soon, but not that fast. Not until they got every last thing out of its hard drive.

FIFTY-TWO

Lafaye had always assumed that her years of emails with sam66942@yahoo.com were an anonymous exchange of information. She didn't know Stoltz had discovered her identity three years ago and after doing so had made a point of learning everything he could about her. The email he sent her this afternoon read simply, 'I have information you'll want. It took work to get and cost me some money. Interested in splitting the costs?'

'What is it?'

'Found where she's living.'

'Confirmed?'

'Very close to. If you're in, you're in for ten grand.'

'Too much for me.'

'OK.'

She expected him to write more, he always did. But after two hours had passed and he'd left it with the one word, she wrote back, 'OK.'

'It's not easy for me to meet. Where are you?'

'San Francisco.'

Though she didn't know where he lived, she'd surmised from previous emails that he lived in the Bay Area at least part of the year.

'I am interested; just don't know about shelling out ten thousand without proof.'

'Will show you some proof. Meeting would have to be San Francisco at the Marina dock. I have a boat. Five p.m. today. I leave town tomorrow.'

She wrote back a few minutes later, and he gave her the berth number and where to find a hidden key to the dock gate. Neither of them had ever revealed their true reasons for trying to find Quinn. They'd both gone to websites and chat rooms where credit information is bought, sold, and traded. So that said something mutual was understood, but all they'd traded were leads.

Shortly before 5:00 p.m. he saw her Audi pull into the lot. She looked nervous and uncomfortable as she walked to the dock gate. She was probably afraid. She'd always tried online to milk him for information, and maybe she knew he'd figured out that she had a lot of information about Erin already. He watched her find the key, get in, wander down to the lower dock, and with his face hidden behind glasses and a cap, he waved to her and untied the boat as she boarded.

'We'll do a lap around the bay,' he said.

'Why not here?'

'Because I feel safer out there, and you don't need to be afraid of me. I wish you wouldn't act like you are. It makes me nervous.'

Once he'd gone to hear her talk, just to see what she looked like, and he watched how she changed her posture now, nothing like the lack of confidence she'd showed as she'd looked for the boat.

'Strange to meet after all these years,' she said.

'Are you going to show me your face when we get out on the bay?'

'I am, and don't think I'm crazy for doing it this way. Erin once tried to kill me and for all I knew, you were her.'

She warmed up to that idea. She'd once had the same fear herself and said, 'All these years you were afraid you were talking to her online?'

'Yeah, could have been and it's another reason I wanted to see you walk down the dock.'

He kept his face turned away as he steered the boat out. He kept the sunglasses and hat on, his coat collar turned up. But she acted like this was all good fun now. She had to be scared but appeared to be enjoying this, asking, 'If you've found her why are you sharing it?'

'Because I owe money and I've got to get paid off. I can't do it alone. Besides, you're going to get her arrested, right? I can't do that, so I may as well help you and get help with the costs.'

She could see his back and that wasn't going to be enough, no matter how much TV she'd been watching.

'She tried to kill you?'

'Stole all my money and then tried to kill me.' Stoltz made it up on the spot. 'She ran off with another guy and all my money, and they thought I was dead but they'd killed the wrong person.' He let a beat pass and then let her know. 'I recognize you.'

'That's what I didn't want to have happen.'

'I think what you do with your foundation is cool.'

'Thank you.'

They were well out into the bay now and he turned the wheel slightly before reaching in his pocket and pulling the gun as he turned.

'Nothing is going to happen to you, and this isn't a rape or a trick.'

She was much quicker than he would have ever guessed and tried to get out on the deck. He had to drag her down from behind, grabbing her hair, wrenching her head sideways and slamming her down. He spun a roll of duct tape around her mouth as she fought him. He had the handcuffs ready and clicked those on, ran the chain through the eye hook and snapped the lock.

'We're going to talk, and depending on what you say, you'll be fine. Otherwise we'll go outside the Gate ten miles and you can swim in.'

He took the duct tape off her after he got around to the east side of Angel Island and cut the speed to nothing. Without forward speed the boat wallowed, but the bay was calm and would be dark soon enough. As long as he moved occasionally no one would pay that much attention to them. He took her purse into the forward cabin and went through it, found a small gun, what looked like a .25 caliber. He removed the bullets and put them in his coat pocket, then walked out on the forward deck, debated throwing her phone in the water and put that in his pocket also. He didn't find any money and walked back to the stern cabin.

'You forgot to bring money.'

'After we make a deal, I'll wire it to you.'

He looked at her, handcuffed, chained down,

and still talking like that.

'You brought a gun.'

'For self defense, but I want the information. I want to make a deal.'

'You're going to get one chance to.'

He took his sunglasses off now and the hat. He turned the collar down.

'Now, your turn. Recognize me?'

She shook her head.

'Cody Stoltz.'

She recognized the name. She couldn't hide that and quickly said, 'The person the police are framing.'

He almost smiled.

'You should be scared, but there's a way out of this for you. I know you're smart and tough, but nothing will save you if you don't have what I need.'

'Will you free at least one of my hands? It hurts so much I can't think.'

He freed her left hand and then told her, 'I want to know how you ended up with her identity and why you're looking for her still.'

'I'm looking because she's blackmailed me for more money. We are on the same side here and I know the police have been framing you. Everyone knows and—'

'Do not play any games with me. I don't want any of your bullshit. I want what you know about Erin and if you don't give it to me I'm going to kill you. That's why you're on the boat. But you don't have to die.'

'Obviously, I don't know where she is.'

He thought about her last three responses and

asking to have her hand freed. He'd thrown her on the deck, taped her mouth, and handcuffed her, but she didn't seem scared enough. He leaned over. 'I'm offering you a chance to live.'

'OK, she's come back asking for a lot more money. Either that or she'll make sure it gets known that I've traveled under a false passport and credit cards and all the things that have a good explanation but that people wouldn't understand, particularly my directors. I'd have to step down.'

'She's contacted you.'

'Yes, through the foundation website. I have a phone number I'm supposed to call no later than midnight tonight. You don't have to kill me and I don't care that the police are after you. Police have never done me any favors. We both want her found. We want the same thing, so why can't we work together on this? I have plenty of money; I can help you.'

'Where's the number?'

'I need my phone.'

Stoltz handed her the phone and she asked, 'Do I say I'll pay and set up a meeting?'

He had to think about that. She was bluffing, lying, somehow manipulating him, but he let her call. When no one answered she left a message and he steered the boat under the Richmond–San Rafael Bridge. Twilight came and still no call back, and Stoltz realized that if a call did come from Erin, and Erin agreed to meet, then he was done with this woman here. An hour later he said, 'I don't believe that was her number.'

And then the phone rang and on the screen was

the number. He handed her the phone and heard Erin's voice, scratchy but her.

'I'll agree to your terms,' Lafaye said. 'But I want to meet and know it's never going to happen again.'

'No meeting,' he heard Erin say. Definitely her, and it affected him in ways he didn't know it could. He turned Lafaye's head with his hand and mouthed, tomorrow. Tomorrow, tomorrow, tomorrow, he knew she understood but instead she said, 'I'll double the offer if we meet. It can be anywhere you want, but if we don't meet I'm not going through with it. I'll take my story to the press. I don't care what happens at that point. If I lose my foundation, I'll start another one. I'll point the finger at you.'

He heard Erin agree and then name the meeting time and place. When Lafaye hung up, he told her, 'I'm going to let you go now. That's all I want. It was never you. I don't want anything from you. Take your clothes off. I want you to leave your clothes.'

'What do you mean?'

He aimed the gun at her head. 'You're going to swim in.'

'I can't swim well enough, I'll drown.'

'I have a way for you. You'll be fine.'

'No, please, I did what you asked. I got her to call, I set up the meeting, but I can't swim well.'

She took her clothes off and he had her throw them over the side. Under a bench seat were life preservers and Stoltz pulled one out.

'Please don't do this. I don't care what happens to her. I'll never say anything.'

261

He threw a life vest at her.

'Put it on. It'll keep you afloat and it's not that cold. Swim toward those lights. The tide will help you. You just float in the vest and kick.'

'Why can't you drop me near the shore somewhere?'

He stopped listening and watched her cinch the vest tight. Its reflective stripes would be easy to locate. The vest would keep her bobbing on the surface. He shoved her and her leg slapped against the railing as she fell into the water. Right away, she started thrashing and he heard her cry, 'Help, help, please, help me.'

Stoltz found her in the water with one of the boat's lights, then went to the cabin and brought the heavy boat around. He wanted good speed but as he accelerated he saw the vest floating but not her. The boat went over the vest and he swung around again. He risked using the searchlight, found the vest bobbing and began a methodical search. The straps were tight when she went in. It couldn't slip off her, could it? Where is she?

His circling and the searchlight attracted another boat and as it came toward him, Stoltz cut the light. He pushed the throttle forward and moved away. He drove back to the marina furious at himself for not having just knocked her out and pushed her in the water. Still, she had to be gone. She'd drowned. By the time he got back to the dock he'd convinced himself.

FIFTY-THREE

Raveneau and la Rosa sat in an interview room eating Chinese to-go. It was late. It was good to eat and they did so without talking as the smells of ginger, cooking oil, and steamed rice filled the room. After the initial success of getting through Stoltz's password and into his emails, the computer techs ran into a second firewall. That's where things stalled and they were pessimistic about getting through it tonight. One tech wondered aloud if they ever would. When they finished eating, Raveneau checked with them again. Then he and la Rosa cleaned up the little round table in the interview box and left with the understanding that if anything changed they'd be called.

When the phone rang late in the night, Raveneau was deep in a dream where he was fifteen again and up in Presidio Heights on a night the fog was blowing low over the Julius Kahn playground. His older brother, Donny, was in trees off to the edge of the playground making out with a new girlfriend while he waited for them. He felt like a tag-along and leaned back against the rock wall, listening to sirens that at first were a faraway, hollow, lonely sound and then raw as they got closer.

He left the rock wall, moved out on to Cherry Street, feeling the sound now along his spine. He looked back for Donny and the new girlfriend, but they didn't come out. He expected a fire or a car accident and looked up into the fog along the row of houses, listening for the snapping of wood burning and the pop of glass exploding and the orange light in the sky, or voices around a car wreck, but heard only a muffled sound of a heavy footfall, and then saw a man running toward him down Cherry Street, and not really running, but chugging along the way heavy guys do.

Just before a police car rounded the corner the guy slowed to a walk. The cops pulled in fast alongside him but they didn't jump out and take him down, instead looked like they were asking directions. The man pointed the other way and the cop car did a U-turn. When they were gone the man started down the sidewalk straight at him.

Raveneau rolled in the bed and reached for the phone, answering even as the other images stayed with him. It was a dream he knew every frame of. The man would follow him back into the park and come within five feet of him. In those days he'd been a tall skinny kid, putting on a leather jacket every day and bell-bottomed jeans with holes at the knees. He had hair down to his shoulders that his dad mocked. The guy would go face to face with him and there would be a moment he'd carry the rest of his life, a moment when everything hung in the balance.

A motorcycle cop would interrupt that by

racing down Cherry Street. The street dead-ended at the playground and the motorcycle's headlights would cut an arc through the fog as the officer slowed to make a U-turn. When the light touched the man he'd run in the dream as he had in life, as if the light burned his skin. He'd go crashing through the brush down into the Presidio.

'Inspector Raveneau,' a tech said.

'I've got him,' Raveneau said. 'I see where he's going.'

'Inspector?'

'Oh, yeah, OK, this is Raveneau, go ahead, what have you got?'

Raveneau couldn't place the voice on the other end. When you first come on as a homicide inspector and you're learning how to solve a case and the officers out there on the street in the radio units are learning you, you find out that calls can come in the middle of the night from an excited patrol officer, someone you may have talked to weeks or months before and asked to watch for a suspect or witness, and now they've found that individual. It could be 3:30 in the morning when they call you, but you'd better be enthused and let them know how much you appreciate it, or else word gets around and your urgent requests start taking a backseat.

But now it clicked it was the computer geek calling about Stoltz's encryption. They must be through the second firewall.

'You said call you no matter what the hour.'

'Yeah, and thanks for calling. Did you get through?'

'We got through but I've never seen anything like this. We can read stuff, but it doesn't stick. It's like the program is a living thing and it adapts to us. We're reading sentences and then they start scrambling, you know, going away again.'

'What have you read?'

'Things that are like observations of people and feelings he had, maybe after killing someone. We can only get it to hold for five seconds or so and then the program takes over again. I need somebody better than me to look at this.'

'I'll come in.'

'No, I mean someone that understands encryption.'

'I mean I'm coming in to read what I can.'

Streetlights blurred a syrupy yellow-orange in fog and his car climbed from shadow into light and the streets were empty as he drove toward Bryant. He called la Rosa.

'They're through the firewall, but there are problems still.'

And maybe it was the fog, but as he waited briefly for la Rosa downstairs at the Hall, the dream returned and Donny and the new girl-friend, Elena, came out of the trees. He told them about the heavyset guy who'd run when the motorcycle cop drove up and Elena put her arm around him and said, you're so cute. He closed and with Donny leading and Elena behind him, they dropped down off the Heights, hugging the rock wall, staying on the Presidio side.

Raveneau shook the dream off but remembered how it had gone. The next day, Sunday, there'd been news about a cab driver murdered at the corner of Washington and Cherry Streets. He'd heard it first on his clock radio, on KFRC, before watching a TV report. Whoever the cab driver had picked up had probably killed him, and later that night after their dad got off his shift he told them that the police were initially given the wrong description, which was why the killer had gotten away. They'd been looking for a NMA, a Negro Male Adult, when they should have been looking for a Caucasian.

He'd debated telling his dad about the guy who'd come into the Julius Kahn playground, but he and Donny weren't supposed to be out and they'd just gone a month of being grounded for a six-pack of Hamm's beer their mom had found in their room. He would have grounded them for another couple of months, so Raveneau had written an anonymous letter to the homicide detail. He mailed it Monday morning before school and years later realized that was the moment he'd started toward a homicide career.

The next day, Tuesday, October 14, 1969, a different letter had arrived, this one to the *San Francisco Chronicle*, and Raveneau didn't hold that letter in his hand until after he had his homicide star and his father had retired and Donny was dead. The envelope had been addressed with blue felt tip. Where the return address should have been was a crossed circle. That letter was still with the Zodiac binders. Raveneau had pored over all of them, but knew that particular letter word for word. It started this way:

FIFTY-FOUR

'This is the most recent entry,' the tech said. 'Ready to question her.'

As Raveneau read the phrase vanished and reassembled as numbers.

'Wild, huh, look how it morphs, weird,' the tech said, and his fingers went rapidly over the keyboard. He glanced up several times at the screen and then was in the file again and quickly scrolled.

'I'll come back for her. I'll come back when the time is right. She's unfinished business.'

Raveneau read the date of the entry as it began to fade away.

'That could be you he's writing about,' he said to la Rosa. 'This is a recent entry.'

La Rosa had just walked in. She stood behind him reading over his shoulder.

'I get that, but what's up with it fading away?' and the tech launched into the spiel he'd given Raveneau about living encryption.

'Like an organism reacting to stimuli,' he said and chuckled, adding, 'we're causing it pain.'

He seemed more interested in that than what he'd found and Raveneau cut off the riff and asked, 'Can you keep getting us in?'

'I can get you in no problem, but it's getting

faster at getting me out. I don't have a clue how it's learning.'

He got them in forty-two times over the next two and a half hours and they experimented, tried printing out when the screen held letters, but the paper came out blank. The tech called friends of his and they didn't seem to be able to help, and he mumbled something about needing the government guys.

They drank more coffee, read more, and dawn came. Some of the entries were only a few words and it was hard to make sense of why he even bothered. 'Tomorrow is go night,' read one entered the day before Whitacre died. They read 'He will be the last,' and Raveneau wondered aloud, 'Who gets the honor?'

'You're the one he missed,' she said. 'I think it should be you.'

'For waking you up tonight?'

'For that and other reasons.'

'To take care of that retirement problem.'

'Yeah, that's it, and then I'll catch him and bring him in. From there it'll be an easy rise to chief.'

'What if you find out you want to stay on the homicide detail?'

She didn't answer that. Another entry read, 'It's probable she knows something about where she is.'

Was he talking about Jurika? That entry jumped out at him. He copied down each as they read them. More techs arrived and Raveneau and la Rosa broke from the computer and put together a new search warrant app. They expanded

270

it to all vehicles owned by Cody Stoltz and listed computers in both his and his mother's house, citing the encryption as a reason he might commandeer his mother's computer without her knowledge. They faxed it to the judge on-call this weekend.

Later that morning, Walnut Creek police got the DNA match they were looking for and charged the ex-boyfriend with Alan Becker's murder. Raveneau phoned the Walnut Creek detective who'd called SF Homicide with his news.

He asked, 'How strong is your DNA connection?'

'It's not the best but we've got him either way.'

'Did you get a confession?'

'No, but we will. Becker humiliated him in an argument over the daughter. He admits to that and to taking a swing before Becker decked him.'

'We have some new information that plays in.'

'We've already got our guy, but whatever you have I'd like to hear it.'

'You may have the wrong guy. You may want to go slow on it.'

'I don't know about that, but I'm all ears.'

'It won't be until later today, but I can tell you we found a laptop yesterday and what we've seen so far suggests it was Cody Stoltz in Walnut Creek.'

'Like I said, show me.'

'What's a good number to reach you at?'

He copied down the detective's cell number and then drove over to Lafaye's office to re-

271

interview her. Her office was one block off Sacramento in an upscale area down the hill and west of Pacific Heights. A gray redwood gate faced the street. On it was a brass plaque listing the businesses inside, and beyond the gate was a shady brick courtyard with a koi pond and a garden of succulent plants. Lafaye's office was up a flight of stairs in the back. He knew from their lunch together that her office wasn't in the main foundation building. This office was a perk the foundation directors allowed her and the main foundation headquarters on Mason were considerably more austere. She had talked about the garden here and how it calmed her.

When he saw the splintered door jamb he didn't bother to knock. He pushed the door open and stepped into a carpeted reception area with a lot of maple paneling and cabinets. Nothing looked out of place and he walked through into a conference room, and then what he guessed was Lafaye's office, where a computer lay on its side, panel off, hard drive missing. Two file cabinets had been pried open and when he tried calling her house and cell both went to voice mail. Then he called it in as a burglary and took several photos as he talked with la Rosa.

'I've got to wait here for the burglary guys,' he said. 'And I called her foundation. No one has talked to her since yesterday afternoon. We need to swing by her house. Why don't you go by there and then meet me here? Get a patrol unit to back you up.'

'They're going to be waiting for us in Los Altos.'

'We can leave from here.'

'OK, but we're tight for time and I'm not sure I need to see a break-in. I worked Burglary for three years and I'm looking at the photos you sent. I'll go by her house, call you, and if she's home, I'll drive down to Los Altos ahead of you.'

'Yeah, you're right. One of us should be on time.'

He was forty minutes behind la Rosa when he left for Los Altos. La Rosa was inside with Mrs Stoltz and had already let her know that they had new evidence, and that her son could be facing multiple murder charges. That was a pretty big exaggeration given where they were right now. But it was the way they had agreed to play it.

As Raveneau arrived and sat down, he realized Mrs Stoltz didn't know any more than they did about where to look for Cody. Neither did the SID team. SID guessed that after dumping the car and crawling into the storm drainage pipe he'd exited through some fallback escape route.

Stoltz's mother looked much older this morning. She rose now from her chair and asked her housekeeper for a coat. When she returned she said, 'He was a gifted child, really very, very gifted, the kind of child everyone marvels at. He had the gift of music as well as math.' She turned to Raveneau. 'Are you absolutely sure?'

'Not of everything, but enough to put out an All Points Bulletin and make an arrest. We're going to charge him, Mrs Stoltz.'

She nodded and said, 'I want to go alone to the guest house.'

'We can't let you do that,' la Rosa said and Raveneau added, 'We should go with you.'

'It means a great deal to me to go alone. I'm seventy-five years old. If what you're telling me is true, I won't see him again outside a jail or prison.'

La Rosa shook her head but Raveneau knew there was almost no chance Stoltz was home. He touched la Rosa, said, 'I think we can do this.'

Mrs Stoltz had already stood. Along the back of her house was a wall of eight glass doors that folded open to expose the garden. They allowed Raveneau and la Rosa to watch her follow the brick path through hundreds of roses to the portico and entry at the guest house. She unlocked the front door and went in. Fifteen minutes passed before she came out and then invited them to search.

He wasn't home and a broader search was underway in the hills behind. By the time he and la Rosa got there, they'd lowered a handler and a dog into the storm drainage system and were snaking video cameras down the smaller pipes.

Now Raveneau's cell rang and he learned that half a mile away one of the SID team and a Public Works foreman had found sheared bolts on a storm drain grate. When he and la Rosa got there, he ran his thumb over the cut thread and drew blood.

'You could use a battery-powered Sawzall and a metal cutting blade,' the foreman said.

'How big is that tool?'

The foreman held his hands apart maybe a foot and a half, and said, 'That's with the blade.'

'How often do you inspect these?'

The man smiled as if Raveneau had just told a good joke. 'We do fire drills, not inspections. You only see us when there's a problem.'

An hour later Lafaye's car was found in the lot adjacent to the marina where Stoltz's boat was berthed, and then someone put that together with a report of an unidentified naked Caucasian woman suffering from hypothermia found by two fishermen early this morning along a stretch of rocky shoreline east of the Richmond Bridge. That woman was airlifted to John Muir Hospital in Walnut Creek, where apparently she was now in a stable condition. Raveneau called John Muir. He gave a description of Lafaye and waited for the head nurse to finish telling him for the third time that they didn't have any way to identify the unknown woman.

'You said she's middle-aged.'

'Yes, I would guess early fifties.'

'Is she able to talk?'

'She's not coherent.'

'Do you have a phone with a camera?'

'Of course, do you want me to take her picture?'

'Yes.'

'I'm not sure that's allowed. I'll have to call you back.'

'How about if you transfer me to who it is you're going to ask?'

'I'm sorry, Inspector, our privacy policies are very strict.'

He was driving back up the peninsula toward San Francisco behind la Rosa when the photo came through from John Muir. He forwarded it to la Rosa and then called her.

'Let's drop a car in the city and head out there.'

They dropped Raveneau's car outside the Hall and la Rosa's tires squealed as she roared up the on-ramp. Raveneau didn't look up as they crossed the bridge. He studied the image of Lafaye on his phone screen and tried to make it all connect.

276

FIFTY-FIVE

On the way there la Rosa took a call from her roommate. She listened a moment and then said, 'Karin, I'm going to put you on speaker phone. My partner is in the car with me. I want him to hear this.'

Karin the roommate, Raveneau knew only by name. He knew also she was an X-ray tech and someone la Rosa had known for years. She sounded level-headed.

'Can you hear me OK?'

'We can hear you,' la Rosa answered.

'You told me to watch, right?'

'Yes.'

'So there's a white van two blocks down the street this morning – the same one I saw two days ago and I know, so what, there are a lot of white vans, but it did the same thing as two days ago. It pulled out as I walked toward it.'

'How far away were you when it pulled out?'

'That's really why I'm calling. You know how I walk to the bus, right?'

'Sure.'

'I go down a block and then cross the street. Two days ago as I crossed the street it pulled out and drove away. I know, that's a big so what, except that it did the same thing today and the

277

way it pulled out was the same.'

'Was the van alone or did it have a driver?'

Karin laughed. She had a light cheerful laugh and la Rosa chuckled.

'That's why you're the cop,' Karin said. 'I couldn't see.'

'What kind of van?'

'I went online and looked at vans. I think it's a Dodge van, the kind with two doors in the back.'

'Could you tell if it was a man or woman driving?'

'No, it was faced away from me.'

Raveneau cut in. 'Karin, this is Ben Raveneau, Elizabeth's partner.'

'Oh, hi, I've heard a lot about you.'

'Yeah, but Elizabeth probably exaggerates. She's builds me up too much.'

That got even more laughter.

'I want to ask you about how the van pulls away and how far you are from it when it does.'

'Well, that's the whole thing, that's why I called. It's this weird thing where it's about a block away facing down the street not toward me—'

'So, on the right side of the street?'

'Yes, and it does this kind of hitching motion, pulls out part-way and sort of stops and waits, and then goes forward.'

'The camcorder,' Raveneau said. 'The hitch is so he can film down the street.'

'What?' Karin asked, and la Rosa answered her, saying, 'Karin, we have an idea about who it might be.'

'So I'm not crazy?'

'Oh, you're still crazy. This doesn't change that.'

Karin laughed again, though this time much more subdued, and la Rosa said, 'I'll call you later.'

As the connection broke, Raveneau voiced it. 'Heilbron is stalking you. You're why he came in to confess. It wasn't just to taunt us. He wanted to meet you. Remember how he knew it was your first week and all; you're his target.'

'We could be getting ahead of ourselves here.'

'True.'

FIFTY-SIX

Three hours earlier, Lafaye didn't know her own name. Now she spoke in a forceful if hoarse whisper, her eyes fixed on Raveneau.

'I'm not afraid of anyone. I publish the names of known traffickers on my website and push the police, and lobby the UN and aid groups. Young men in poor areas are selling their kidneys for eight thousand dollars and I go after those buying.'

Sunlight slanted through the window to her right. High on the wall beyond her feet a TV blared. A nurse came and went. She went on about her foundation and Raveneau read it as stalling, as obfuscation. She didn't want to talk about how she came to be on a boat with Stoltz. She was fine talking about how he tried to kill her, but not why she was there in the first place.

He found the TV remote and killed the sound as la Rosa went to retrieve a photo of Stoltz they'd left in their car. She shut the door and Raveneau was alone with Lafaye. Until they'd arrived Lafaye hadn't given the hospital staff her last name, and as he asked her about that she coughed hard and brought a knee up as she rolled away and reached for Kleenex. The sheet slid off exposing her naked back and ass. When she rolled on to her back again she looked at his eyes, gauging him as she said, 'Sorry, somewhere in the night I lost my clothes.'

'You must be a pretty good swimmer.'

'I broke the girls' breaststroke records in high school, but that was a long time ago and I swallowed a lot of water last night. I don't like the taste of the sea as much as I used to and I've never been so glad to crawl on my knees over rocks.'

'How did you come to meet Stoltz on a boat on a dock in San Francisco?'

'He proposed the meeting in an email, though I didn't know it was him, obviously. I've corresponded in a chat room with a person who turned out to be him. That's because I've searched for Erin Quinn. He's also looking for her and somehow learned that I was Alex's friend, and that's probably where he got the idea I knew where the real Quinn is.'

She coughed again and her face reddened as she tried to suppress it, then gave up and spat whatever it was into the Kleenex. She was weaker after that bout. The nurse had warned Lafaye had gotten some water in her lungs. The worry was pneumonia. They didn't think she could talk for long. Other than the cough, it seemed to Raveneau she was doing pretty good.

'Inspector, I don't want your partner shoving a photo in my face, so when she gets back I'd appreciate it if you'd slow her. What's she doing working anyway? I thought she got shot.'

'The bullet grazed her.'

'She's pretty tough.'

281

'So are you.'

'You bet I am.'

'You said he wrote you an email. I'd like you to forward those emails to me.'

'I have to talk with my attorney first.'

'Why is that?'

'To make sure I'm not overlooking anything. When will you press kidnapping and attempted murder charges? He tried to run me over with the boat.'

She lifted an arm and as she did the door opened and la Rosa walked back in.

'I knew he would try to run me over. I dove under the boat. That's not luck. Then I swam toward lights. I swim nearly every day at a club and I don't think the distance is much different, and it really wasn't any colder than the workouts used to feel. I'm tired though, very tired. It's all I can do to talk to you.'

'We understand and we're going to let you sleep. We'll leave soon, but a few more things first. I went to your office this morning. Remember, we were going to meet.'

'Oh, yes, of course,' but her attention was on la Rosa now. 'Let me see the photo,' she said, and la Rosa showed her six photos. She pointed at Stoltz immediately.

'Your office was broken into. Is there something there Stoltz might want to steal?'

'I don't think so, but I believe he intends to kill Erin Quinn when he finds her.'

She coughed hard again. When she finished Raveneau asked, 'Did he say that?'

'No.'

'Did he have reason from the emails you've exchanged with him to think you knew where she was?'

'None that I can think of, and clearly I had no idea this person I've talked to online for years was this man you're looking for.'

'You drove there. You boarded the boat, but you didn't know it was Cody Stoltz until you were out on the water?'

'He hid his features.'

'Like a spy,' la Rosa offered. 'He fooled you.'

She smiled at la Rosa, as though smiling at a mildly amusing comment by a child. Raveneau bored in.

'So this guy was in a disguise and you went for a boat ride with him anyway?'

Lafaye stared, debated, and then said, 'Correct. For years I've exchanged email messages with an unknown someone who had a grudge against Erin Quinn. Online he said she'd stolen thousands of dollars from him. I had the impression they'd planned to get married and she'd cleaned out a joint bank account and run off. Neither of us revealed our true identities, so it wasn't strange to me that he'd want to keep hiding his on the boat.'

'You didn't know who he was, but you figured you were OK to take a boat ride with him.'

'All right, Ben, I'll plead guilty to being stupid or eager, or whatever it is you want to charge me with, except anything criminal, which I'm not guilty of. Frankly, I'm lucky to be alive.'

'We're glad you're alive and I'm sure it was very frightening.'

'Why don't you find him first and then we'll talk about the emails.'

They talked another twenty minutes with her and then left unsure if kidnapping could be filed today. As they passed Lafayette on the drive back, Raveneau looked at the field of white crosses on the face of a hill to his right. There were many crosses bright in sunlight on the hillside.

'What's that about?' la Rosa asked.

'They're a reminder and a memorial for soldiers who died in Iraq and Afghanistan. There's a cross for each one.'

They lost the sun as they came back through the Caldecott Tunnel to the bay side. Gray clouds sat at horizon.

'Looks like rain,' Raveneau said, and then took a call from the office.

'Inspector, a woman called for you a few minutes ago and said she had new information on the John Reinert murder. Do you want her phone number?'

'The John Reinert murder?' La Rosa turned her head immediately. 'Yes, give me the number.'

When he hung up, la Rosa said, 'That's probably another kook, another nut feeding on all this. Why is it the kooks all come here?'

'Goes back to the Gold Rush, I think. San Francisco was where you went to start all over again. I'm going to call the number.'

He did and a woman answered. She said softly but with some irony, 'I thought that would get your attention.'

'John Reinert died thirteen years ago,' Raven-eau said. 'What can you tell me?'

'Thirteen years, two months, and sixteen days, but I don't really keep track like that any more.'

Then he knew. He reached for a pen and something to write on.

'In those days I was Erin Reinert.'

'Where are you now, Erin?'

'In San Francisco, here to talk to you and your partner.'

'And we'd very much like to talk to you. Can you meet us at the Hall of Justice on Bryant Street?'

'No, I want to meet you in China Basin. I want you to show me where Alex Jurika died.'

'Did you know Alex Jurika?'

'Once, I knew her very well.'

'We'll meet you in China Basin. We'll be there in fifteen minutes.'

He gave her the address and hung up.

FIFTY-SEVEN

Erin Quinn wore a black leather coat and jeans. Her face was fuller, her hands chapped, hair streaked with gray, eyes distant, haunted. She looked away as she talked. She looked through the chain link at the bay as Raveneau unlocked the gate. Inside, the interior still smelled strongly of new paint and carpet.

'She was killed upstairs,' la Rosa said, talking as she led the way up. 'Tell us about yourself. Where are you living?'

'In the Sierras, but I don't want to say where until after you arrest Cody. I don't want any publicity. I don't want anyone to know about me, especially him.'

'Do you live alone?'

'I've never thought I had the right to remarry. I had my chance and I ruined it.'

'Do you believe Cody Stoltz has kept looking for you all these years?'

'Yes, and he blames me.'

'Why does he blame you?'

'Show me where Alex was killed.'

They had reached the room anyway, but it was nothing like that night. A row of cheap new fluorescent lights hung on pendants from the ceiling. The floor had a low-grade commercial carpet and the walls new white paint. La Rosa resumed her soft questioning.

'Tell us more about you and Alex.'

'I was with Alex when I met my husband. I met Cody the same night.' She looked down at the floor, asked, 'How did Alex die?'

'She was strangled,' la Rosa said. 'She was bound and strangled.'

'In this room?'

La Rosa glanced at Raveneau, then described the murder scene before asking, 'Did you keep in touch with Alex?'

'Yes, but we didn't talk often.'

'What about email?' Raveneau asked, thinking about the qnn@yahoo.com emails.

'Never, because I was afraid of him hacking into her computer, and then finding me.' She turned to la Rosa. 'Who do you think killed her?'

'Who would kill her?' Quinn asked. 'Who do you think killed her?'

La Rosa glanced at Raveneau again before answering, 'We don't know yet. We're hoping you can help us.'

When Quinn was silent Raveneau asked, 'Could Cody have gone to Alex to try to find you?'

She exhaled hard and said, 'Anything is possible with him. He wouldn't know unless he figured some things out, but he might have done that.'

'What things?' La Rosa asked.

'How does revenge sound?'

Raveneau caught his partner's eye. This is where it got tricky. She was about to give them motive.

'Cody wanted to be known as very bright, as the guy that thinks up the ideas that change things. He thought he was going to be famous but I don't think money ever really mattered to him.'

'Because he already had it,' la Rosa threw out, and Quinn didn't respond. She held herself as though she was cold and stared at the floor until Raveneau said, 'We'd like to go back to our office with you.'

'I don't want to go to a police station. Can we talk in your car?'

'Sure.'

Raveneau sat in the backseat with her. In the front la Rosa took notes, her pen scratching on the pad she carried. Quinn spoke in a flat voice tinged by sadness.

'In those days Alex was pretty wild and I was the more conservative one, but we both partied a lot. John and Cody were best friends and they were in a hotel bar together the night we met them. We were out cruising. Everything that happened after was my fault and I'm going to tell you why. I've made up my mind to tell you.

'We met in a bar on Spear Street that isn't there any more. That night Alex sort of paired off with Cody and I went with John. Alex and Cody ended up going home together. Cody was very aggressive with women. He was very good looking. They went home together and did whatever they did, and John and I talked until late, and then we took this long walk along the Embarcadero and past Fisherman's Wharf and all the way out to Fort Mason and the Golden Gate

288

Bridge.'

'Pretty good walk,' Raveneau said.

'Yeah, and we saw the sunrise from under the bridge and then had this great breakfast, but what we had was more intellectual than anything else and we were too young to realize it wasn't enough. We would have made great friends but we weren't meant to be married. Do you know what I mean?'

'I do,' la Rosa said from the front seat.

'We got married six months later. By the time the affair started with Cody I was very angry with John, and the marriage was less than a year old and failing. John had started snorting a lot of cocaine and his temper was totally out of control. He was also drinking too much, and there was the gun thing. I don't remember what started it. I think it was because of a carjacking in San Francisco. This was right when all that sort of stuff started to happen and Cody and John had sports cars they worried about getting stolen.

'Cody already knew how to shoot. John didn't. They went shopping and bought guns one Saturday so no one could take their precious cars. I didn't want the guns in the apartment, so they kept them in their cars. The day John got killed they'd been out to a shooting range in the afternoon.'

That was in the murder file. Raveneau had read it. Whitacre and Bates confirmed that Stoltz and Reinert had been at in indoor range in Fremont.

'I really fell in love with Cody. John's new

289

cocaine habit and his jealousy and insecurity were oppressive. I hated coming home. But Cody was all energy and fun. I didn't know then how angry he could get. He had a beautiful body and he was so bright. He was already well known in certain circles for the work he was doing. John looked up to him and I thought he was a god.'

'What were you doing for work at the time?'

'I quit my job when we got married. I wasn't doing anything and that was part of the problem. I was living off my husband and sort of despised myself for staying with him just because I had no job or place to go.'

'And what about Alex? What was she doing for work?'

'She did temp work but always had plenty of money. She told me once that she'd inherited money. Another time it was because she'd come up with an idea for online bookkeeping that got patented, but I'm sure that wasn't true, and I'm sure you know by now she was into credit fraud.'

'When did you know?'

'Not until after John was dead, but she never really ever talked to me about the credit cards. I just sort of figured it out when she offered to get me a new identity. After Cody went to prison Alex made me into someone else.'

She paused and looked down at her hands. Raveneau looked at la Rosa's eyes.

'With Cody and me it built up to a boiling point, and then one afternoon we just tore each other's clothes off, and then there was no going back. After that everything either of us said to John was a lie. We were lying as routinely as breathing and I made excuses so John and I didn't sleep together any more. I kept myself chaste by avoiding sleeping with my husband. How's that for classy?'

'It happens,' la Rosa said. 'You're not alone there and we understand.'

'I only wanted to be with Cody but I didn't have the courage to leave John.'

Her right hand came up now, touched her forehead in an odd gesture and then returned to her lap. She shook her head.

'I didn't see Alex much after I got married. It seemed like it was Cody, John, and I hanging out together all the time. Everybody liked Alex but it was as though some part of right and wrong was never taught to her. I remember once she used the phone in our apartment to call a friend in London. They talked for two hours and she never told me. I tracked it down through the phone company and the guy in London said he'd been on the phone to Alex. She was like that. She'd apologize and offer to pay but that didn't mean she wouldn't do it again tomorrow. Have you ever known anyone like that?'

'Those are the only people we know,' Raveneau said. 'That's who we hang out with every day.'

That got the faintest smile.

'Alex had this charisma, this kind of crazy impulsive streak and she'd get you to do things you wouldn't otherwise. I was jealous of her because guys gravitated toward her. I'm trying to think of an example ... OK, here's one. We go to a hotel up on Nob Hill, one of the stuffy ones, you know, boring, and as we're leaving some woman is dropping her Mercedes with the valet. I remember she had this perfect blonde hair and the Mercedes was this gold-colored two-seater. The doorman was helping somebody else and when this woman got out of her car she wanted the valet to carry a package in. Her car was sitting there with the driver's door open and the engine still running and Alex turned to me and said, "We don't need a cab after all. We'll just borrow this. Get in."

'We drove it to within a couple of blocks of another bar on Union Street and then left it with the keys in it and walked away.'

Her chest heaved as she sighed and said, 'Now comes the part that's not in your police files on John's murder. You know we went to dinner and then went back to the apartment. We'd all done lines of coke. We drank more and John fell asleep. The inspectors asked if we'd done any drugs and I said only John had. If they'd tested me or Cody we would have come back positive. But those inspectors wanted to believe me.'

'Inspectors Whitacre and Bates.'

'Yes. We'd been talking about a weekend trip that we'd planned to take together to Mendocino; or rather Cody and I were talking. We were holding each other in the kitchen because we thought John was asleep and then he walked in and caught us. When he did, Cody pretended it was nothing, but John wigged out. The marriage ended when he walked in. Everything ended.

Then Cody said he was leaving and John asked if he wanted to kiss me goodbye first. He should have left right then, but he didn't. He kissed me long and hard and then walked out the door. That's Cody, and of course John went crazy and followed him down. Cody wanted the confrontation. He knew John would follow and he knew the guns were in the cars. I was supposed to back up his story about the mugger, but I couldn't do it.'

Raveneau saw it now. He knew what she'd say next. 'So you came up with your own.'

'That's right; I came up with my own version. How did you know that?'

'Tell us what happened.'

'I don't know what was said in the parking lot, but Cody was ready. Earlier in the night he told me he was going to be ready if something happened later. Somehow he made it happen and I know he must have shot John. I heard the shots, and when I went downstairs Cody was kneeling next to John who was lying between two cars in this little back parking lot. He was alive. He might not have died. He was having a very hard time breathing, but he was breathing. He was still alive and we didn't do anything. Cody leaned over him and he told me what to say about a mugger. If John was conscious he heard it. It was that horrible and you should arrest me, but at least I don't have to hold it inside any more.'

'Did Cody ask if you'd seen the shooting?'

'No, he just told me what to say, and there's something else I have to tell you. I had nothing to do with John getting murdered, but I did lie

293

afterwards and that's why Cody has looked for me all these years. He knows I lied.'

'Let's go back to the conversation with Cody after John was on the ground shot. What did Cody tell you to do?'

'He said to tell the police there was a mugger who'd tried to rob them and shot John and run, and that no matter what to stick with that story.'

'Did he tell you he'd shot John?'

'Yes, and he wanted me to get the story right. He was holding the gun he'd shot John with and I was supposed to call 911 and tell the police that he had gone looking for the killer. He said he'd turn up after crashing his car.'

Her voice broke. A gasp came out of her as she said, 'And then John died. He was telling all this to me in a whisper as John was trying to breath. If I'd run and called 911, maybe he would have lived.' Tears ran down her face. 'He made this noise, this sort of sound from his lungs and then he died, and Cody looked at me and said, "He's over with. He doesn't exist any more. You don't ever have to think about him again." Those were his exact words.'

Her shoulders shook as she wept.

'I am so sorry. I so wish it had never happened. I wish it had been me. I wish everything that came after never happened. It should have been me instead of John. It should have been me.'

Raveneau waited, then asked quietly, 'And you didn't see the shooting?'

'No.'

'Is there something more to tell us about that?'

She wept uncontrollably before saying, 'Yes.'

FIFTY-EIGHT

They brought her back to the homicide office and she made her statement in an interview room.

'I wasn't at the window. I never saw Cody shoot him. I was outside on the landing. But everything else was true. Cody shot John and there wasn't any mugger.'

'Are you telling us you lied to Inspectors Whitacre and Bates about what you witnessed?' Raveneau asked.

She nodded and after a pause said, 'Yes, I lied. I couldn't do what Cody wanted.'

'Did Cody know you didn't see the shooting?'

'Yes, he knew. When I came down I asked him over and over, what happened, what happened, and he told me John had gotten his gun out and shot at him. The shot missed and he was able to get his own gun out of the glove compartment. He said he didn't shoot until John raised the gun and started to aim at him. Right after that he asked me, what did you see, and I remember saying, I didn't see anything, I only heard the shots. I came down because I knew they were gunshots and John had been talking about getting his gun out of the car. I knew something very bad had happened.'

'How did Cody respond when you told him you hadn't seen anything?'

'He said I did see and it was a mugger. He said listen closely because I'm going to tell you what you saw. He was completely calm and John wasn't even dead yet. He said, this is what we're going to tell people. There was a mugger.'

She recounted a long back and forth dialogue about the mugger who'd stepped out of the bushes when John and Cody were arguing, and then said, 'I talked to Alex a lot afterwards but I never told her I'd lied to make sure Cody got locked up. I said I was afraid of him and wanted a new identity, and Alex got me one. She sold my real name and info that goes with it. It seemed like a great idea since I knew Cody wouldn't hurt whoever bought it. He might question them, but they wouldn't know me.'

'Who did she sell your identity to?'

'A woman named Deborah Lafaye. She started and runs this international charity and I don't really know what she's done with my name. But I wanted to know who was buying it. I've never met her but you can google her name and come up with a lot. I thought it was perfect because I figured she was traveling a lot and would leave a trail that went everywhere. When I gave Alex the go-ahead I wanted it to go to someone who needed it for a good purpose. I was thinking of a woman hiding from an abusive ex-husband, but she found Lafaye in a chat room and after she'd gone back and forth with her, Lafaye made it clear she would only use it in foreign countries and that I should never make contact with her, so

I haven't.'

She seemed unaware that Jurika had worked for Lafaye and they left it that way. Maybe Jurika thought that would blow the deal so hadn't told her. Or maybe she had other motives.

'How much were you paid for it?' Raveneau asked.

'Five thousand dollars.'

'And then you became someone else?'

'Yes. Alex got me a new identity.'

Raveneau wrote down $5000, drew a dash and left a zero standing by itself. Lafaye had told them she'd paid fifty thousand dollars to Alex Jurika for the name. Jurika may have pocketed the balance.

'Do you know if Alex had any continuing contact with Deborah Lafaye?'

'No, but I didn't talk to Alex much after that. I had made up my mind to disappear. I think it was probably more than a year before I talked to her again.'

Raveneau accepted that Erin felt she had to come forward now. He understood that. But it felt like something was still missing in her confession. That she had lied to Whitacre and Bates said plenty about her. He was weighing that as well.

Unprompted now, she said, 'I know how wrong what I did was, but it doesn't change anything. Cody still killed John.'

Raveneau nodded. 'We know he did.' He paused and added, 'Inspector la Rosa and I are going to step outside for a few minutes.'

'I don't want to be left alone in here.'

'Have you been in an interview room before, Erin?'

'Yes, I was arrested twice when I was nineteen.'

And once when you were twenty-two, but all three were out of state and we haven't been able to get the prints, which was what he wanted to talk to la Rosa about. He told her again they'd be back in a few minutes.

Outside, he told la Rosa, 'I think we ask her for her fingerprints so we can confirm she is Erin Quinn. Then we'll run her prints and see what happens. But we don't want to stop her from talking, and it seems to me she's getting more skittish. But I also think she's holding something still. What do you think?'

'I agree.'

'If we press her about the name she's living under now she may want to walk out. She's not going to give us her current alias. Let's leave that alone for the moment.'

On the screen they saw her start to move around. She looked agitated and Raveneau said, 'Keep her here. I'm going to run to the bathroom and I'll be right back.'

Raveneau was standing at the urinal when his cell rang.

'She walked. She's at the elevator. Do I let her go down?'

His voice echoed in the bathroom.

'Stay with her. She needs a ride back to her car so give it to her and I'll follow.'

La Rosa dropped her on a corner in China Basin and reported that Quinn wouldn't let her take her to her car.

'I've got her, I see her,' Raveneau said. 'She's walked back up to Third Street and looks like she's going to cross.'

But it was another forty-five minutes before Quinn unlocked a white Enterprise rental car. He watched her pull away and then trailed her. Ten minutes later he read off the license plate to la Rosa. It took la Rosa another fifteen to find out the car was rented yesterday afternoon in Sacramento by a Corinne Maher.

'That's got to be her identity,' la Rosa said. 'They required her to show a driver's license. I'm running Corinne Maher through DMV. Where is she now?'

'About to cross Van Ness and driving a little erratically, a little bit of speed up and slowdown, but not watching her rear-view mirror, in fact, she's hardly looking in it. It shouldn't be hard to stay with her.'

After seeming to drive with no real direction, she drove out to Ocean Beach, where she parked and walked the sand, her hair blowing sideways in the wind.

'She's either killing time or doesn't know where she's going to go next. I don't think she faked being distraught.'

Now she came back to the car and sat there. Finally, the brake lights flashed and then she backed out. She started tracking back through the city and once again it seemed aimless.

La Rosa came back with a driver's license address for a PO Box at Bucks Lake.

'Where in the hell is that?' she asked.

'North of Tahoe along the Feather River. There are places up there you could hole up.'

Quinn drove toward the southwestern corner of San Francisco and parked in the big lot above Lake Merced. In the late afternoon the lot had a modest amount of cars, not many, and she was up against the railing, looking across the lake at the golf course that rimmed the far side. Down at the end of the gray-green lake was a boathouse. The lake rippled with wind. Raveneau got the feeling she was waiting for somebody and scanned the vehicles in the lot again, working from one to the next with his binoculars. There were only three vehicles he couldn't see into.

Off to his right an elderly Chinese couple came up the stairs from the path below that ran around Lake Merced. They moved slowly toward their car. Less than a minute later a young woman with black hair almost down to her waist backed a baby stroller up the stairs, working the stroller on two wheels as though it was luggage. She rested at the top, leaned over and talked to the child in the stroller. Quinn didn't pay any attention to her. Then a dark blue chopped Honda Accord with chrome wheels pulled in and drove toward the railing. She turned and looked at it but the Honda driver didn't stop. He wheeled around and left.

Another ten minutes passed. Raveneau talked with la Rosa and then picked up on a mountain biker coming in from his left. The rider wore a red helmet, bike gear, wraparound sunglasses, and got Raveneau's attention as he slowed near Quinn. He checked out the rest of the lot as he got off his bike. Quinn turned and stared at him as he slid a small pack off his back and unzipped it.

Now Quinn started to back up and Raveneau said, 'It's the mountain biker. He's made contact and she's scared. She backed up as he approached her.'

'Is it him?'

'Body is right, it could be, but I need him to turn. He's standing very close to her. He may have a gun or a knife. I'm going to have to get closer.'

Raveneau's view was blocked as Quinn and the man moved away from the guard rail, the man standing too close to her as they came alongside a car and then disappeared alongside a new GMC van. When the bike rider came into view again he was alone and Raveneau called out, 'It's Stoltz! He's got her in a van and he's getting in. I'll stay behind him but we're going to need everybody. I think he's armed and I don't think she wanted to go with him. We don't want this to turn into a chase. They've got to shut the road down. I'm southbound on Lake Merced Boulevard.' He looked over at the sign.

'Just passing Brotherhood Way and accelerating. He's jumping on it. Get me backup, get them out here fast. He's on his way somewhere.'

He said the next more to himself than her. 'We should have seen this,' he added, and then focused on the road.

FIFTY-NINE

She sat on the floor of the van, knees drawn up, head bowed but refusing to answer him. At the lake she didn't run or scream. She did exactly what he told her to, as if she'd expected him, as if she always knew it would happen like this, and that both angered him and gave him confidence. He turned to look through the steel mesh. The van's tall rear doors had no interior handles and were heavy duty and reinforced against theft. The mesh behind his head was sturdy. She really was his now.

'Erin.'

She said nothing.

'We're going to talk,' he said, and pulled off the road, drove to the corner of a shopping mall lot.

'You're going to talk to me. It's going to be a long drive and I want you to talk.'

'Why don't you just kill me here?'

'Because I have a house for us; we're going to live together. It's in the mountains and very beautiful, the kind of place you'll like.'

'You're kidnapping me, Cody. That's what's happening, and you're going to kill me.'

'No, I didn't search for you to hurt you. I know you got scared that night. I know you did what

302

you did because you were scared.'

'You shot John.'

'John got himself killed. He tried to shoot me first. He got his gun out and—'

'And then you made up that lie.'

'It was a mistake to have asked you to lie. I admit that.' He turned and looked through the mesh again. 'But what you did was worse.'

'Just admit it, you shot John! You wrecked our lives!'

She yelled and he liked that. It was better to get it out now and get it done. She turned to look at her again and said, 'I want to know everything about you. I want to know everything that's happened to you.'

'What happened is I had to get a new identity to hide from you. You shot John, then you made up a story to try to hide what you did, and when that didn't work you blamed other people. But you want to know about my life. You want to play out this fantasy, OK, here's my life, here's how it's been.'

It just spilled out of her and he knew she wanted to be with him again. He heard it in her voice. She told him about living in a cabin near a lake and then he told her about the mountains where they were going now.

'It's dry and remote but the there's a creek and a beautiful canyon. There are coyotes and bobcats and some mountain lion. We're going to start over.'

She didn't say anything to that, but he meant it. There were three rooms for her, and later, in a year or so, if everything went well, if she was good, he'd let her out on a chain in the yard. There was the room she'd sleep in at night and where he'd visit her. He did not plan to ever tell her where she lived or ever let her talk to anyone else. Or at least not for a very long time and there was no landline phone or even a paved road yet. His cell phone didn't even work up there. If he was away on a trip she would have the long chain and ankle bracelet, and no knives or anything she could hurt herself with. She would have food and the TV until he got back. The mail already came to the PO Box down in Brantley and there were no neighbors, just the dirt road and the locked gate and the signs warning trespassers.

She'd fall in love with him again. It was a matter of being together and having time, but first things had to be even. She had to make up for the five years he did in prison. She needed to know what it felt like to be locked up. That was important.

He checked the rear-view mirror. Not far from the freeway now and the long drive south. They would need to make a stop at the warehouse for supplies for her first few months, and then they would be on their way.

'Did you like living at Bucks Lake?'

'It's was always pretty, but there wasn't any real way to make any money and I was always afraid you were going to find me.'

Just like her to be so frank. That was the Erin he remembered and he smiled at that. For the first time it seemed like her.

'You don't have to watch out any more, and I

took care of Lafaye too. She's gone.'

'You killed her?'

'No, she jumped off my boat and drowned. I drove around looking for her but I couldn't find her. She was looking for you. That's how I found you. I found you through her. She told me you were going to meet her at Lake Merced. You were blackmailing her.' He turned and smiled. 'So I said I'd meet you instead.'

He thought that was kind of funny but she didn't and started to cry.

'Don't cry. It would spoil everything and we have so many things to talk about.'

'I'm not going to spoil anything. You were once all I had.'

She moved up to the mesh and he could smell her, the warm heat from her face as he turned and leaned toward her and swerved the van toward the shoulder.

'I want to try to kiss you through the mesh,' he said. 'We're going to have to get to know each other again. Try turning your head toward me again. Do it quickly.'

She didn't really try but there would be time to get to know each other again. There were rules he wanted her to memorize but those could wait until they were at the house.

Now the traffic up ahead slowed. It distracted and agitated him. He wanted the timing to be very clean today. The drive south was long. They slowed to a stop and he saw police and emergency vehicle lights.

'An accident,' he said and felt her breath on the back of his neck. She was already working on him. He loved it how quickly she adapted. There were other police vehicles up there and if he'd been alone he would have turned on traffic radio to make sure it was an accident.

'I was out of money,' she said. 'That's why I was after her. She must have told you.'

'She did.' He turned. 'Money isn't going to be a problem any more.'

She didn't answer and then said, 'Money probably doesn't matter any more.'

'You think I'm going to hurt you? Is that why you say that?'

'You've hunted me for years. You've kidnapped me. You ordered me into a van at gunpoint. Is that the person I knew once? Or were you always that person?'

'I spent five years in a cage.'

'I'm sorry about that but I couldn't pretend there was a mugger.'

'It's OK, but it has to be even.'

'What has to be even?'

'We're not going to talk about that yet.'

'That's fine, and I'm OK dying, I really am.' Her voice quavered. 'There won't be any satisfaction in it for you and maybe God will forgive me for what we did to John.'

'You aren't going to die but it has to be even.'

She didn't say anything for over a minute and they barely moved forward.

'Cody?'

'What?'

'Are we really going to live together?'

'Yes.'

'You're going to keep me somewhere.'

'For five years and then we'll travel all over the world.'

'Five years to match your five years?'

'Yes.'

'OK.'

More police cars now and a fire engine, but no smoke and no ambulance and they sat for ten minutes before the cars ahead started to move slowly forward. He questioned her more about the lost years and she told him she caught fish out of Bucks Lake and worked as a waitress, and did other seasonal stuff for employers who preferred to pay her under the table.

Then she asked, 'Did you kill the San Francisco homicide inspector, the tall one, the one who arrested you?'

He gave her the same frankness she'd given him. It was the right way to start again and every word spoken at this stage was important.

'I did.'

'What about the wife of the other one?'

'Are you going to ask me about Alex Jurika next?'

'I am.'

'After the first time we make love I'll tell you everything that's happened.' He pointed through the windshield. 'Looks like it's moving again.'

It was but everything was flowing into one lane and there were more police cars. Must have been something else, he thought, not an accident, but whatever it was looked like it was over. When they got closer and he saw two cops standing directing the flow he said, 'Get back and get down.' When she lay on her side in the back he asked, 'Do you want to be with me?'

'I don't know yet. You've got to give me time.'

'I'm the same Cody.'

'Then after what I did, why wouldn't you just kill me?'

'I've thought about killing you.'

'Then just do it.'

'I had a long time to think about it. I know you got scared that night. I knew ahead of time exactly what was going to happen so I wasn't scared. But you didn't have a chance to prepare. The cops knew you were lying. Did you know they knew?'

Even though they were getting close to the cops directing traffic, he turned and looked at her. He wanted to see her answer.

'I couldn't tell anything,' she said.

'Well, they knew you didn't see me shoot John, but they also knew if they didn't have you they wouldn't be able to make the case stand.'

Stoltz checked her once more, and then pulled his cap down and blocked part of his face from view with his elbow resting on his driver's door as the cop impatiently waved him forward. Behind him the whole line of cars got stopped and as he crossed the intersection they let cars start from the other direction. He neared three police cars parked in a line and another cop car swung in behind him. As soon as he saw that he knew something was wrong, but it was too late. Just like that they boxed him in and stopped their cars.

He went for his cell phone. He had Raveneau in there on speed dial and called him as he jumped the van up on to the sidewalk and started driving. He hit a light pole and the van rocked sideways but kept moving.

'Get them to back the fuck off or I'll kill her,' he said as Raveneau answered.

'You don't want to do—'

'Goddamn you, I'm going to fucking shoot her right now.'

'I'm walking up to talk to you. Let me talk to you, Stoltz, you don't have to get yourself killed.'

He saw the SWAT fuckers and Raveneau rushing through ahead of them. A bullhorn voice ordered him out of the van and he was blocked. He couldn't drive any farther without ramming one of them. He saw Raveneau break from someone trying to hold him and then start down the sidewalk. Stoltz opened the van door, laid the gun on his seat, showed his hands, and put one foot out on the sidewalk with all the guns pointed at him and people yelling. He ignored the order to get down and just before they rushed him he turned, grabbed the gun, and in a quick motion aimed through the mesh at Erin.

But his legs gave away. He heard a sharp crack and another sharp pain flowed up his side as he fell, bouncing off the van and sliding to the ground. He heard Raveneau's voice close to him, saying, 'Try to keep him alive,' and then, 'Hang in there, Stoltz, we're going to get you to a hospital.'

Then the sidewalk turned gray and the voices moved far away. He heard Erin. He wanted Erin. He tried to say her name.

SIXTY

Quinn was ghostly pale but oddly composed for someone who'd just been abducted and lived through a violent rescue. At first she didn't seem to want to come out of the van and told Raveneau, 'He was taking me to a house where we were going to live together.'

'That's over, give me your hand and I'll help you get out.'

'Is he dead?'

'No, but he's in bad shape.'

She refused a ride to the hospital to get checked out, said it was ridiculous, that all she'd done was ride in the back of a van. He hadn't hurt her.

'Why did you get into the van at Lake Merced?'

'He had a gun.'

'Did he pull it out of his pack?'

'Yes. So you saw?'

'I was there.'

Quinn paused on that, probably quickly realizing they'd followed her after la Rosa dropped her near her car. Whatever she thought about that she hid.

'I drove there because I remembered the lake was pretty and I couldn't think very well after I talked with you and your partner. He came up to me on a bike when I was standing looking at the water. He must have been following me. He must have had the bike in the van.' Her voice wavered. 'He said he was taking me to a house in the mountains, where for five years I wouldn't be allowed to leave so that I would be even with him for his prison sentence.'

'That's over with.' He waited a beat. 'How did he know you'd be at Lake Merced?'

'Maybe because he was following you he saw me today. He's been stalking homicide inspectors. He told me he killed Inspector Whitacre.'

'He told you that today?'

'Yes.'

'Did he say anything about following me or Inspector la Rosa?'

'I don't know. I'm so cloudy right now I don't remember. He talked a lot but I don't think he said anything about you. Will you take me to my car?'

'Are you sure you're good to drive?'

'I feel nothing but relief. I'm fine to drive.'

'We're going to need you to come in. I can have someone pick your car up.'

'No, I need my car. I'll come in tomorrow.'

'You're very brave and tough. I think most of us would be shaking like a leaf after what you just went through. There are counselors who can help you with it. I can get someone who'll talk it through with you this afternoon.'

'I don't need to talk to anybody and I don't want to go to a police station.'

'There's no way around that. You're going to

311

need to make a statement today about what happened this afternoon. You can follow me back.'

'But I told them back there what happened.'

'There's more to it.'

'I don't want to be interrogated.'

'No one is going to interrogate you, but you're going to need to answer some questions.'

Raveneau turned on to the big lot above Lake Merced and drove toward her car. As he slowed to a stop, he asked, 'Were you meeting Deborah Lafaye here?'

'Who?'

'Deborah Lafaye.'

'Oh, her, no, and I didn't even know she lives in San Francisco.' She looked puzzled or tried to. 'Why would she want to meet me?'

Raveneau took a chance now and said, 'She told us she was going to make an additional payment to you.'

'You're kidding.'

'There's a path around the lake here. Why don't we walk and talk a little before we go downtown and you get recorded on videotape? It might make you feel better to walk first.'

'I've told you the truth. I came forward so I didn't have to carry it around any more. I've told you the complete truth.'

'I know you have. There are just loose ends.'

Steps led down to an asphalted path and they went left and followed the path across a wooden bridge over a finger of the lake. Along the shoreline below were tule reeds and stands of willow trees. The wind blowing in was clean and heavy with the coming rain and seemed to revive her.

She got some color back and a little flash in her eyes and a smile.

'I'm alive,' she said. 'I'm lucky.'

'Yeah, I think you're very lucky and it's over with Cody. He won't ever come after you again.'

'His legs were all twisted around.'

'His back is broken. He may not make it, Erin.'

'If you want the truth, it all still makes me feel sad.'

'Because way back when you could never have imagined this?'

'That's right.' She bit her lower lip. 'It's such a mess. He wanted me to talk to him and I started to. I told him the truth about everything, where I hid and why. I was lying on the floor of the back of the van and not even really afraid, though I felt certain his plan was to eventually kill me. He told me he had to kill Inspector Whitacre. Why would he have to kill him?'

'I don't know. I do know he didn't follow you here. His van was here when you pulled in. I was behind you.

'Think about that as we drive to the Hall of Justice, OK. We need all the loose ends and I think everyone appreciates what you've done in coming forward.'

They walked back up to the cars and she followed him to Bryant Street. He put his pass on her dashboard so she wouldn't get towed out of the red zone out front, and upstairs la Rosa was waiting. In the interview room she recounted it just as Raveneau had seen it and filled in many more details about the conversation with Stoltz. Then Raveneau took the conversation

313

back to Stoltz finding her.

'Did he say anything at all about how he knew to be at Lake Merced?'

'Didn't we already talk about this?'

'Yeah, and you've got to forgive me on this. Sometimes I'm going to repeat myself and I know it's exasperating and annoying, but you've got to roll with it. Did he mention Deborah Lafaye?'

She pursed her lips, seemed to be trying to remember, and said, 'A woman jumped or was pushed off his boat last night. I think he said it was her. He said she was dead, that she drowned.'

'She didn't drown, Erin. She swam to shore. We talked with her this afternoon.'

Now they waited. When the wait got awkward la Rosa stood and said, 'I'm going to get another tea. Would you like one, Erin?'

They did the tea thing and Quinn stalled; Raveneau brought her back to the question.

'Who were you meeting?'

She answered oddly, saying, 'I know every inch of Cody's boat. When we were having our affair we would meet at the dock because the boat was safe. It took a key to get through the dock gate and the boat had a bed, and sometimes we'd go out on the bay. I can picture the gold colored paneling, the dark wood of the wheel and the white and blue paint like it was yesterday.'

So they touched on the relationship with Cody again, and then revisited Lafaye.

'Was the meeting today with her?'

'You've asked that so many times! I don't know how Cody knew to go to Lake Merced. I have no idea. I wasn't meeting anybody.'

Raveneau nodded. He went back through her statement about the abduction today and then took her downstairs. In the elevator he said, 'We need you to stay in town for a few days. The department will pay for lodging.'

'I really don't want to do that.'

'We need you to do that. I've got to ask you to. You're our best link to several open cases.'

'Is that a standard procedure?'

'This is a very unusual situation. I can make you a reservation at a motel we use on Lombard Street. It's not the swankiest but it's clean and fairly nice.'

'You're not really answering my question.'

'And you haven't answered mine about the meeting at Lake Merced.'

She held his gaze now, none of the furtive glances he'd seen when they'd first met. She didn't want to stay in San Francisco and he knew she was debating telling him she was leaving. Raveneau pulled out his cell.

'I'll call the motel. It's a good place and I'll lead you over there.'

She watched him as he talked to the motel. Then he led her over, and after she'd checked in, he drove to the hospital and learned that one of the two bullets had severed Stoltz's spinal cord, and that if he lived he'd be a quadriplegic.

The doctor Raveneau spoke to said, 'There's absolutely no way he'll ever walk or use his arms again. I doubt he'll be able to move his

315

head or even talk, and I'd only give him a fifty-fifty chance of living. He's got a helluva fight ahead of him. Was he the cop killer?'

The question had a hard ring to it.

'It looks that way.'

When he left the hospital it was dusk. He called la Rosa.

'How soon before you get back?' she asked. 'The techs are through the third firewall. They're ready for us.'

'I'm going to make one stop.'

'Don't you want to see what they found?'

'Yeah, I can't wait to see it, but I'm going to stop by the Reinert's old apartment first.'

'What are you going out there for?'

'Go see what the techs found and I'll catch up to you.'

'They want me to handle a press conference. I'll probably be doing that when you get back.'

'No sweat.'

When he got to the apartment building he saw they'd stripped a lot of the exterior skin, removed windows and gutted several of the units in the last two weeks. Much of the pink stucco and rococo style ornamentation along the roofline was gone. Unit 5, where the Reinerts had lived, was one of those that had been completely gutted. He figured a way to get around the construction fencing and walked up the stairs with a flashlight. The exterior walls were stripped so all he had to do was squeeze between the two-by-four studs. Once in the Reinerts' unit he found where the kitchen had been by looking at the plumbing pipes in the wall.

Then he heard footsteps coming up the stairs, someone who knew how to walk quietly and that turned out to be a security guard who clicked his flashlight on Raveneau's face. Then he moved the beam to the homicide star Raveneau held up for him to see. He told the guard the story of what had happened here.

'You're talking about the man the police shot today, had the woman in back?'

'Yeah, and there wasn't much choice but to shoot him.'

'Never is.'

Some social comment there but Raveneau let it slide. He looked through the hole in the exterior wall where a kitchen window had been centered above the sink and figured this must have been the window where Quinn had told Whitacre and Bates that she'd seen the shooting from. He studied what you could see. The parking lot in back, but it was small. Some cars, but not all. Part of the stairs. Less of everything at night and you'd have a real hard time identifying anybody or what they were doing in the lot. Yet Whitacre and Bates had accepted her version.

He'd have to go back and reread the file yet again. Maybe she'd only claimed to have seen muzzle flashes, though what he remembered was her stating she'd seen Cody Stoltz shoot her husband. Or maybe the lighting was better in those days, but he doubted that, and it was certain the parking lot hadn't been any closer.

'I've been thinking of applying to the police,' the guard said. 'How long would it take me to get into Homicide?'

317

'Might take you ten years, maybe a little longer, though my partner got there in less.'

'Get out of here, man, you're messing with me. Ten years?'

'There aren't many openings and the homicide detail isn't big.'

'How long you been there?'

'Forever.'

'Did you watch *CSI*?'

'At least once.'

'What do you think?'

'That if we had those people working for the city we could probably get by with just a couple of inspectors, maybe only one.'

He thanked the guard and left him looking out the hole where the kitchen window had been. When he got back to the Hall the press conference was almost over. He passed by it and went up and opened the Reinert murder file to Quinn's witness statement. It was as he'd remembered. She'd told Whitacre and Bates where her husband had stood and where Stoltz was, and that hadn't been possible. Not even if she had stood at the window.

He went to see the computer techs and they couldn't show him what they'd found without first telling him how they'd broken through. But their pride was earned and understandable and he put his impatience aside. What they'd found on the other side of the last firewall was a list of contact names, such as who he'd bought the stolen pickup from in LA, and where he purchased guns, and a list of all the vehicles and aliases, including passport and driver's license info. There were two houses, one in the town of Brantley in southern California, where he was taking Quinn, and one in the north. Both houses were owned by the same LLC. The house up here was on the road from Calistoga over to Santa Rosa. He read a San Jose address just as la Rosa walked in ebullient from the press conference.

She asked, 'When did you get back?'

'A half hour ago, and you were already winding down so I came up here to see what they found.'

'Did you hear any of the press conference?'

'No.'

'They told me I was live on CNN.'

'That's great, take a look at this.'

He showed her an address of a building in San Jose and put his coat on.

'This must be where the cars and whatever else is stored.'

'The bat cave you were talking about.'

'Yeah.'

She looked at the address and at Raveneau adjusting his coat and said, 'Let me tell Ramirez I can't go to dinner.'

'Meet you downstairs.'

SIXTY-ONE

A nondescript building, gray stucco walls, flat roof, unpainted sheet metal caps at the parapets, two steel man doors, no windows, and two heavy gauge metal roll-up doors in an industrial section of South San Jose. The sidewalk was wet from showers and the wind was cold as Raveneau walked over to the locksmith's truck and tapped on the guy's window, while la Rosa dealt with the alarm company.

Within fifteen minutes they were inside where it was warm and quiet and clean. Cars, trucks, and SUVs sat on a floor of waxed concrete. La Rosa pointed at a boxy blue Volvo wagon and then took a step back.

'That it?' he asked.

'Yes.'

'We'll probably want to impound it tomorrow, not tonight.'

She walked over and moved slowly around it, looking in through the windows, her shoes squeaking on the wax floor. They went from vehicle to vehicle, and then through an apartment and an office. Close to fifteen thousand square feet and many automotive mechanical tools. He didn't know anyone that worked on their own car any more, but it looked like Stoltz assembled engines. When they found a locked storage room door he wished they'd kept the locksmith here longer.

They used a battering ram instead, punched out the lock and found rows of guns and boxes of ammo. They found maps with notes written on them, lines in different colored ink, and Raveneau took a guess.

'We're looking at us, the homicide detail, our patterns of habits. He mapped our lives.' Raveneau spread some of the maps and looked at the notations. 'Looks to me like he studied all of us at one point, I mean, look at this, that's Jacobi's house and McKinley right there, Stewart, Garcia, I'll be damned.'

They found a big stainless-faced Sub-Zero refrigerator with beer and some fresh vegetables, and a photo board in the office off the apartment that had seven or eight photos of a well maintained ranch house, and varying shots of the driveway sloping up to it and a carport.

'That's Becker's brother's house in Walnut Creek,' he said.

'But he didn't shoot Becker's brother. They got a DNA hit and charged the kid.'

'They want to revisit their case.'

Before leaving they returned to the blue Volvo wagon and la Rosa stood in front of it with her arms crossed. 'I didn't think we'd find this. I didn't expect to see it again, and I'm surprised it affects me so much. I thought it was Heilbron.'

Raveneau nodded.

'And I didn't know seeing the car would be this emotional.'

'It was that close.'

When they left it was three in the morning and raining. It rained harder as they drove back and they were too tired to talk any more. He fell into bed and asleep to the sound of rain against the windows. At dawn he woke to a phone call from an exuberant Bates.

'Where you at, Ben? I'm coming into the city ready to buy you breakfast. I want to thank you in person.'

He met Bates at a place on Potrero Hill that Bates and Whitacre used to frequent. The sidewalk in front of the café and the sliding door to the patio was plastered with dry plane leaves that were sodden with last night's rain. It was the morning after the first true storm off the Pacific and you could feel the change. He found Bates inside at a corner table, a plate of home fries, eggs, bacon, and sourdough toast in front of him.

'I take twenty milligrams of Lipitor every day so the eggs don't hurt me. Man, these are good. I miss this place. You know, Ted and I used to come here all the time.'

'I remember.'

'I wanted to thank you in person because they were right on the edge of charging me. They'd already gotten a warrant and gone through my house. I came home to that two days ago. How'd you get him? I heard he showed up.'

'He did but I don't know how he knew to be there.'

'So it's not over?'

'Not quite, but pretty close. We've got everything we need to charge him for three murders.

We got a lot off a laptop.'

Raveneau watched to see how he reacted to that and Bates stopped eating. One of the three was Jacie and he laid the toast he'd bitten into back down on the plate.

'Jacie, too?'

'Yeah, it was Stoltz.'

'How sure are you?'

'Everything about the truck is there. We got enough off the laptop and from photos and diagrams out of a warehouse in San Jose to charge him. He did a lot of planning, but do you really want to hear this?'

'Pictures of Jacie?'

Should he tell Bates that? Was it really necessary?

'Hey, hand me that menu.'

Bates reached across the table and gripped Raveneau's wrist. 'I want to know.'

'There were photos. He studied his targets, recorded what happened, and analyzed his mistakes. He killed her, Charles.'

A waitress showed and Raveneau ordered coffee and toast. The waitress wasn't the one clearing tables but Bates handed her his plate, and then seemed to forget where he was and stared at the wall behind Raveneau.

'How long did he follow her?'

'I don't know, a couple of months, a year, longer, and there's no way to say whether he was really after you or Jacie, or evaluating both of you. Given Becker's brother I'd say he was after Jacie.'

'So Ted was right and I was wrong.'

'Ted was right.'

'Fucking Ted was always right.'

'Not always.'

Raveneau watched him pick up the coffee cup and then set it back down. His face seemed to have aged in the ten minutes Raveneau had been here. The short distance Bates had gotten from his initial grief was lost.

'I've got something I want to ask you,' Raveneau said, and Bates tried to find a balance again, waved weakly at the table, said, 'You should eat. I want to buy you breakfast.'

'I'm OK, and maybe this goes back to Whitacre worrying so much about Stoltz. I went out to the Reinerts' old apartment yesterday.'

'First time you've been there?'

'First time inside.'

'You got inside their apartment?'

'Yeah.'

'What did you do, knock on the door?'

'No, the building is being renovated. It's stripped to the studs.'

'Nice old building, isn't it?'

Raveneau didn't care about the building this morning. He watched Bates.

'The Reinerts' former apartment has been gutted. At the kitchen sink the cabinets are gone and there's just the opening where the window was. I stood where she would have been had she seen Stoltz shoot her husband.'

Raveneau didn't really believe they meant to do anything wrong. He had studied the Reinert murder files and there was no question Stoltz had fled the scene. Not much doubt that Stoltz had shot John Reinert.

'What do you mean, had she seen?'

'She lied to you and Whitacre. She told us yesterday that she never saw the shooting. She heard a popping sound she knew was gunfire. She may have seen a flash of light. Then a second shot and she ran down the stairs. She wasn't afraid to run downstairs because Stoltz had warned her something could happen that night. When I was there I realized it didn't matter whether she'd been at the window or not. At that distance and angle and at night, no one could have seen the shooting or told who was who.'

'I stood there and I could tell. So could Ted.'

'A good defense lawyer would have eaten you up, but it didn't matter, you had him every other which way.'

'I don't like this, Ben.'

'I'm not really asking for you to like it. The place is being remodeled. Go back and take a look yourself.'

'I don't need to. If she lied, then why did she lie?'

'Because she knew Stoltz had killed her husband. She was supposed to back his mugger story and not only did she not do that, she came up with an eye witness account to help take him down.'

'And you're telling me we should have called her on that eye witness account?'

'What I'm telling you is I stood at that window and I couldn't see buying her story, and if I had to guess I'd say Stoltz who was in love with her

325

at the time for his own reasons, took the plea bargain and didn't start his attorney on her. And like you said, he would have gone down anyway. But somewhere later on he probably started dwelling on her lie.'

'Stoltz had remnants of powder burns on his right hand.'

'He cleaned his hands. He didn't have enough on them. It wouldn't have stood up and you and Ted knew it.'

'He fired that gun. He should have told us he'd taken shots at the mugger.'

'Oh, he killed John Reinert. That's not the question. The question is why you believed she saw it. I know you. You stood at that window.'

'You can see the parking lot clearly from that window. I can easily remember that.'

'But you wouldn't be able to make out who was who, and it was night. Stoltz knew she hadn't seen it. He—'

'How do you know that? You don't know that.'

'He started to write you letters. He was dwelling on her lie. He wrote about it. It's in the letters to Whitacre that got filed, but you were more careful. You made sure you lost the letters. I'm betting he brought it up again and again to you.'

'He killed the man, so what's your point?'

'This is what I'm seeing. He shot and killed Reinert, but if he hadn't had the window testimony to dwell on he'd have only himself and Erin to think about.'

'You can go fuck yourself, Raveneau. We did it exactly by the book.'

Raveneau got to his feet.

'Those Oakland detectives were locked on you, but so you know, I never believed any of it, and I'm very sorry about Jacie.'

Raveneau walked out and his face felt flushed as he got out in the cooler air. He knew Bates would go back and look out that window, and he'd probably see just what he saw that night. Bates would never admit it but both he and Whitacre must have known her account was bullshit.

He was in his car when his phone rang, figured it was probably Bates. But it was the nurse he'd given his card to at the hospital where Stoltz was. A decision had gotten made yesterday that Stoltz didn't need a police officer guarding his door and on the off chance someone might show and want to get in to see him, Raveneau had written his cell number on the back of his card and asked the nurse to call if there was anything unusual. As he listened to her explanation he guessed it was Erin Quinn who'd showed up.

'She said she knew him and needed to make sure he really was paralyzed and wouldn't be coming after her any more.'

The nurse thought that was very strange, but more than that she was outraged they'd found the woman in the room leaning over him.

'She sneaked in. No one saw her and she didn't check in with us.'

'But she said call me?'

'She did say that, she said call Inspector Raveneau. I don't know what she was up to but I didn't get a good feeling.'

'Describe her again.'

As she did, he realized his guess that it was Quinn was wrong.

'Thank you. I think I know who it is.'

He called la Rosa.

'Stoltz had a visitor sneak into his room this morning. A woman who told the head nurse that she just wanted to make sure he was paralyzed.'

'Geez, you'd think she'd had enough of him.'

'It was Lafaye. I think we go see her this morning. When are you getting in?'

'I'm just parking, I'm here.'

He signed in and then left again with la Rosa, drove to Lafaye's house on Fulton Street. They went up the stairs and Lafaye opened the door like she'd seen them coming for fourteen blocks.

She said, 'I love the way you follow up. Come in, both of you.'

SIXTY-TWO

Lafaye led them into a high-ceilinged room with paintings hanging from picture moldings and tall double-hung windows that looked out across Fulton Street into the trees of Golden Gate Park. A curved sofa arrangement faced the windows and she urged them to sit down and have tea with her. A silver teapot she said she brought home from Thailand sat on the thick glass of the coffee table. Lafaye lit a cigarette and when la Rosa frowned, blew a stream of smoke her direction.

'This is my house and as far as I know they haven't banned smoking at home yet.'

'You visited Cody Stoltz in the hospital,' Raveneau said. 'Let's talk about that.'

'Well, if you're here to confront me about it, it's true. They discharged me early this morning and I drove straight to the hospital where he is. Then I lied my way in. I told them downstairs that I was his half-sister from Indiana and I'd flown all night to get here. Then they were kind enough to tell me what floor and room he was in.'

'The nurse said that when she walked in you were messing with the equipment they've got him hooked up to.'

'You're really loaded for bear this morning,

329

Ben. You'd think you'd take the day off and get down on your knees in a chapel and thank God you got him.'

She took a long pull on the cigarette but this time exhaled away from la Rosa. She turned back to Raveneau.

'I was leaning over him hoping he was awake and conscious enough to recognize me.'

'She heard you talking to him.'

'I was talking to him. Did he hear me? I have no idea. I hope he did. I told him what they probably haven't told him yet, that if he lives, and I made sure he understood that's a big medical "if" right now, but if he does live the only thing he'll ever be able to move will be his eyes. Now here's the good part, he opened his eyes as I was saying that. I said it twice and slowly, and then added, but no one really expects you to live. Pretty awful of me, isn't it?' She stared hard at la Rosa. 'He tried to run me over with a boat. On TV they're saying he's the one that shot at you. How do you feel about him?'

'I think making a trip to the hospital to do that is disgusting,' la Rosa answered.

'That's what you're trained to feel, but what do you really feel?' She tried to stare la Rosa down but that wasn't working, so she added, 'Are you going to tell me I didn't have the right to tell him what I think?'

'Let me tell you why we're here,' Raveneau said.

He let several seconds go by before continuing and Lafaye interrupted his timing, saying, 'Oh, I'm such a terrible host. All I've made is tea.

Would you like some coffee? Isn't that what homicide inspectors drink? And what else do you serve at the homicide detail, soda pop, water? What can I get you?'

'You can ease up a little,' Raveneau said, 'we weren't expecting lunch. We're here to talk with you about some things we've learned after going through files. We got a lot of information, including emails relating to his search for Erin Quinn.'

'How exciting, but will any of it matter if he dies?'

'We think so. Under one of his email identities he corresponded with you. Both of you were using aliases but he'd figured out who you were.'

'Well, obviously, Inspector, if he lured me to his boat.'

'How do you you think he discovered who you really were?'

'I'll never be able to give you that answer.'

'Did he learn about your Erin Quinn identity and work backwards?'

She gave the smallest shrug and sipped tea.

'Now we're behind the third firewall and reading more emails.'

He paused again. Whether or not she knew it was Stoltz she was talking to in the chat rooms, she had certainly learned it on the boat. She wouldn't say what had lured her to the boat, but he must have had something she wanted. And Raveneau suspected a shared search for Quinn, and that to get her to the marina and on the boat he either offered something or threatened her in some way. If it was a bodily threat then they would have heard about it by now, and if the threat was as Lafaye had suggested earlier – to reveal to the media that she had a false identity that she used in foreign countries and that was going to somehow create a scandal – Raveneau wasn't buying. He doubted anyone would fault her, given what she was doing.

Lafaye leaned forward now, as if to speak in confidence.

'All he wanted was a way to find the real Erin Quinn and I couldn't give him that.'

'You did give him that. You led him to her.'

'Excuse me.'

'You told him about the meeting at Lake Merced and he met her instead of you.'

'Oh, please, this is like a B movie. I didn't collude with that monster.'

'How else could Cody Stoltz know to be at Lake Merced at three in the afternoon? Maybe you were on the boat, maybe you were scared and he forced it from you, but he learned it from you.'

'Now I'm losing patience.'

'Or maybe you made a deal with him and he dropped you near the shore and you swam in.'

'I made the swim I told you about and he tried to run me over with the boat. You can believe that or not believe it, I really don't care. Why don't you ask the doctors if I really had hypothermia?'

'You need to come clean with us on this.'

'Then I'll feel much better, right? Nothing will change but I'll feel better to get the burden off my soul and more to the point, your case will be tidied up. What did the lovely Ms Quinn tell you about a meeting? Obviously, not much, or you wouldn't be here. What else did you find behind the mythical third firewall?'

Lafaye tapped out another cigarette from the pack on the table. She glanced at la Rosa and said, 'You were good on TV last night. If you get tired of working murder cases come see me, because you can bullshit with the best of them. Anyone watching last night would have thought the case was solved. I guess it's not.' She lit the cigarette and nodded toward Raveneau. 'You're so lucky to be learning at his knee. Is there anything else before we end this?'

'There is,' Raveneau said, 'we don't want you to make any travel plans.'

'Really, Ben, that's a little vindictive, isn't it? I think you're trying to tie things up a little too neatly. You've already got enough to satisfy everyone.'

Raveneau leaned toward her. 'Here's my big problem. We happened to follow Quinn to Lake Merced. We could just as easily not have. If we hadn't, Stoltz would have taken her and probably not been apprehended. So let's say you made a deal with Stoltz and gave him the meeting time, and like I said earlier, maybe you had to. But, if so, you could easily have told us when we came to see you in the hospital. But you didn't do that. That bothers me. That means the case is still ongoing.'

'Well then, that means my lawyer needs to take over. This will be the last interview we have without him.'

She stood up but Raveneau remained sitting.

'One more thing, we also believe you're hiding information that could make you a suspect in the murder of Alex Jurika.'

Raveneau waved the stack of papers he'd brought in.

'It's all here.'

'That's preposterous.'

'Is it?'

Lafaye snorted and said, 'You answer a question for me. I swam in and survived, and you caught him and he was the cop killer. Why is it not enough for you that I've given most of my adult life to trying to save lives? Why doesn't that buy me any credibility?'

When he'd had lunch with her she'd told him she did for overpriced medical supplies what Amazon had done for books. She found a way to get cheap bandages and staple generic drugs delivered to third world countries for pennies. She had alliances with firms producing drugs in China and India and her foundation worked out methods to teach doctors and dentists on a massive scale, webcasting dental and medical procedures as they were performed live. Those watching could email their questions. People called her a visionary.

'We don't question that you've done good deeds on a large scale, but none of that has anything to do with this investigation. What's the real reason you went to the boat?'

Lafaye got up and walked over to the windows. She looked out at the park as she answered.

'I went to buy Erin Quinn's home address for ten thousand dollars.'

'And do what with it?' la Rosa asked.

'Give it to my attorney who would work quietly with law enforcement authorities to build a case against Erin Quinn for extortion. You have to understand that this woman has threatened me. She's a nightmare to me. And I had no idea that the man I was going to meet at the boat was Cody Stoltz. I thought that he was an individual like me that Quinn had cheated or was extorting. For separate and unspoken reasons we were both looking for her. But of course I didn't know who I'd been chatting with all those years. You can imagine my shock when he took off his disguise and said he was Cody Stoltz. He tricked me.'

'How did he know to be at Lake Merced the next day?' Raveneau asked.

'Ask him.'

Her foundation was everything to her. It was her life, her ego, her everything, and so he played that last, after she'd ordered them to leave.

'You're going to force us to go public with this.'

'I don't see why that would be, but I'll take it as the threat you intend it as, and I have some advice for you, don't do anything until you talk to my attorney. He'll call you this morning.'

He did.

'What can I do to help solve this misunderstanding?' the attorney asked.

'We have information that could cause us to view your client as a suspect in an unsolved murder in China Basin. We need her to fill in some gaps in her account to us. That may clear her of any suspicion.'

'I know that she would like to clear this up.'

'She needs to tell us how Cody Stoltz knew to be at Lake Merced.'

'That's it?'

'That's it, right now. We'll give her the rest of the day and I'll give you another phone number you can reach me at this afternoon.'

'After all she's been through, do you really think you can twist her arm this way?'

'Use my cell number, that's going to be more reliable. Are you ready for the number?' Raveneau waited a beat and then read the number off. After the lawyer repeated the number, Raveneau said, 'I'll talk to you this afternoon,' and hung up.

SIXTY-THREE

In the mid afternoon la Rosa called him over to her computer.

'This Lafaye's foundation website – look at this. She's supposed to be in Seattle tonight at a dinner honoring the most significant donors to her foundation. They're giving her an award at the dinner.' La Rosa threw him a wicked smile. 'Think she'd pass up an award?'

The award was to be given at a restaurant Raveneau vaguely remembered reading about as cutting edge with a rising star of a chef, a dinner more likely to draw wealthy donors, the type of people she wouldn't want to disappoint.

'What do you think?' la Rosa asked.

'I think you're on to something here.'

At four thirty that afternoon a driver showed up at Lafaye's house and took her to SFO. They watched her check in and pass through security, and waited until United was ready to board the first class passengers before approaching her. Raveneau pulled his homicide star and made sure the people nearby could read it. Her face reddened with embarrassment and humiliation. One of her aides, a young blonde woman with heavy black glasses, stood dumbfounded nearby. La Rosa turned to her and said, 'Better board or you might miss your flight. Your boss won't be coming.'

'You can't do this,' Lafaye said.

'Step away from the line, Ms Lafaye,' la Rosa said, and Raveneau just watched her, saw her fumble with her phone and call her lawyer, who demanded to speak to him and then told Raveneau he had two choices, charge her with a crime or let her on the plane.

'Do you really want us to charge her?'

'Let me talk to my client.'

He handed the phone back to Lafaye who sat down now, her face pale, her worried aide hovering nearby as the plane boarded.

'Please don't do this. You don't know how important this dinner is.'

She pleaded and Raveneau asked, 'Do you want to come downtown and tell us what happened? Your lawyer can meet us there.'

The warning about unattended luggage drowned out what she said next. The United Seattle flight finished loading and a gate near them streamed passengers unloading.

'If we had more information it might look different, but I'm afraid where things stand right now, we're very close to charging you,' he said.

'Do that and you may ruin your career, Inspector.'

'I don't need your help to ruin it.'

He came close to saying, you went to Alex Jurika's apartment and she lied to you, and the next night you killed her. Almost said it, but held back, and she seemed to read his mind.

'You know very well I didn't kill her.'

338

'We know that you've been lying to us. That much we've figured out, and that's what we're operating off right now, and you're gambling you can back us down and that you've got the juice to keep us from pressuring you. Maybe you're right, then again, maybe you're not. This is our offer. Security here at the airport is under SFPD, so if you want we can go to a room and you can tell us the truth, and maybe we can work this out and you still catch a flight. Otherwise, your lawyer can meet us at Bryant. It's your call.'

She didn't make that call for a long minute, and after she did they led her to the airport security office, got her a chair, and shut the door. In that room she finally gave it up.

'I didn't go to her apartment for a drink the Wednesday before she was killed. I went because she was a thief and a liar and I needed to talk alone with her. And I don't care that she's dead. Good riddance, and as to the bitch who sold me her identity, Erin Quinn, she was a friend of Jurika's and she's been extorting me with Jurika's help for too many years.'

'You've paid Erin Quinn money.'

'You need to carry your notebook more often. I've been telling you that Quinn has extorted me. Those payments were made through Jurika. I've paid her more money every year since the foundation became more successful. At first it was another twenty thousand. She said she hadn't been given enough for her identity and then it was more, and so forth.'

'And why didn't you go—'

339

'To the police and tell them I'd bought some-one's identity and there are places where I travel under a false passport, and that I've paid money to keep the woman whose true name is Erin Quinn quiet. The mistake I made was paying anything in the first place, but at the time I thought the alternate identity would have very negative repercussions. Besides, Quinn let me know through Jurika that she considered her identity stolen and that's what she was going to go out with. Jurika, of course, would deny having ever sold it to me. How do you think my board of directors would react to that in this age we live in, where no one has the patience any more to wait for the truth?'

She paused, then added, 'The day I met Jurika at her apartment she asked for another twenty-five thousand. I stalled and hired a private investigator.'

'Give us a name and a way to reach this investigator,' la Rosa said, and Lafaye pulled a card from her purse as Raveneau asked, 'Why did you lie about what happened on the boat?'

'I told you the God's truth.'

'Stoltz knew when to be at Lake Merced.'

'I set up a meeting through Jurika. I was to meet Quinn there, pay her the twenty-five thou-sand, and the private investigator was going to follow her when she left, and then with the help of the authorities we were going to go after her. But I was in the hospital. I didn't make it to the meeting.'

'Was the investigator there?'

'Yes.'

Raveneau studied her a moment and then stepped out of the room with la Rosa.

'Let's get her to call the investigator and we'll go talk to him. She can go on to Seattle with the understanding this isn't over.'

La Rosa's answer was, 'If we do that we may never get the answer.'

'I'll try her one more time after she calls this investigator and gives him the go to talk to us.'

Lafaye was very willing to do that as soon as they got in the room. Her aide had already found another flight. There was still time for them to make the dinner. Raveneau sat down next to Lafaye and la Rosa steered the aide away. He spoke quietly.

'Jurika's murder is still an open question. That's where this investigation started and where it'll finish. So nothing I'm going to say to you now clears you on that.'

'I would never kill any—'

'Just listen. In order to go forward I need to know how Stoltz knew to be at Lake Merced. If you told him about the meeting with Quinn, tell me now. If it was on the boat you were under severe duress and maybe you weren't coherent enough the next day to put it all together.'

'But if there's a trial I'll get called to the stand.'

'There won't be a trial. I got a call from a doctor an hour ago. Stoltz's kidneys and liver are shutting down. He's not going to make it. It'll stay with us. But I have to know.'

Lafaye looked down at the carpet. She looked saddened, as if disappointed in herself.

341

'I'm sorry,' she whispered. 'I'm truly sorry. But, yes, that's what happened. He frightened it out of me on the boat and I didn't tell you when I had a chance. Is that what you needed?'

'Yes.'

'I really am sorry.'

Raveneau nodded. 'We'll still have questions,' he said. 'There'll be plenty of questions about how it worked with Jurika and Quinn and you.' He stood. 'We'll talk when you get back.'

The private investigator had a few things for them, not a lot but a few things that mattered. The Quinn woman – his words – he believed lived in the Bucks Lake area, was only seeing a trickle of the payments made through Jurika. His client, Lafaye, had paid over two hundred thousand dollars in six years, an amount he considered foolish and unnecessary. It was also enough money to give Lafaye motive to kill Jurika and hope that Stoltz killed Quinn at Lake Merced. But that wasn't the conclusion Raveneau was coming to.

When the private investigator finished, Raveneau left a message for Erin Quinn at the motel on Lombard, and when she didn't answer a second message they drove over to the motel and the manager opened her door, showed them all her things were still there, so they decided to wait. When Celeste phoned he left la Rosa and stood outside in the cool air talking to her.

'What are you doing tonight?' she asked.

'Watching a motel. So far it hasn't moved.'

'Will you be around later?'

'I don't know, but things are moving. I'll see

342

you soon.'

At midnight they called in and got a combination of an undercover officer in an unmarked and a radio car to cover until six in the morning, when Raveneau said he'd be back. If she returned during the night a call would go to la Rosa and him. He returned just before six and brought coffees with him for the officers in the radio unit. He told them they could take off. Ten minutes after they did, Quinn showed up. She left her car running and the headlights on as she went into her motel room. She didn't carry anything out of the room and left the motel room door open as she got back in her car. Later, Raveneau realized that the open motel room door was a signal that he should have seen. But he was finally seeing the Jurika killing. He was too caught up in that.

SIXTY-FOUR

Quinn drove the San Francisco waterfront as though sightseeing or looking for someone on the street. She passed the ballpark, crossed the Lefty O'Doul Bridge over Mission Creek and continued south into China Basin. It didn't surprise him that she drove past the building where Alex Jurika died, or that after passing the building she turned and went back toward the downtown.

Raveneau gave her distance. In a separate car, la Rosa did the same. Morning commuter traffic fed into the city and at this hour many had their headlights on. Raveneau turned his off as the sky lightened and Quinn drove toward Golden Gate Park, and then to the apartment complex where her husband died. As she slowed there, he nodded to himself. He picked up his cell and called la Rosa.

'Lafaye gave Stoltz Quinn and hoped Stoltz would kill her and that would be the end of her problem. I think her problem is bigger than she told us. I have a feeling it's more than her board of directors disapproving of her using someone else's identity to do good works. My bet is she used the Quinn identity for things other than saving the world. I'm guessing she made money

344

with it in a way she now doesn't want to admit and that's why she kept paying the extortion money. She paid two hundred thousand dollars and didn't call the police. Who does that without a solid reason?'

Quinn led them through the Presidio and then on to the Golden Gate Bridge. As she started to climb up the steep grade into Marin County, la Rosa asked, 'What do you think, is she starting to drive home?'

'Let's give her another few miles.'

As he called her cell, Raveneau watched Quinn move over two lanes and take the next exit. When she picked up she said, 'You want to meet with me, don't you?'

'We do. We'd like to meet this morning.'

'And after that can I go back home?'

'We can talk about that too. Where are you now?'

'I'm in Marin in the car and close to the freeway. Can we meet at the motel?'

'Sure, and we may take you back downtown.'

'Are you going to arrest me?'

'What we really want to do right now is talk with you.'

'I'm sure you do.'

'Tell me more about Lafaye. Where did she get the money for those first payments?'

'Where do you think? She took it from the foundation.'

'Did Alex know that's what would happen?'

'Alex was very clever. Alex was a very good reader of people.'

'That's what I'm gathering. I'm thinking Alex

345

wouldn't have gone into a rundown building in China Basin at night with someone she didn't know.'

Raveneau saw her get on 101 southbound back toward San Francisco and pulled back on behind her. He narrowed the gap between them and kept talking. She listened then abruptly interrupted him with an anxious edge in her voice.

'A private investigator was asking questions about me in a town called Quincy not that far from where I live. He told people the woman he was looking for had extorted large amounts of money from his client. That's what he was saying to people in Quincy and I knew he wouldn't be there for just a couple of thousand dollars, so I knew Alex had lied to me. I needed to question her. I had to question her. What else could I do?'

'You called her and came down to visit and talk it out.'

'Yes.'

'Did you get the Ketamine from a veterinarian up where you live?'

She didn't answer, and he thought again about Lafaye continuing to pay and not going to the police, but searching for Quinn on her own, and Quinn following the money trail back through the questions of the private investigator. Then she'd gone back to Jurika.

'Alex wanted to show me a rundown building she was thinking of buying into. She wanted me to buy in also and made up a story about how we would own it together. She said she had a way to make it happen, so I said I'd come down and stay with her a few days and we'd go see the

346

building. She was sleeping with the realtor and had a key, so we could go anytime.

'She had a key and false papers to show me that I was half owner in this building. She had a whole new identity for me as the building owner: Alex and me, the credit thief and unemployed middle-aged woman buying a commercial building in San Francisco. She wanted me to sign these false papers and feel like I had two hundred thousand in equity. She claimed there was no mortgage. She got the realtor on the phone and he told me Alex had paid cash for the building.'

'You must have been very angry.'

'I wanted revenge. I needed to make things fair. I've lived very quietly and paid cash for everything, or done things for trade. I've lived poor. I never had one credit card. I cancelled everything when Cody went to jail because I knew what he'd do when he got out.'

'Where are the papers Alex showed you?'

'With me.'

'I'd like to see them.'

'You'll see everything.' She paused and then spoke too quietly for him to hear, but something passed along the edge of his consciousness, something he should realize, something missed. He was twenty seconds behind her as they went through the Waldo Tunnel. He watched her car going out the other side. As she started down toward the Golden Gate Bridge, her voice was much slower.

'You're right, I got the Ketamine from a vet I know. When did you figure it out?'

'Last night.'

'I just wanted to question Alex. I didn't mean for anything else to happen.'

Having seen the marks on Jurika's neck he didn't believe her.

'Where is the rope you used to strangle her?'

'I threw it in a garbage can at a rest stop on the drive back home.'

As bridge traffic slowed to a crawl and her brake lights came on she described the room and the mattress, and moving a chair over and Alex convulsing on the mattress.

'We were going to go out and celebrate after she showed me through the building. That's why she was dressed up.'

Raveneau decided to close in and radio for backup. He carried a second phone, an emergency phone, and used that to text la Rosa, 'Quinn confessing to Jurika murder. Call for backup.' La Rosa could see him but probably not Quinn, but she'd figure it out.

'Are you still there?' he asked, and Quinn wasn't. He tried calling her back and didn't get an answer. He tried again as he reached the first tower of the Golden Gate. At this hour there were four lanes running into the city. Later, they'd move the cones and the other side would have more lanes for the reverse commute. Up ahead, the right-hand lane stopped moving and Raveneau changed to the cone lane, the center lane.

It was Quinn holding up traffic in the right lane, her car barely moving forward, cars bleeding out of that lane and honking. When she came to a stop Raveneau forced his way over, hitting his horn hard. He came close to an accident and then just stopped his car and got out. He ran toward her and he almost got there.

He got within ten feet. 'Erin, no, Erin wait!'

She turned. She looked at him and then went over the rail before he could grab her. Raveneau saw her tumble, clothing fluttering, flapping, and the ocean foaming as she hit. Then he could barely keep his hand from shaking as he called for help. A Coast Guard rescue team from Fort Baker was there within minutes and they found her, but she was dead when they pulled her out.

Raveneau and la Rosa drove down to Fort Baker and identified her after the guard brought her into the dock, and in the car they found a written confession.

'I should have known,' Raveneau told la Rosa later. 'I saw the open motel door and had a feeling when I came out of the Waldo Tunnel that I needed to catch her. I just didn't put it together fast enough.'

'We did everything we could.'

He didn't answer that. He knew he should have seen it. He could have kept her from killing herself and the feeling stayed with him through the night.

Cody Stoltz died that same morning and late in the afternoon Lafaye's lawyer called, and she and the lawyer came to the homicide office. There, she recounted the extortion in detail and told of her anguish and suffering, explaining that the risk to the foundation's credibility had been too great for her to come forward.

She brought a record of almost all the payments she'd made.

'I don't have the very earliest,' she said. 'I paid those with cash I had saved.'

'How much were they?'

'Too much, and I don't like to think about those first ones. I've blocked them from my memory.'

'Do you think an audit of the foundation's books would turn them up?'

She smiled at him. She said, 'You and I are alike. You say just what you're thinking, but to answer your question, no, I don't think an audit will ever turn up anything.'

Raveneau didn't either, but he held her gaze for a while. It rained most of that night but by dawn, when Raveneau went out to the Guadalcanal Memorial, the rain had stopped. He laid flowers at the base of the memorial for the men his father had served with and for Chris, and then stood near the front of the bow section looking out at the ocean. When the sun broke through the water turned from gray to greenblue. He watched a line of pelicans fly from shadow into sunlight and work their way south.

He knew the city would remember the story of Cody Stoltz and those he murdered, but few would remember Alex Jurika or Erin Quinn. Lafaye's star would continue to rise. She was already walking with celebrities and showing up on bigger TV talk shows. But there was a reason the boy pushed from the helicopter haunted her and maybe her missing fingernails were to remind her not of the evil out there but within, and to keep her focused on what she wanted to be.

And maybe that's where redemption lies, in what we someday could become. He touched the flowers, felt their soft petals between his fingers, then pressed his palm against the cold steel of the memorial and held it there a long moment before walking back to his car.